C000192738

THE STORM BRINGER

DOUG LIVERSIDGE

First published in the UK by RMC Books in 2011
www.rmcbooks.co.uk
RMC Books (0114) 250 6300

RMC Books is a division of
the Regional Magazine Company Ltd
6 Broadfield Business Park
Sheffield S8 0XF

Front cover: Paul Cocker
Edited by: Martin Edwards, Chris Brierley, Emma Robson

Copyright© Doug Liversidge

The moral rights of the author has been asserted. Without limiting
the rights under copyright list below. No part of this publication may
be reproduced, stored in a retreival system or transmitted in any
form or by any means, electronic, mechanical, photocopying,
recording or otherwise, without the prior written consent of the
copyright owner.

ISBN 978-1-907998-03

Printed and bound in the UK by Thomson Litho

Conditions of sale
This book is sold subject to the condition that it shall not, by way of trade
or otherwise, be lent, re-sold, hired out or otherwise circulated without the
publisher's prior consent in any form, binding or cover other than that in
which it is published and without a similar condition including this condition
being imposed on the subsequent purchaser.

All rights reserved.

This book is dedicated to my Grandson Charlie
who died in a car accident on 21st April 2008,
a few days before his eighth birthday.

ACKNOWLEDGEMENTS

*I am indebted to Sue Vicars Smith and to Natalie Wilkinson
for all their hard work typing my longhand manuscript.
I also owe a huge debt to Martin Edwards for all his help
with editing and particularly his encouragement.
Finally I could not have managed to write this book without
the unquestioning support of Pam my wife.
She had to put up with my obsession for my writing
every time we went on holiday to our home in Florida,
followed by me talking about it over dinner*

INTRODUCTION

When I began this book two years ago I could hardly have imagined the sudden turn of events in Libya.

Now, even as I write, Colonel Gadaffi is under siege. Part of the country is in revolt, and the western coalition is using air power to bomb him into submission. How distant this seems from the perspective of 50 years ago. In the Libya I knew, as a British officer on military service, King Idris still reigned and Gadaffi was no more than a corporal in the Libyan army. But even then the tribes of the east in Cyrenacia had a fear and dislike of the tribes in the western half of the country. It has taken nearly half a century for these feelings to surface into a civil war that no one can win. Gadaffi and his sons admired much about the west, not least its lifestyle, but any hopes of better relations are now extinguished. All that remains is a fight to the finish in a country once more torn by war.

As I write this introduction at my desk in Florida I am reminded in the most dramatic way of the central theme of the book. The Mid-West of the USA is being battered by the worst tornados in living memory. Already 400 people are reported dead. The use of the weather as a deadly weapon must be on the agenda of many countries. I can only hope it is not to be the warmongers who succeed in that new arms race.

Doug Liversidge
May 2011

PART ONE

CHAPTER ONE

Saida turned over and glanced at the bedside clock for the third time that night. The stark red figures were a lone point of light in a room not yet touched by the first hint of sunlight through the heavy blinds. 4.17am. She lay back on the bed, eyes wide open, her ears attuned to the hum of the ceiling fan. How could she sleep with so much resting on this day? Before the clock showed 5, she was dressed in a sheer white blouse and a black knee-length skirt, as if for a day at the office. But the office was the last place she wanted to be. Today of all days she had to be at the beach.

Her third floor apartment was six miles inland from North Miami Beach and it would only take her fifteen minutes to get there on the deserted highways. Her Ford Mustang would be one of the very few cars moving in the city today. Only the bright yellow official pass inside her windshield would save her from being immediately arrested as a looter.

Her thoughts were of nothing but Zoe. WIOD's early morning news told of more casualties in Afghanistan. Helmand Province. A roadside bomb. America assures the world that it remains committed... it was only when she heard the final evacuation warning that reality struck home. This was no dream.

But the reality of the lifeless seafront was stranger still. The car trailed a cloud of dust and sand in its wake as it came to a halt in the empty beach parking lot. A forlorn cluster of small clapboard shops, their shutters closed, creaked and groaned as their awnings were whipped by the stiff sea breeze that brought cool relief to her face. At the height of the season, they plied their trade selling sun tan lotion and cold drinks to the carefree high school students who idled away their summer here. But for now they resembled the set of a ghost town in one of those old movies about the American West. Saida took her shoes off and carried them in her hand as she walked onto the beach. The soft sand yielded under her feet as she sought a spot to rest her back against the sea wall. Her gaze was drawn to the east, to the Atlantic.

The sun was now full in the sky, the air already heavy with the steamy humidity she found so uncomfortable. It was a world apart from the dry desert heat of her native Libya.

She looked out eastwards anxiously. Nothing. Perhaps this would after all be just another day.

"Come on Zoe, where are you?" she mouthed.

The absurdity of her situation struck her. Should she fall to her knees and pray to Mecca to unleash a disaster on this place, just to prove her right? She would ask Allah to forgive her for such vanity later. For now, all her training, her reputation, her life's work, was being carried along somewhere out there on the sea. Of course she was right. This is where Hurricane Zoe was going to hit.

A week earlier, the inhabitants of Port-Gentil in West Africa had paid scant attention to the late afternoon rain shower. Eight miles further out off the coast of Gabon, among the sea lanes where container ships carried on their ceaseless procession, rising humidity from the water had met the offshore breeze to prompt the downpour. Small spirals of wind and rain pattered the sea and initially faded away. But the combination was the right one. From the union of wind, humidity and water temperature, Zoe was conceived.

The storm's path, and very existence, fed on air and sea conditions as it made its way across the Atlantic. So complex and volatile was this mixture that it was now almost impossible to predict its path and intensity.

The National Weather Bureau in Miami took its accustomed cautious view when satellite data first showed the atmospheric disturbance that was Zoe. So the standard general warning went out, predicting a storm front hundreds of miles wide and estimating the intensity on the Saffir-Simpson scale, the Richter scale for hurricanes. Where exactly it would hit, no-one could yet say. No-one perhaps, except Saida.

It was accepted that a large part of the American coastline would be put on needless alert several times a year. Better safe than sorry. Even then, the forecasters still got it wrong occasionally, with sometimes devastating consequences. The onslaught of Hurricane Katrina on New Orleans was not foreseen until the last moment, and the city paid a heavy price.

Saida Sanussi had never believed anything was impossible. Whether that was the scientist in her, forever seeking to explain rationale where there appeared none, or just an inborn, obdurate determination, she didn't know.

But it had served her well. Here she was, at the age of 28, barely six years out of MIT and already a senior figure in the Weather Bureau. Even as the outstanding student of her year and winner of the Chancellor's Medal of Excellence, her career progress was meteoric.

There were greater challenges to overcome than academic conquest. Being a Muslim from Libya marked her out in a country reeling from the shock of 9/11. She had become accustomed to the insults and occasional physical threats from Americans seeking a target for their anger and grief.

But the country had given her an opportunity and she loved it in return, learning to accept the American ways she found hard to come to terms with, and never expressing strident opinions on world events. There were after all world-shaping forces to be found in her own personal field of fascination, the hurricane.

Her boss John William Jnr had made her the Head of the Severe Weather Unit after only three years working there. To her colleagues in the bureau, she had everything. She was gifted, and not only with intelligence.

It was true Saida was by any standards beautiful. Her black shoulder-length hair framed her intense dark, eyes with their searching, inquisitorial quality. Her natural confidence added to her presence, often prompting all to turn and look as she walked into a room. Like her, John had risen to a position of influence at a young age. Still only 31, his blonde hair and all-American boyish good looks concealed a capacity for cold, carefully-considered, and invariably correct judgement.

In Saida he had found one of his own kind, a scientist with a passion to piece together the apparently random elements that governed natural forces, as if assembling a jigsaw puzzle.

His confidence in her had been well-rewarded. She had not been long in her new post before embarking on a promising study of hurricanes and storms.

Throwing herself into her work, she examined every record she could get her hands on, no matter from what part of the earth. In the Far East they called them typhoons or cyclones, but whatever their name, they all begin in the same way. A slight depression starts inland and meets the coastline; the warm moist air rising from the sea reacts with the depression, causing a small whirlwind. As the depression moves over the sea it picks up more warm moisture and when conditions are right, it feeds the whirlwind so that it intensifies, growing stronger and more dangerous as it passes across the sea. When it reaches landfall the moist air is reduced and the hurricane slows down, eventually diminishing to a tropical storm.

Deep inside the bureau's hurricane-proof headquarters in the Miami International University campus, she worked with a passion. Neural networks and fuzzy logic had become the tools of many sciences over the last decade as computers had become more powerful and the writing of complex programmes simplified. But to apply them to explain the secrets of storms was something new.

She reasoned that neural networks act just like the human brain, sieving and measuring information and using it to deliver likely outcomes.

Days, weeks had been spent at the computer screen, as fuzzy logic had built patterns around the information, learning from each experience before delivering a judgement. The implications of the process were beyond imagination. Could she, Saida, be edging ever nearer to solving the mysteries that had defied explanation for thousands of years?

The thought left her awestruck. She might be on the brink of unlocking the secrets of storms. She, of all people, could be the first to understand the forces unleashed by nature, the forces that sweep aside like so many ants any of humankind foolish enough to stand in their path.

She could be about to come face-to-face with the wrath of God.

CHAPTER TWO

With a huge sense of relief, Saida pressed the send button and the report was on its way. It was now up to others to decide. The storm was on its way, whatever happened. If she was right and it was now possible to predict its exact landfall, she would make scientific history.

"Insh'Allah"

God willing or not, the task was done. The past weeks had been a blur of testing and retesting the data, pitting science against self-doubt. Someone, somewhere higher up the bureau would decide whether her claims about predicting the exact landfall and storm surge of the hurricane was a breakthrough or just another theory.

She flicked the screen onto the latest bureau weather reports. Zoe would most likely be the last hurricane of the season. It was now late October and unusual for severe hurricanes to hit Florida any later in the year. Not since 2005 had they been called on to deal with a major hurricane. But the damage Wilma had wreaked resulted in South West Florida being named a National Disaster Area. The last three years had been mercifully free of drama. But this year was different. The warming of the seas increased the threat of hurricanes. And the power of Zoe was growing as she approached the coast.

She was due to hit the East coast in under two weeks. Here was the chance for the bureau to prove its worth.

Saida was sitting in her office two hours later when the

phone rang.

"Saida, it's John Williams".

"Good morning Dr Williams," she responded respectfully.

"Please, call me John. I was hoping to discuss your work on point determination. Are you utterly confident in your conclusions"?

"Yes," she said, a hesitant note in her voice, "it still needs to be tested on a real storm but the research I've carried out so far looks positive."

"Great! If it's convenient I'd like to come in to review your work in about ten minutes."

"Of, of course," she stuttered as the phone went dead.

Saida thought for a moment, unsure whether she should have been more cautious. She frantically started to tidy her office, removing the computer printouts scattered across the floor and pulling up a chair for him. She ran her fingers through her hair and smoothed down her skirt, noticing a stain on the front. Damn! she thought. Mayonnaise. She was feverishly trying to rub it off when John knocked on the open door. She smiled a nervous greeting. Their eyes held each other's for a split second, but stopped short of discomfort. Turning her attention to the piles of paper on her desk, she began to pass him sheets and graphs. They sat close together, their arms touching occasionally.

Absorbed in contemplation of the data sheets, he quickly grasped the basis of her theory. It took a further hour of searching questioning and analysis before he was satisfied. He stood up and stretched.

"I'll get back to you. I've more people to see" he said.

With that he was gone leaving Saida a little breathless and wondering what he was thinking.

Her answer came two days later when John called her again. He offered no introduction, expecting her to recognise his voice.

"Very impressed with your work Saida. Very impressed indeed. I would like you to present your work to the main board tomorrow. Do you think you can handle it?"

Her heart beat faster in spite of her natural self-confidence. She had only met one board member in the six years she had been at the bureau.

"Well I was convinced, so all you have to do is repeat what you said to me and it would be helpful if you had some sort of PowerPoint presentation available. The meeting is in the main conference room at 2pm so I will meet you there at 1.45 to help you set up."

With that he was gone. Saida didn't have such a presentation ready. Panic set in for a few moments before her logical mind started to take over. She worked late into the night, checking and rechecking every detail.

When John met Saida the next day he noticed her nervously shifting in her seat. Despite conviction in her work, she couldn't help but worry the other meteorologists would discard her ideas. She realised that it wasn't just work that was making her nervous. She'd met John many times before but the impromptu meeting yesterday and his easy manner had been different somehow. He was a handsome, intelligent man. Now she was distracted, thinking of him. Focus! She said to herself, mind snapping back to her data.

"Relax Saida. Just be yourself," he tried to reassure her, assuming her nerves were based purely on the presentation.

"Just wait here while I go join them, we'll call you in right away".

Minutes later the door opened and she was met by the collective gaze of the sober-suited board members. John broke off his exchange of pleasantries with the board chairman, Ralph Watts.

"Ok Ralph, guess we're ready".

"Miss Sanussi, I'm going to ask John here to introduce you and your work before we hear from you".

All eyes fixed on John, who had clearly prepared for this moment.

"Gentlemen," he began, "as you know we are always striving to improve our forecasting. Our work can help save many lives. For the last three years Miss Saida Sanussi has been working on a new and complex method of prediction, using neural networks and fuzzy logic. Miss Sanussi may be relatively new here but she is the best mathematician we've had in the bureau for a long time."

Saida blushed at his compliment as John gestured for her to take over. She slowly stood and began to speak with an authority that belied her anxiety.

"Gentlemen, you will know that hurricane Zoe is fast approaching the East Coast. My objective today is to show you that we can very accurately predict her landfall point."

Now she was on familiar territory, the reams of calculations that were her safe refuge and fuel for her confidence. The board members sat impassively, betraying none of their inner thoughts.

Using graphics and a vast array of data, Saida explained her theories and why she was pinpointing North Miami as the point of land fall for the Force 5 hurricane. She was also predicting a storm surge of eighteen feet which would cover over one hundred square miles of the surrounding area in water.

It was done. The presentation over, the questions began. She dealt with most of them without hesitation. When they were satisfied, she waited for someone to break the silence. John motioned for her to sit.

"I have to admit gentlemen," he said, "I'm impressed with Miss Sanussi's findings. The data she's presented appears credible, if lacking in field-testing. I realize that to use her work would mean evacuating 100 square miles in the Miami area. It could leave us vulnerable in other areas if Zoe hit land elsewhere. There are risks, without doubt. But let me remind you that Zoe is due to meet the American coast in the next twelve days. We need to make a decision as soon as possible. I suggest that Miss Sanussi leaves whilst we discuss the best possible course of action". The board members nodded in agreement as Saida left the room.

After she left, controversy raged around the boardroom table. The consequences of accepting Saida's theories were daunting. The area she was predicting for landfall would have to be evacuated without exception. A mandatory order would have to be issued and the police warned of possible public disorder caused by those who refused to leave. The storm surge – a tidal wave of considerable force – would also inflict terrible damage on top of the havoc wrought by the wind. It was all or nothing. If they accepted the findings, restrictions in other areas would be lowered, allowing police and other volunteer organisations to concentrate on the North Miami area.

With immense relief, Saida made her way back to her place of refuge, her private office. She could only speculate on the exchanges within the room. The decision they had to take was momentous.

John felt torn. He had come to have faith in Saida's work but the doubt expressed by his more experienced colleagues troubled him. His role in the decision was crucial and he would bear the responsibility if she was wrong. He would have to look more closely at her data before committing to her plan.

He left the meeting to deliver the verdict to Saida personally at her office just across the campus. The door was ajar. Knocking politely, he peered inside. Three computer screens lit the otherwise gloomy room. The floor was covered in scattered sheets of paper. Immersed in a calculation, she suddenly looked up, startled at the unexpected interruption. John's silhouette filled the doorframe in the bright light; she could only just make out his face. She instantly regretted having kicked off her shoes and let down her hair after the meeting.

"You were excellent," he said, "and they were impressed. There was reluctance at first, but after reviewing your supporting evidence more closely we determined that you and I should work on the data again before deciding."

"That's fantastic!" Saida exclaimed, jumping out of her chair, "I'm so pleased, I might get to test my ideas on a real hurricane! Although, that leaves quite a responsibility on my shoulders," she added slowly.

"I realise that," John replied, "we've got about a week before evacuations need to take place. I propose we start running computer models tomorrow."

With Zoe drawing ever closer, everyone grew increasingly anxious. Saida and John spent their time reviewing the neural network data she had compiled. They looked over past hurricanes, working out the exact conditions that had caused the most ferocious storms. Hurricane Fran had hit North Carolina in September 1996. She had only been a Category 3 storm but had still killed 34 people and caused over $3 billion in damage. According to Saida's predictions, Zoe was going to prove far worse. Hurricane Galveston, which devastated Texas in 1900, had exhibited similar initial conditions. It caused a storm surge of 15 feet, killed 8000 people and decimated the city. If Zoe behaved in the same way as Galveston, she could be deadly. The responsibility Saida felt for protecting the people of Miami weighed heavily on her. She was also desperate not to disappoint John. They had worked tirelessly, often late into the night. Saida felt her attraction for him growing. She looked over at him now. He was sitting back in his chair, legs outstretched, the purple smudges under his eyes, tousled hair and faint hint of stubble attesting to their hard work. Neither had found much time to get home and freshen up. John's head was lolling to one side, his hand supporting it. His eyes, which had been starting to close as he sleepily slumped in his chair, snapped open. She drew a sharp breath in anticipation. He was going to make his decision, she thought to her herself, suddenly filled with apprehension.

"I'm going with your prediction," he announced confidently. Saida smiled in relief.

"Let's treat ourselves to lunch, to celebrate. I can't remember the last time we left this office!" he added.

Grabbing her handbag and coat, they walked through the rain towards the deli in comfortable silence. Saida felt in a strange way she would be almost disappointed when Zoe had finally arrived. She had enjoyed being so close to him.

Days later, she watched in fascination through her office window at the chaos outside. With under 48 hours to go before Zoe hit, they were evacuating the city, traffic jamming the freeways. Horns blared as lines of traffic crept slowly out of the city centre. The gas station on the corner was closed. There was no fuel left to sell. Everywhere there were angry clashes over bottled water, tinned food and petrol. She looked on, awestruck by how many lives had been changed, just by the calculations in her notebook. As if to fuel her worst fears, her mind leapt to a postcard she kept pinned to the wall in her room at MIT. The words on it came from Einstein. "Mathematics is well and good. But nature keeps dragging us around by the nose".

And so nature had brought her to the beach on this day of reckoning. Saida stood on the sand, her mind still filled with the events of the last few days.

The path of Zoe had been erratic. At one point, the storm abruptly moved south as if heading for the Caribbean, causing Saida to fear she had been wrong. Yet within a few hours, the satellite tracking showed it following an inexorable and ominous path northwards. And it was picking up speed.

The Miami Herald had led a chorus of media criticism of the drastic measures being taken by the authorities. But as it became clearer that Zoe was heading straight for Florida, the headlines were overtaken with warnings of the civil emergency to come

The streets were deserted. The only signs of life were a handful of policemen and the odd television crew. Waiting. Saida was standing on the beach, on the spot where she expected Zoe to hit. In defiance of danger, she had to be certain that her predictions had been right. She had to see it for herself. It was not long in coming.

Clouds slowly filled the sky and the first heavy drops of rain hit her cheek, stinging her skin. The temperature was dropping rapidly and the wind was picking up, ripping at her clothes. The waves were tumbling violently, the surf spraying in bursts. Her eyes streamed as they fought to stay open against the gusts. Within minutes she was soaked, her clothes sticking to her. From the beach it was all too easy to feel the growing intensity of the storm. Tiles on a nearby restaurant began to rattle on the roof. Saida was filled with both excitement and fear. She peered out into the storm, elated that her predictions had come true.

The noise suddenly rose in intensity, the darkness penetrated only by the flashes of lighting offshore. She was completely alone.

Fear took over. A tile was wrenched from the roof, flying through the air. She looked around wildly. How had she let the storm come so close without realizing? Peering out through the rain, she could see the black and grey turmoil of the hurricane looming towards the coast. She had to run. The thin trilling of a cellphone reached her through the roar as she struggled across the heavy sand, heading back towards the sanctuary of her car. She scrabbled in her pocket, her wet fingers unable to grasp it. Missed call – the ninth. It rang again.

"Where the hell are you?" he shouted down the phone.

"On the beach," she screamed back, racing up the concrete slope, tears streaming down her face.

"What? You've got to get away. I'm tracking Zoe on the computer – she's going to hit in a couple of minutes!" he exclaimed breathlessly.

"She's here now!" Saida yelled.

Pressing the phone back in her pocket, she sprinted through the deserted car park, blinded by the rain. Where the shops had stood, there was nothing but ruined and splintered wreckage. Through the hail of flying debris, she saw the outline of her car, rocking violently in the wind. Throwing herself behind the wheel, she stuffed the keys into the ignition.

The wind was blowing straight into the car. The screen! What's happened to the screen? Diamonds of broken glass littered the seats, the remnants of the windshield jutting over the bonnet like jagged teeth. The thick tree branch that had shattered it intruded into the car. She put the car in reverse and backed away, the branch twisting and bursting the passenger window before finally, mercifully, breaking free. She raced towards the bridge that would take her inland. Torrents of water gushed down the roads, filling gutters. Shards of glass broke away from the exposed screen, cutting her face as the wind rushed towards her. She ignored the pain and the blood streaming down. Although gripped by fear, her instinct told her to keep calm to survive. She couldn't panic on the flooded road. If she drove too fast the car could easily take in water. It could blow up the engine.

She reached the bridge, wrestling with the steering as the rain pelted down on her. No-one was in sight. As she raced across it her phone rang again.

"The freeway's blocked," John shouted down the phone, "you'll have to take the inter-coastal." The suspended traffic lights ahead swung erratically in the wind, the red light a beacon in the darkness. Suddenly they lurched violently skywards, crashing to the ground their debris blocking her path. She braked hard and whipped the steering wheel to avoid the wreckage, slewing the car sideways.

"I'm on Sunset Boulevard," she yelled at the phone.

"Find some shelter, I'm coming to get you".

Shelter. Anything would do. Through the hail of windborne debris, a wall next to the 7-11 Store. She cowered under the partial protection of the wall. Minutes passed.

She desperately tried to call John. The digital display showed no reception. How could he hope to find her?

Mercifully the phone flickered back to life. It was John.

"I'm on Sunset and 9th", she shouted, close to tears.

An SUV screeched round the corner, John behind the wheel. Leaping from the car, he led her away, cradling her against the wind. Clinging to one another, they battled to stand, staggering to the vehicle. At last they were inside, the door closing on the fury of nature outside. They sped away. Saida looked up, her hair in strands around her face. He saw the blood smeared across her cheeks.

"We've got to get you to hospital".

She was reluctant to let go, the intensity of their closeness making her light headed. Suddenly the howl outside changed to a new note. They realised the wind had dropped and the sky was brightening. They were in the eye of the storm. A dream-like quiet descended as the wind subsided. They knew only too well that if the eye of the storm had reached them, it was wouldn't be long before the storm surge that inevitably followed would engulf the city. Saida and John knew now was not a time to dawdle. They could hear the sound of water roaring onto the beach. The wind had started to pick up again and they knew that where they stood would be under at least six feet of sea water within the next hour.

"Let's get out of here" he urged. As they sped away from the beach, swerving around fallen trees and broken glass. Saida reeled from the shock of the past 20 minutes.

The phone display showed the bureau was on the line. Zoe was now flooding the beach, the team tracking its every movement. So far, more than ten square miles had been submerged. The streets were empty. Even the emergency services had abandoned the area.

The storm had hit exactly as she predicted.

"Please do something for me will you Saida?" he said as he put down the phone.

"Don't try and prove your theories like that ever again".

John took Saida to the Memorial Hospital located on the outskirts of the city. The hospital was quiet with very few people about and just the occasional patient. Saida sat patiently as the doctor worked on the wounds on her face. Nothing serious he said and the scars will disappear in a matter of months. John looked at her face and felt a sudden urge to stroke her cheeks; instead he reached out and held her hand. Her hands were small and delicate and he detected a slight tremble. He looked into her dark brown eyes which opened wide and he thought that she was suffering from shock. In reality she was coming to terms with the enormity of the decision she had made in advising on the storm path. If she had been wrong hundreds of lives could have been lost but what she couldn't understand was why she felt so frightened now when before she had been so confident especially as she had been proved right.

John whispered gently in her ear. "I will take you home. You're all in. Take a couple of days off. I'll keep you in touch with the office".

The concerned look on John's face was enough for Saida to simply say "OK' 'and with that he drove her home.

She was exhausted and after a quick check to see that her apartment was undamaged, he left her to rest and get some sleep.

"I'll see you in a couple of days at the office" he called as he quickly closed the door and made his way back to the

Weather Bureau. The wind was still howling but now it was coming from a northerly direction and already he could feel that Zoe was losing her strength as she crossed over land.

Saida switched on the television to get the latest news, but Zoe had done her work. The Miami television station was off air, its buildings flooded and for the time being abandoned. The weather channel did have some pictures but even their crews had been evacuated from the area. She took more than the usual professional interest in the satellite images of the hurricane and even more terrifying pictures from an aircraft that had flown into the eye of the storm. The plane was one of the "hurricane hunters" of the US Air Force, which often flew into the very heart of storms to measure wind speed and barometric pressure. They were more widely renowned for the dramatic photographs they sent back, often taken directly down the eye of the storm with the ground clearly visible beneath.

Saida suddenly jarred awake. She had fallen asleep in front of the television. An unlatched door had closed with a bang. It unnerved her, and she guessed that in similar circumstances a westerner would resort to alcohol to steady her nerves. She had never knowingly drunk alcohol and had no desire to try. Her brother, Abdulla, had tried it once when he was a teenager and she had seen the effect on him. He had lost control of himself and acted so violently that she was scared out of her wits. Alcohol would never be part of her life.

She lay on her bed. The trembling inside slowly subsided and complete exhaustion overcame her. She opened her eyes to see it was 3am. A window had slammed shut. In the darkness she explored the wounds on her face, fearful they would become scars. The wail of the police and ambulance sirens could be heard in the distance. Their task was clearly not over. She struggled to stay awake, to contemplate the success of her work. Of the moment that had passed between John and herself. It was no good. Exhaustion overcame her. She slept, dreaming of how she had come to be here.

CHAPTER THREE

Unlike the rest of the insular Arab world, the port of
Benghazi has always looked outwards to other nations.
And in turn, the people of those nations, be they British,
Italian or Greek, have come there to rule over it or simply
to find a new life there.

Saida's father Ridi was in a very real sense a King among
men. To Libyans, the very name Sanussi suggests noble
ancestry. And indeed he was a descendant of King Idris I.
It was Idris, Emir of Cyrenaica who had led the Libyan
resistance to the Italian Occupation between the two
World Wars.

King Idris had ruled the country after the Germans and
Italians were defeated in 1945. After the war, Tripolitania
and Cyrenaica the two major divisions of Libya were under
the control of the British and military personnel from both
the UK and the USA were stationed there. The King had
spent the war exiled in Egypt and took up residence in
Benghazi when, through the 1947 Peace Treaty, Italy gave
up all its claims to Libya. On November 21st 1949 the
United Nations General Assembly passed a resolution
stating that Libya would become independent by January
1st 1952 and the United Kingdom of Libya was born, a
constitutional and hereditary monarchy under King Idris.
The King was adamant about the hereditary nature of his
role and decreed one of his two nephews would one day
inherit his title. Idris did not have any sons and had taken
his nephew, Samyia Hasan, under his wing. His other

nephew had five children and the eldest was Ridi, Saida's father.

The family were wealthy, having benefited from the discovery of oil in the desert in 1959. This discovery had changed the lives of the ruling classes in Libya and the country became one of the wealthiest in Africa almost overnight. The wealth resided with only a small proportion of the five million population, and Ridi was one of the lucky ones

But he had earned distinction in other ways. A respected surgeon, Ridi had trained in England and the USA before returning to Libya, part of a family with undoubted wealth and influence. His choice of wife could scarcely have been more appropriate.

The talented young physician's training in England had taken him to St Bartholomew's Hospital in London. It was there that he had his first experiences with women. An affair with a nurse had been a torrid and emotional relationship, but it was ultimately doomed. Ridi's lack of commitment and complications caused by his religious beliefs spelled its end.

His career next took him to the USA and North Shore Hospital on Long Island. It was here in America, in New York, that he met the woman who would become his wife and the mother of Saida.

A Libyan delegation to the United Nations was visiting the city and the Ambassador invited Ridi to a reception at the embassy. Among the other guests was Alisha, already a tall and striking woman who commanded attention. She was from a wealthy Libyan family and had studied law at Oxford University. Now embarked on a career in International Law, she was appointed to the chief supporting role to the Libyan representative to the UN.

During the evening Ridi had made his way towards Alisha, nervously thinking of the best way to introduce himself. At that moment she looked up and walked towards him, holding out her hand.

"It's Dr Ridi Sanussi, is it not?" she asked. Ridi was taken aback. Libyan women rarely initiated conversation with men. And she spoke in English. She felt less awkward about such a direct approach than she would have done in Arabic. They talked for the rest of the evening. Both felt an immediate attraction. Ridi was a devout Sunni Muslim and his family were keen that he married well. His meeting with Alisha was the start of a true romance.

Their attraction for each other was obvious to all around them. Alisha confessed later that she had already heard of Ridi before the reception and had been determined to seek him out. Her advance was born out of desperation not to miss her chance, and in the years to come she would often fondly remember her embarrassment at ever being so forward.

Over the next few weeks they spent many evenings together, mostly discussing the crisis that was gripping their country. In that year of 1969 a group of military officers led by Muammar Abu Minyar al-Gaddafi had staged a coup d'etat. The Monarchy was abolished and the new Libyan Arab Republic formed under the distinctive symbol of the plain green flag that would fly for decades to come. Gaddafi was named Brother Leader and Guide of the Revolution. His firmly anti-Western stance would cause a rift between Libya and the West that would not be healed over the coming years.

And yet Ridi and Alisha had found success in America. So they were torn by the thought of returning to a country that now opposed the USA. Events in their home country soon made their decision that much easier. Gaddafi quickly established a twelve person revolutionary council that could not be voted out of office. He shrewdly saw that, stripped of its former ruling class, the country would lose much of its senior business and professional talent. He wasted no time in contacting the Sanussi family. His assurances were much to the relief of Ridi and the rest of his family. The country's oil reserves were enormous and King Idris had always been pro-Western, forging close ties to Britain and the USA. Both countries maintained military bases in Libya.

It was not to last. Gaddafi soon closed the bases and nationalized all foreign oil and commercial interests.

Against such a backdrop of turmoil, the Sanussis came back to their native country. Adamant in their belief that Libya was still the best place to raise a family, they set up home in the outskirts of Benghazi. Ridi used his influence to buy the deserted British officers' mess, known locally as D'Austa House.

The British army had been compelled to leave in haste, such that many of the married quarters still had their furniture.

Before becoming an officers' mess, the building had been part of the estate of the ex-King's relatives. It had eight bedrooms and numerous other grand rooms as well as stables. The British had built a small church in the grounds and Ridi quickly had this converted to a family mosque. Alisha was not asked for her opinion of the house before Ridi bought it. He followed the Arab tradition of being the provider of the home.

For her part, Alisha was delighted with D'Aosta, a house she remembered visiting as a child learning to ride. When she asked Ridi why he had bought such a large house he calmly explained that his plan was to have several children. Alisha was still working as an international lawyer and Ridi had settled into his role as the foremost paediatric surgeon in the country. It was not long after they were married that Alisha became pregnant and over the course of seven years she gave birth to sons, Abadallah and Jamal, who soon had a sister in Saida.

From an early age, she knew she was her father's favourite. She enjoyed a carefree childhood, benefiting from the family's privileged position. As she was growing up, Saida was only vaguely aware of the political turmoil that had gripped Libya. But the reality of her country's standing in the wider world was soon all too apparent.

In 1984 her mother had taken her to visit Roedean, a girls' boarding school near Brighton favoured by wealthy and influential British families. Only a month earlier the Libyan embassy had shot and killed a policewoman controlling anti-Gaddafi protesters outside.

At Heathrow, immigration officers detained them. Their Libyan nationality marked them out as a potential security threat, and the authorities were in no mood to believe otherwise. Three armed security guards marched them through the crowded airport terminal. They held hands tightly, Saida growing increasingly distraught at the anxiety of her normally imperturbable mother. She remembered shrieking, tears streaming down her face, clinging to her mother as they were forcibly parted. Alisha had tried to appear calm in the face of her daughter's distress. Saida was left in a small office. All her family's influence, their money, their noble ancestry, counted for nothing here. She would never forget the slightly damp smell, the beige carpets and stained material on her seat. She had sat in that room for what felt like hours. The light that struggled past the blinds at the window began to fade, leaving her in partial darkness. She was too afraid to stand up and switch on the light.

They were eventually released after ten hours. Only her mother's persuasive skills had saved them from an even longer ordeal. She was no under no illusions about Libya's standing in the eyes of the world she now aspired to be part of. It shocked her to discover back in Benghazi that there was no mention of the embassy shooting. Gaddafi controlled the media.

Despite the actions of the dictator who now ruled there, it pained Saida that her country was so disliked. Nor could she share in the hatred of the west that manifested itself in carefully-incited demonstrations of anger by ordinary Libyans. She was eventually sent to study in Switzerland at the age of twelve. It was there that she developed her remarkable understanding of mathematics, which has become apparent at an early age and soon led to her surpassing the achievement of her two elder brothers. Her education in Switzerland had improved it even further and she became fluent in German, English and Russian. Most people liked Saida, but her detractors saw in her an arrogance. Her lifestyle and family wealth marked her out even in an environment peopled by the privileged. Her developing beauty had not helped matters. As she entered her teenage years, she grew to resemble her mother.

As she matured, her eyes were opened to Libya's problems. She saw the poverty outside the gates of their great house. The country had oil. But its climate, in particular its unreliable rainfall, meant that many Libyans often lived hand to mouth. She was aware that millions of years ago the desert had been fertile, that even now water lay deep below the sand. It occasionally came to the surface and formed the many oases that were dotted across Cyrenaica. Once, on a trip with her father in the desert she had been caught in a rare downpour, the first in twenty years. The following day the desert was transformed. The desert was covered in small, green plants. The heat – this was the desert that could lay claim to the highest temperature ever recorded on earth – meant the plants had not survived for long. She reasoned that if only they could somehow harvest water, her country would be far better placed to support itself. The country would be transformed and its reliance on American oil dollars, and all that entailed, could be overcome. It was a naïve thought but it set her on a track that would influence the rest of her life.

After her eighteenth birthday a major family discussion

took place on the matter of Saida's next step in education. Her two brothers had gone to European universities but Saida's thoughts turned to the USA. She wanted to learn more about mathematics, to study with others who would challenge her and to work under outstanding teachers. Moscow State University had a world-class reputation for mathematics. There would be the opportunity to study under Andrey Kolmogorov, who had developed the theory of probability. Saida recognised that as an Arab she would be more welcome in Russia than in the USA, where prejudice against Muslims was at an all-time high.

Ridi gently helped her to make the right decision. He found much to admire in America. He had himself been educated there. When one of his numerous visits took him to a medical conference at the Massachusetts Institute of Technology, he liked what he saw. Likewise, Saida was excited at the prospect of going to MIT, above all the thought of meeting Edward Lorenz, professor of meteorology and a renowned mathematician. Lorenz's development of weather forecasting programs had already made him one of the foremost authorities in his field. It was the thought of meeting him that tipped the balance for Saida and the decision was made.

Gaining a place proved no obstacle for Saida. Her family connections saw to it. There was still the hurdle of a visa to overcome but the timing was in her favour. Her mother's legal expertise came into play just as relations between Gaddafi and the USA thawed slightly – commercial flights began again and the Libyan leader had even allowed American military bases to be re-established, despite opposition from more radical Libyans. Gaddafi's sense of insecurity had become so great as he approached old age that he had invited the Americans to re-establish military bases in Tripoli and Benghazi.

The USA had seized at the chance not only for defence reasons but to spell out the message it sent to the rest of the Middle East. Israel was still the thorn in the side of many Muslims. They felt a minority of American Jews wielded such influence that the USA propped up Israel by equipping it with the most powerful military in the Middle East. It was the only country in the region armed with weapons of mass destruction. Gaddafi sensed that moods in the USA were changing. A Democrat President had very quickly reduced the military presence in Iraq and was taking a harder line with the Israeli Knesset over the lack of progress with the peace process. The Colonel was aware that some sporadic fighting had broken out between the governing body of Cyrenaica and some local tribesmen and that much needed to be done to prevent a growth in the terrorist movement in his own country. The re-establishment of the American military base had not gone down well with the more radical Muslims and unrest was growing, particularly in the outlying districts of Tobruk.

Saida's departure for university was a family affair. Cousins, aunts, uncles and grandparents gathered at the Berenici Hotel in downtown Benghazi, to share one last meal together. The hotel itself was an impressive sight: built in the 1930s during the Italian occupation, it had a distinctly Renaissance feel, with twin domes that dominated the skyline. The table was piled high with food in a private room for the 40 guests. Lebrak, Shorba and Saida's favourite, mb'atten (potatoes stuffed with minced lamb and herbs) sat alongside flat breads and dates. The family prayed together before eating heartily and celebrating Saida's university success. It was only after the meal, when everyone drank tea together, that Saida was able to talk to all of her relatives. Habib, her cousin, was standing alone on the opposite side of the room. He was one person she was eager to speak to. Although he was older than her and already studying law, they had always felt like equals. Saida suspected that Habib had hoped for more than friendship between them – she had caught him glancing at her when he thought she wasn't looking. He was dressed in the traditional Libyan style, with a long white gown over a shirt and trousers. Although many young people in Benghazi wore Western clothes as she did, for special occasions some wore traditional dress. Even she had covered her head with a scarf to acknowledge their custom. She walked up to him and to his surprise kissed him on each cheek. He blushed. Contact between men and women was highly regulated in Muslim culture. As her mother had done, her western education and liberal attitude made her comfortable in breaking with the norm. Ridi stood up, calling for everyone's attention. Saida and Habib turned towards him, listening as he wished his youngest daughter well in America. His two sons had gone abroad for their education but Ridi felt that Saida's departure from home would feel different. She was the youngest child and she might never return home from America. There were tears in his eyes as he spoke.

As the time for departure drew closer, Saida started to feel anxious. She had been to the USA before, but always with her family. She was worried about travelling by herself. In the end, the flight had gone to plan but her arrival at university was more distressing. As she arrived, an angry crowd was blocking the entrance to the main registration hall. Struggling through them, she realised she had walked into a clash between two opposing rallies – one protesting against the war and the other anti-Islam. She was startled at the violence, silently thanking her mother for advising her to wear jeans and a t-shirt. At this of all times she didn't want to draw attention to her Muslim heritage.

She was sharing a room with Mary, a loud blonde girl whose stated aim was to get married to a rich man and live a life of luxury. Although she was by no means thought of as pretty, she nevertheless had a string of boyfriends within the first few months of the first term. Saida, shocked and somewhat disgusted by Mary's moral standards, threw herself into her studies.

Saida flourished at university. She met with Edward Lorenz many times, their conversation often dwelling on the need to somehow create a sustainable water source for the Libyan Desert. They speculated that the water cycle might be manipulated to create rainfall. It was a possibility that fascinated them both.

Edward Lorenz had trained as a mathematician at Harvard and later at Massachusetts Institute of Technology. He had been called up to serve in the US Army

Air Corps as a weather forecaster. It was there that he started putting his maths to use in predicting the weather. Upon his return to MIT, he continued to develop his computer programmes. He found himself baffled why, after repeated attempts at predicting outcomes of weather conditions, the same input data gave variable results. He subsequently realised that the set of numbers were always the same – it was only the number of decimal places that altered. The professor realised with alarming clarity that very slight variations of the input data gave dramatically different results. From this he rapidly developed the Theory of Chaos, for which he became world famous. He would illustrate it by asking his audience to imagine a ball at the top of a hill and trying to predict the position of the ball when it rolled down and came to rest at the bottom. The lecture for which the world will always remember him was delivered in Washington at the annual meeting of the American Association for the Advancement of Science. He remarked that a butterfly flapping its wings in Brazil could cause a tornado in Texas. The Butterfly Effect had been born.

The tutorials with the now 90-year-old Professor Lorenz were inspirational to Saida and for his part he found her the most able student he had worked with. At times her thinking ran ahead of the Professor as she explained to him her burning ambition to find ways of creating rain in her own country. He was sceptical. There had been several attempts at rain-making such as using seeding with ice particles dropped from aircraft but nothing, as far as he knew, had worked over an extended period of time.

As expected, she graduated with Honours and won the Chancellor's Prize for the Best Mathematician of the Year. Her education complete, her father tried to persuade her to return home and work for the government agency that controlled the environment and mineral resources of the country and even arranged for her to be interviewed by a senior government official. The interview turned into an argument as Saida recognised that as a woman her role would have limitations that would not exist in the USA. Her brothers, like her father had stayed in Benghazi, where all three worked at the hospital. But her time at MIT had shaped her life. It was a natural progression to live in America and pursue a career in meteorology there. She had grown to love the American way of life, particularly the freedom it allowed women. Ridi quickly acknowledged he could not win this battle. And Professor Lorenz had secured her an interview with the US Weather Bureau. She was soon the new Assistant Scientist in its Hurricane-Tracking department.

CHAPTER FOUR

Saida woke with a start; someone was knocking on her door. She jumped off the bed, checking the bedside clock. Eight o'clock – why was it still dark? She suddenly realised that it was 8pm and she had slept the sleep of one exhausted for nearly twenty-four hours. The banging on the door grew more insistent. Grabbing her dressing gown, she ran her fingers through her hair and went to the door's video display. It was John.

She opened the door, pulling her dressing gown tightly around her. She felt a mess but too late to do anything now. He studied her face with concern and a momentary urge to embrace came over them, as if to awaken the memory of their closeness when they met in the eye of the storm.

"I've been calling for the last four hours but your phone has been busy."

Saida remembered she had taken it off the hook the previous evening. His expression brightened.

"I've been calling to tell you that Good Morning America wants to interview me tomorrow morning but I've said that I will only do the interview if you come with me. We need to be at the Miami studio for 7am tomorrow. I'll pick you up at 6.15".

Saida knew the difference between a command and a request, and clearly she had no say in this. Nevertheless she felt a twinge of excitement to be asked to appear on a major television channel. Suddenly remembering her face, she ran to the mirror and was horrified by what she saw. Little cuts and nicks were dotted across both cheeks and an inch-long cut across her forehead had been neatly stitched.

"I can't appear on television like this" she exclaimed "I look grotesque." She was aware of him standing behind her, looking at her reflection in the mirror; he was smiling and had a look of open admiration.

"You look great to me, a little make-up and you will look your usual beautiful self." She noted the compliment but let it pass. Surely any man would try to reassure her. She had barely put the phone back on the hook when it started to ring. It was a reporter from the Miami Herald. He wanted to know her background and hear about the part she had played in forecasting the storm track. She hesitated. All communication with the press was vetted by the bureau. She took the easy way out and passed the phone to John. He was the voice of the bureau, and adept at getting over the message he wanted to send. She left him talking as she slipped into the bathroom, pointing at the coffee pot as she passed him. He nodded and smiled, but continued in full flow with the conversation. She showered, dressed and used make-up to cover the marks on her face.

When she emerged from the bathroom John had made the coffee. She wondered why he had stayed but she was glad he had. He poured the coffee and leaned forward, handing her the cup. Their hands momentarily touched and she felt a tingle of excitement run through her body. She looked at John but he was clearly in thought about something else

"I'm not sure I should have agreed to this television interview" he said, more to himself than to Saida. He turned to her. "Have you ever done an interview before?"

"No, never".

"Well it's not as easy as it looks and one small wrong word can be misinterpreted. Before you know it you have to explain yourself in a negative way." His mind went back to his television training.

"If you can, ask the interviewer before the interview what the first question will be, then at least you can start off in a positive manner. Bear in mind that you will be nervous. Fortunately the interviewer tomorrow will be either Diane Sawyer or Robin Roberts and I'm sure both will be very understanding, but watch out for the googly."

"What's a googly?" asked Saida.

He explained it was a word he had picked up at Oxford, during his time in England,

"It's a cricket term. I never understood the game but apparently the man who throws the ball at the batter can spin it so that when it touches the ground it shoots off at an angle. If the ball comes out of the back of the hand it spins the other way and spooks the batter. So tomorrow watch out for the googly".

With that John stood up and went to the door. Saida felt she should kiss him goodbye but with a quick smile he opened the door and was gone.

She sat by the window thinking of him. Never before had she felt like this, and she could sense her body reacting to just the thought of him touching her. Pushing those thoughts to one side her mind turned to the interview. She decided she would say as little as possible, that would be safest. She suddenly realised how hungry she was and prepared herself scrambled eggs and toast. Having just slept for so long she wasn't tired. She switched on the television, realising she hadn't seen the results of the storm, other than at first hand. The local news came on at 10pm and led with the devastation of North Miami but was full of praise for the emergency services. Not a single person had died in the massive storm surge that had covered nearly one hundred square miles. The damage to property would run to hundreds of millions of dollars and the President was already being pressed to make the district a disaster area. Little mention was made of the Bureau's role in forecasting the path of the hurricane. Saida flicked to the Weather Channel but they had already moved on to the next storm. Zoe had run out of steam over Florida but was now over the Gulf of Mexico and picking up speed.

It was now nearly 6.15 and it had taken her an hour to get ready in what would normally have taken only fifteen minutes. The strangeness of the situation struck her as she dressed in her best business suit, a dark two-piece.

A few days ago I was an unknown somewhere in the weather bureau. Today I'm going to be on national television, in front of millions.

She added a multi-coloured scarf around her neck then decided against it, instead putting on a flat gold necklace, a farewell present from her parents. Perhaps it would bring her good luck. But those bruises! Not even carefully-applied make-up could entirely conceal them. Saida's stomach was turning over with nerves. She wasn't usually shy when it came to facing an audience, but the prospect that lay ahead made her anxious. It was hard to decide which was worse – John turning up unannounced and seeing her in such a mess, or appearing on screen before the nation. The moment that had passed between them in the storm had played on her mind. There was a connection with him; they'd shared something.

At that moment John called from his cellphone to say he would meet her outside her apartment in two minutes. A quick brush of the hair and a second look in the mirror and she ran down the stairs nearly tripping over with her unaccustomed to high heels. John was waiting in the car and as she got in the smell of his aftershave brought back all the feelings she had the night before. He gave her a broad smile and touched her on the hand. Fifteen minutes later they arrived at the TV studio. They'd been told the interview would be carried out by tele-link to the studio in New York. But there, standing in the studio, was Diane Sawyer herself. She had come to Miami to report directly on the disaster. Looking up, she saw John and Saida and smiled

"We're going on at 7.40; you've time for a coffee and Saida, if you would like to avail yourself of the make-up department it's down the hall. As she left Diane called out after her "do you mind if I refer to your face?"

"No" said Saida "but what's that got to do with the hurricane?"

Diane was now engrossed with her script but she seemed to have warmed to John. The two of them sat in the Green Room watching the show on the television. They hardly spoke to each other, both lost in their own thoughts. In what seemed an instant, they were on air. John was an accomplished performer, answering questions without hesitation, playing down his own role and occasionally referring to Saida's work. Diane turned to Saida and asked a few gentle questions. Clearly the interview was coming to an end when suddenly she held Saida with a gentle quizzical look.

"What would have happened if your theory didn't come good?" she asked, her tone more aggressive. "Isn't it true that people could have died if you got your math wrong?"

Saida stuttered, unsure how to answer. Sawyer had hit her with the googly. John jumped in.

"There was little risk involved in our decision. We had the greatest confidence in Saida's work. Of course, we had a very clear plan B so that we could have, if necessary, deployed the emergency services to other areas very rapidly. In the end though, her theory was proved one hundred percent accurate."

The interview was wrapped up, the theme tune sounded as the credits rolled. Saida sat back in her chair, the adrenalin of the last ten minutes subsiding. She felt frustrated that she hadn't defended herself. Lucky she'd had John to rely on.

"You did great," John offered once they'd shaken hands with Sawyer and made their way off set. "Annoying about the googly at the end but at least the bureau came off well."

"Thanks. I felt a bit useless to be honest. But I can add it to the list of things I've done in America!"

"I think we deserve some breakfast after that," John said

as they headed out of the studio.

They found a small café not far from the office; John ordered eggs and bacon and Saida had a pancake smothered in whipped cream. It was the quick fix she needed after the adrenalin rush of the last hour. Over breakfast, for the first time, John asked about her personal life.

"Where's your home town?" he asked, waving to the waitress to bring more coffee.

"Benghazi, in Libya. Do you know where it is?" she replied.

"Of course," John said, "it's at the top of Africa." She smiled.

"That's closer than most Americans get!"

"Does your family still live there?" he asked.

"Yes, my parents and my two brothers are still living in the city. Sometimes I wish I lived closer to them. What about your family?" she asked.

"I come from Dallas. Mom and Dad still live there, but my brother and sister live some way out of town. My father owns an engineering company that supplies the oil business." The conversation batted to and fro, John intrigued by their different cultures. He enquired about her friends and her beliefs. Was she a strict Muslim? Did she enjoy living in America? She relaxed, enjoying his company. Suddenly his expression became more serious. He hesitated before speaking

"Saida, I hope you don't mind me asking..."

"Yes?" she asked hesitantly.

"Would you like to have dinner with me?" Saida felt a

rush of excitement fill her.

Her heart raced. Did she hear right? She was being asked out on a date. She hesitated but found herself muttering yes, and before she could say any more John stood up. In an instant, he was the bureau chief again.

"Great. Well, better go. Let's get back to the office".

Back at the bureau she was surprised to see that her colleagues had squeezed themselves into her office. Applause broke out as she entered. She blushed, thanking everyone. Ralph Watts made his way through the crowd to greet her personally, letting her know that the President sent his own congratulations. She felt euphoric. Once the welcome group had dispersed, she sat down to work. It was hard to stay focused as she thought about Saturday. Should she say anything to her colleagues? Dating your boss wasn't the greatest idea. But she felt so comfortable with him, more so than with any other man she'd dated before. No, she decided. She wouldn't let their professional relationship ruin the chance for something between them.

As Saturday approached, she was no less nervous. She hadn't spent much time alone with men – at 28 she was still a virgin. She wanted to stay true to her faith and wait until marriage. Her mind mulled over what she should wear. She decided on a black satin cocktail dress. John arrived at 7. A tailored navy blazer and chinos had replaced the accustomed suit. He took her hand gently as he helped her down to the car.

"You look beautiful," he said. She smiled.

"I am going to be the envy of all the men at the club when they see you," he whispered as they walked through the door. Saida in turn thought she would be the envy of all the women at work if they could see them together.

Over dinner at the sailing club they talked about friends, interests, aspirations. They danced until late. As she felt his arms around her and the feel of his body she started to think to herself how they would part that night. In the event John took her back to her apartment, kissing her gently on her forehead where the stitches had been and saying goodnight.

They met often after that. Staff at the bureau could see there was something between them, and they accepted it. On one particularly fine evening she asked John back to her apartment. John felt he knew what that meant. When he kissed Saida and his hands moved towards her breasts, she pulled back.

"What's wrong?" he asked.

"Nothing. I've had such a wonderful time. It's just…" she hesitated.

"Yes?"

"I need you to know now that I can't give you everything you expect from other women. My faith is really important to me. I believe in no sex before marriage. I understand that you might feel differently about me, knowing this. But I had to tell you before it went any further." She looked deep into his eyes, desperately hoping he would understand.

"Saida, I want to get to know you," he replied slowly. "I respect your beliefs. In fact, I admire them. Too many women rush relationships. I will wait as long as you want." He kissed her cheek again, before walking out to his car and driving away.

CHAPTER FIVE

John Williams Junior had been with the bureau since leaving university and was recognised as one of the leading young climatologists in the country. He worked hard but still liked to have fun: sailing, golfing and surfing whenever he could. He had had several girlfriends, but had only ever been serious with one: Jennifer. He had met her at university. They'd lost touch, but a chance meeting at a hotel in Miami where John was hosting a conference had led to a passionate encounter in a cabana on the beach.

The relationship flourished and John eventually asked Jennifer to come to Miami from Orlando. Moving into his small condo in North Miami, she took a teaching post at the university. For a year, she and John lived for each other.

John's career had taken off and he was quickly promoted to Deputy Director of the Miami division. The promotion meant more travel. Jennifer was unhappy when John was away; she had been slow to make friends at the university and felt isolated in Miami. They began to bicker about things they would have previously laughed off. John had almost given up sailing and surfing because of the demands of work. The serious side of his personality had taken over and Jennifer gently complained he wasn't fun anymore.

They planned an evening together at Fontainebleau Hotel, both hoping they could recapture the passion they had first felt for each other. They needed to talk things over, he told her. A table was waiting in the Starlight Room, overlooking the swimming pool. The trees were covered with a garland of blue lights that cast a gentle hue on the water. He chose the best wine he could afford and they both took refuge in the menu, wondering who was going to speak first. Jennifer was dreading the moment. She still felt that she loved him and brushed aside her doubts.

The main course had been cleared before he spoke about their relationship.

"I feel as if my life, our lives, are incomplete. We love each other but I know it's not enough for you or me and if we carry on like this we will both become very unhappy. She took a large sip from her red wine. John hesitated and looked straight into Jennifer's eyes. This is it, she thought. But nothing could have prepared her for what came next.

"I want us to have a baby."

Jennifer held back despite her sense of disbelief. A baby! At 24! Her head was in a whirl. She could barely hear John as he explained how he felt a great need to be a father. His own father, John William Senior, was a strong family man with two sons and a daughter; he was a committed Christian and had brought John Junior up in an atmosphere of both love and fear of God. They had never even spoken about marriage, still less a family. Jennifer played with her wine glass, holding it against her lips almost as if she could not let out the words her mind was uttering.

She looked at John and could feel his eyes searching, hoping for an answer. In truth she knew she could not go through with it. But somehow to her horror she found herself agreeing.

Having heard what he wanted to hear, John pulled out from his coat a jewellery box and offered her a single three carat diamond ring. Here she was expecting to be dumped and instead John was proposing to her. She let him slip the ring on her finger, a voice not hers saying yes. Here she was, engaged to be married to a man she wasn't sure about and committed to having a baby she didn't want.

John wore a broad smile of elation. As she looked at his face he seemed much older than his years. But now it was too late, she was in it up to her neck and anyway how could she hurt this man when he looked so happy.

John watched Jennifer with loving eyes but he was sensitive enough to feel just a touch of apprehension in her. He told himself it was just shock, that she wasn't prepared for his proposal and that by tomorrow they would be as one again.

That night they made love as if they were back in the cabana.

Even that temporary escape into passion was destroyed as she was reminded of the prison she had built for herself.

"You won't need those birth control pills now", he said, turning over to sleep. Jennifer lay awake. She already knew she couldn't go through with it.

It was several months before she had the courage to tell John her real feelings and even that came about by accident. Searching for his house keys, he looked through Jennifer's handbag. It was then he came across the contraceptive pills, their foil wrapping marked with the days of the week. Today was Wednesday. The pills up to Tuesday were missing.

The break-up was hard on them both and John found himself totally bereft. His parents were coming into town that weekend; they had already met Jennifer and loved her. To them it was the perfect match. Jennifer moved out the next day without saying goodbye. John had dated a few times since Jennifer but had never felt the desire to start another relationship. The hurt had scarred him and he began to feel he would remain alone.

He threw himself into his work. And through his work he'd met Saida. With her he felt restored, truly alive again.

CHAPTER SIX

John's father, John Williams Senior was more than just a prominent businessman in Dallas. An influential figure in the Republican Party, he was publicly being spoken of as a candidate to run for the Senate. His brand of arch-conservative, fiercely Christian politics played well in this part of Texas.

His son grew up according to his father's values. At school John Junior had excelled at both his studies and at sport. It didn't take long at university before he realised many of the ideals his father held received a hostile reception from the more liberal thinking of the academic staff. It was this experience, and his time at Oxford, that influenced a change in his thinking, a reassessment of America's role in the world. Once back home, he often found himself in intense debate with his father about religion, the economy and social injustices in the USA. On one matter John Senior was adamant. The Islamic state was a danger to the free world. He had been an outspoken supporter of the American invasion of Iraq. The bombing of the twin towers had a profound effect on John Senior and he came to believe the USA had to take the initiative, to attack the Middle East before another blow was dealt to the homeland.

As the relationship with Saida developed, John thought about taking her to meet his family. But he knew only too well there was potential for discord, particularly from his father, who would not be able to resist debating world affairs with her. John Senior was formidable in debate and his son was just as apprehensive about the response his father might get from this independently-minded woman. He had already seen her in several situations when the debate about Islam had bordered on anger. She was shocked how little many Americans knew of the Middle East and its people.

Thanksgiving Day was fast approaching and John had traditionally spent a few days with his family on the public holiday. This would be a good time for him to introduce Saida to the whole family; his elder brother and his wife would be there with their three children. His younger sister, Sue, had only recently left home and rumour had it that she had shacked up with some young stud from Memphis much to her mother and father's disapproval.

When he finally invited her, she readily agreed to go with him, knowing how important this step was for both of them. On the last Wednesday in November they took the South West flight from Miami International to Dallas. Saida had some difficulty knowing which clothes to pack. Although she had been in the USA for six years she had never been invited into a family home for Thanksgiving. She was aware of the traditions and how it was a celebration of the first harvest of the original settlers in America in the 1600s. When the first harvest arrived they thanked God and celebrated by feasting. To many younger members of the Weather Bureau, this most American of celebrations just meant time away from work. It reminded her of the limited understanding of Libyan traditions by teenagers in her own country.

John spent much of the time on the four hour flight telling her stories about his own upbringing. He had a very happy childhood. His parents stuck together even though they had married young. Many of his friends' parents were divorced and John considered himself very lucky to have been raised in a loving household. There had been times when the family business had been in trouble and his Grandfather had been called upon to help out financially but that period soon passed. There was never any doubt he was the master of his own household and Amy, his wife, had never worked outside of the home after they married.

They were met by Sam, the family's driver. Leaning against a black Lincoln town car, he smiled fondly when he spotted them. John and Sam embraced like old friends – Sam had been with the family for years, John almost seeing him as a second father figure.

"How's ma boy?" said Sam as he opened the door for them. Then, with a barely –concealed wink at John, he teased him affectionately.

"And I see you got yourself a fine lady too".

Saida laughed along with the pair of them as they recalled stories of John's childhood while the expressionless glass windows of a thousand offices slipped past them. The suburbs of Dallas and their small red-bricked houses gradually gave way to open countryside and the odd secluded mansion. The hour-long drive seemed never-ending and the prospect of meeting John's family made her feel nervous.

The car swung into a broad driveway, its tall iron gates making a clear statement about the grandeur of what lay ahead. An imposing family home was visible in the distance. As they drew nearer she took in the grand columns that flanked the front entrance. Luscious red bougainvillea covered the pale brick walls. Her parents' house in Benghazi was elegant but this American mansion spoke of generations of wealth. She hadn't realised John came from a background quite like this. The car crunched over the gravel and slowed to a stop. John looked over at Saida and squeezed her hand.

"Don't be nervous," he said, "they'll love you."

He stepped out of the car, greeted by the two figures that had emerged through the front door. He strode towards them, hugging them both. For a moment Saida had been forgotten as she stood there hardly moving from the car. Suddenly John realised he had not introduced her.

"Meet the most wonderful girl in the world" he announced to his parents. Saida blushed a little and gently shook hands with his mother. She so wanted them to like her, knowing she'd have to try hard to win over John's father. He didn't care for formality and, to her great surprise, grabbed her in a bear hug.

"It's good to meet you both", she stammered out over his shoulder, still immobilized by the python-like grip of the big man. John and his mother both saw her stunned expression and chuckled.

"Welcome to the family" he boomed, releasing her. "Come on in, I should think you both need a drink after your journey." He ushered them inside.

"Saida, it's nice to be able to put a face to a name. John's told us so much about you but I'm looking forward to getting to know you better."

She smiled, thanking him for the invitation to stay, all the time aware that despite this good start she would have to choose her words carefully.

They settled in the sun-filled conservatory at the back of the house, John's father pouring whiskey into glasses. He handed one to Saida. She politely refused. He looked puzzled.

"I'm sorry, but do you have any soft drinks? I don't drink alcohol, it's forbidden in Islam."

"It's not a big deal Dad," interjected John, alert for the first signs of discord.

"No, of course not. I forgot you Muslims don't drink. I'm sorry, would you like..."

"Some lemonade would be wonderful, thank you."

She accepted the glass. She'd only been here a few minutes and so far everyone was trying hard to be friendly. A large middle-aged African-American woman entered the room.

"Dinner at seven prompt" declared the family's cook, Selina, emphasising the last word and holding her index finger up in a mock-stern gesture "and we are having the traditional Thanksgiving Dinner". John's brother and his wife had arrived and the noise of conversation was growing louder, interrupted by occasional raucous laughter from the two brothers. Saida felt welcome, exchanging pleasantries with every family member. Many had seen the Good Morning America programme. There was much banter about John's performance but it was generally agreed that Saida had been the star of the show.

John showed her to her room; it was the one that John had used when he had lived at home. There were still plenty of memorabilia around the room, particularly of the many sporting events that he had won. Two or three photographs showed John surrounded by girls and she suddenly felt insecure, afraid she might lose him to an American, one of his own. From the window of Saida's room, John pointed out the cabana where he would be sleeping. It was tucked among a copse of Scots pines with a stepping stone path to the brilliant white door.

"How do you like my family?" he asked in hope.

"I love them already, they have made me feel so welcome and I can feel the warmth that everyone seems to have for each other."

"Well, they're not always like that. My brother and I argue about almost everything including politics and occasionally, if Father doesn't get his own way, he gets grumpy. He has strong opinions and gets irritated when people don't agree with him but I'm sure he will always be a gentleman to you. He's already said he thinks you are great, and he hardly knows you."

John left to go and get changed for dinner. She watched him from the window of her room walk up the stepping stone path to the cabana. He suddenly hopped up the last three steps and, in a pantomime gesture, wiggled his behind. He turned to see if she was watching. She was there with a broad grin on her face. Her thoughts were that she loved everything about him.

Saida took her time getting ready for dinner. She brushed her dark brown hair which had grown over the last eight months so that it neatly curled around under her ears. She had selected a summer dress with a discreet floral print that emphasised her slim figure without being immodest. Dinner was a noisy, boisterous affair, the centrepiece an enormous turkey, which John Senior carved at the table. The wine flowed and the eldest of the children was even allowed to have half a glass of wine.

"It will help him get used to drinking so he doesn't make a fool of himself in later life" said John Senior, when the boy's mother protested. The youngster had other ideas, grimacing at the taste and reverting to his Coke.

She was aware of the effect the wine was having on the rest of the party. John Junior became mellow and loving; he kept putting his hand on her leg under the table and at the same time grinning. John Senior became noisier and began to dominate the conversation, his loud voice drowning out his wife's protestations that he had had enough to drink. The conversation turned to politics as John's mother and his sister-in-law left the room to put the children to bed. John's father sat down next to Saida, wine glass in hand.

"I know from John that you're good at what you do…"

She thanked him. He stared into his glass before continuing.

"And please don't take this the wrong way, but you're an intelligent woman who's going places in life and…thing is…I can't understand how you can believe in some of the things Muslims do".

"What exactly did you have in mind?" she replied, steeling herself for what was coming.

"Well you have to say that a lot of trouble in this world is caused by Islam. Bombings, terrorism – it's as though they're angry with the whole world".

She'd heard this kind of thing many times before and listened in polite silence.

"And as for your justice system, how can you support laws like the ones that say people should have their hands cut off and women should be stoned to death?

"Do you know anything about Islam?" she asked quietly.

"I know all I need to know. Wherever it goes, trouble follows it".

John Junior had just come back into the room and saw with dismay the two of them in earnest discussion.

"There are over a billion Muslims in the world and the vast majority are peace-loving people," she said, as John walked up behind her chair and put a protective hand on her shoulder.

"It's the same as Christian people. Most are peaceful people. A few are not".

John's father suddenly prickled.

"Now just hang on here a minute, Saida. I don't see Christians blowing up airports and killing innocent people..."

"Then you should come to the Middle East. There are plenty of them there", she retorted firmly.

"I'll stay right here if you don't mind. I'll stay with America and all it stands for".

She drew in a large breath.

"Mr Williams, let me explain Islam a little better to you. The Koran is the equivalent of your bible and is the cornerstone of Muslim faith. Unlike the West, the religious and political are entwined together. Islam is the Arabic word for submission to God. We believe that our religion should affect everything we do. Some extremists do take the Koran too literally and use it for evil purposes. But that is not what Islam teaches. They are simply misguided men and women."

John's father tried to interrupt, but she was not so easily deflected.

"I admit there are tensions within Islam. I am a Sunni Muslim. I believe that the prophet Muhammad appointed three Caliphs to spread God's word. Shiite Muslims believe Ali, Muhammad's son in law, was the beginning of the holy line of men. Some Muslims are too adamant about their branch of Islam. I am not one of them. If you really think about it, the differences between us are no different to those between Irish Protestants and Catholics."

"So why are the Arabs always fighting each other? They're of the same religion," John Senior muttered.

"Not all Arabs are Muslim and not all Muslims are Arabs. The Arabic peoples make up only a small percentage of the world's Muslims. To group the two together is wrong".

He put his glass down and leaned forward in his chair. He spoke with the assurance of his convictions.

"Look, it was Muslims that attacked the American Embassy in Iran in 1979 and started all our problems, and it was Muslims who blew up the twin towers. We see mosques going up all over the place... and I bet they collect money to help their terrorist friends."

She gasped in shock and disbelief. The rest of the group looked on awkwardly, unsure whether to stop them.

"That is completely ridiculous. The 9/11 attacks were carried out by Saudi terrorists. Saudi Arabia is meant to be one of America's staunchest allies. How can you think that all Muslims would even comprehend killing innocent people?" She stood up, her shaking hands betraying her anger. John, who had not intervened so far, stood with her and spoke.

"Dad, how can you dare to suggest that Saida or her family could be terrorists? You can't invite the woman I love to stay with you and then verbally attack her."

His father thought for a moment.

"Saida, I apologise," he began, "John is right. You're a guest in my house and maybe we let things get kinda out of hand. I won't pretend that we'll ever see eye to eye on any of these things. I've seen plenty to make me believe I'm right. But," he looked down at the floor and then at his son, "my son loves you. I want him to be happy. If that means welcoming you into our family, so be it."

She hesitated, thrown off balance by his change in tone. She couldn't thank him for his words. He still meant everything he said. She replied in the only way she could think of.

"I accept your apology. I think, though, that I will take some air if you will excuse me. Thank you for your hospitality".

The evening breeze was welcoming and even though it was late November, the night temperature was still warm. John and Saida strolled hand in hand around the four acres of land belonging to the house. All of it was neatly landscaped. Eventually they arrived back at the house.

John escorted Saida upstairs to her room.

Nothing had prepared her for what she felt now. Her heart was pounding with expectation, excitement and fear. When they reached her room he held her close and kissed her. She could feel his body and felt his excitement as their bodies pressed close together. He was breathing hard and his heart was pounding but he pulled away – he knew the rules and kissed her once more and quickly said goodnight. She watched him from her bedroom window. Her body had reacted to his. She could feel her breasts pressing against her underwear and she was wet between her legs. She lay on the bed looking around the room and at the photograph and all the girls that surrounded John. He could have his pick of them and none of them had the baggage of being a Muslim. How easily she could lose him. She undressed and her body was still responding to the thought of John. Her nipples were erect and her mind overcome with desire. Rising from her bed she put on her dressing gown, went outside and down the steps to the cabana and gently knocked on the door. John's light was still on; he came to the door halfway through brushing his teeth. She reached for him and no more words were spoken. She kissed him, tasting the toothpaste. John took her into his arms and led her to the bedroom. It could not be stopped now. She was suddenly and ecstatically free; free from fear and inhibitions as she experimented for the first time what she had imagined so many times before. John took his tracksuit top off and threw it on the bed. She looked at his body, fuelling her desire.

She gently slipped back her dressing gown and then let

it fall to the floor. The sight of her naked body brought a gasp of admiration from John. He led her to the bed, and threw off the rest of his clothes. She had never seen an erect penis before and was momentarily fearful. But her apprehension was overcome by her desperate desire. John lay on the bed beside her and gently stroked her body. He rolled on top of her.

"Are you OK?" he asked.

She nodded back, not speaking. He guided himself inside her. The pain that she felt caught her by surprise and she pulled back a little but then wrapped her legs around him, pulling him on to her. They rocked back and forward before John groaned and rolled over panting, with his eyes closed and his arms by his side. Saida was still unfulfilled. John leaned over and tried to bring her to a climax before she took his hand away. She felt afraid and somehow guilty. It wasn't as she had imagined. John gently stroked her hair.

"I just couldn't help it. I've waited so long and I love you so much. The moment overcame me." She carefully put on her nightdress and slowly walked to the door. John held her tightly,

"Please don't be disappointed. It will get better." She held him close and then slowly walked away. When she reached her own room she lay on the bed still with the thought of his body. She slowly stroked herself, feeling her breasts and slowly moving down between her legs. She had done this many times before and this at least was not a sin. The sensation shuddered through her body and she lay back, panting softly. As the moment passed she started to cry. Her sense of guilt growing, she knew she had to carry out the ritual purification before she could pray to Allah. Filling the bath, she washed every part of her body several times. She prayed to God and slowly started to drift into sleep. A thought troubled her.

What if she was pregnant?

A tear ran down her cheek and she prayed to Allah for forgiveness.

PART TWO

CHAPTER SEVEN

Habib Sanussi gazed into the fire of twigs. The embers were slowly dying away and he could feel the chill of the Sub-Saharan desert on his bare arms. It was late evening and he was alone with his thoughts. He felt a growing anger inside. He stirred the embers and suddenly stood up. He knew what he had to do. There was only one path that he could follow and now was the time.

His classical Arab features and intense stare left no-one in doubt that they were seeing an embittered young man. His height, over six feet, only served to strengthen his presence as a leader. It was as a commander that he had come to this place, the Kufra oasis, a thousand miles south of Benghazi in the middle of the Cyrenaica desert.

Habib was the second son of the cousin of King Idris and had proudly kept the Sanussi name. His father, as was permitted then, had two wives at the same time and Habib had been born to the second. As such he was considered to be on the fringe of the family and had on many occasions been overlooked by the more prominent members of the Royal Family. When the King had died Habib offered his help to his cousin the King's successor, but this had been rejected.

His acquaintance with Colonel Gaddafi instilled in him the belief that he could achieve a position of prominence in the new order as a go-between for the Royal Family and the new organisation of the People's Republic of Libyan States. Gaddafi however was already well down the path of embracing the old upper and middle classes and Habib again felt rejected when his overtures were ignored.

Since leaving university, he had worked as a lawyer specialising in commercial work, a career that brought him into contact with senior business leaders and government officials, not only in Libya but also the surrounding Middle Eastern countries. Like his cousin Saida, he had excelled, rising to become the chief executive of Libya's second largest bank. His education in Switzerland had given him a fluency in English, French and German, which had cemented his popularity with women of all nationalities.

He was a devout Muslim and took a traditional view of sex. Over the years, he had had several female partners but he somehow believed that women should remain true to one man. He had never found the woman of his dreams and occasionally wondered about his own sexuality when he found himself admiring the bodies of other men.

His time in Switzerland had also left its mark in another way. A motorcycle accident near Lausanne nearly cost him his life. Only the prompt attention of a doctor dining in the window seat of a nearby restaurant, in full view of the crash, had saved him. All that remained of that day now was a small scar above his left eye, and a pronounced nervous tic which appeared on his face when stressed or angry.

He'd come to Kufra to contemplate, to get away from the increasing Western influence that was invading his country. He had felt a driving need to get away and return to the nomadic roots that were the origins of the Sanussi tribe. He'd travelled the long route across the desert in his Japanese 4x4. The first thirty miles had been over rough rocky terrain that had slowly given way to smooth level sand in a featureless landscape. The route was well marked and he stuck to the track made by the heavy vehicles servicing the oil drilling rigs. Even now the occasional vehicle which strayed from the beaten track could hit an old World War II land mine and meet the same fate that had befallen the German and British soldiers seventy years earlier. Habib had no fear of the desert but respected its power. He had endured many sandstorms and he knew that one could appear at any time. As he travelled to Kufra the flat sand gradually gave way to high dunes that challenge man and machine alike. The dunes, carved by the wind, typically had a gentle slope on one side and almost vertical face on the other. It was not unusual for a vehicle to race confidently up the dune, only to somersault down the precipitous unseen slope, often with fatal consequences for those within.

Habib's 4x4 was well fitted to long journeys across the desert; the fuel tank had been enlarged and space made for extra petrol cans. Attached to the vehicle on both sides were perforated sheets of steel that could be used as sand tracks in cases of emergency. The satellite navigation system was the latest available but Habib often found himself navigating by the sun. In his youth he had spent many happy weeks in the desert with his grandfather. They visited old ruins and relics from the turbulent past of Libya, which over the centuries had been occupied by Greeks, Turks and Italians. His grandfather had taught him the ways of the desert and how to survive the heat and lack of water as well as how to grasp the gift of the occasional downpour of rain. He recalled on one occasion he had been with his grandfather when a storm developed in what seemed an instant. A tiny and innocuous whirlwind of sand suddenly became a ferocious wind, quickly followed by a deluge of rain. The area had not had any rain for over thirty years and, within minutes; wadis of water were formed, cutting paths through the sand. The storm finished almost as quickly as it came. By next morning the desert was a panorama of small green plants punctuated by an occasional flower. They all quickly died in the heat of the day but the episode remained in Habib's memory. The desert could indeed be transformed with water.

The journey had taken him three days travelling only during daylight hours. At night he would make a hollow in the sand, cover his face with his abaya and sleep soundly until the early morning sunlight woke him. He used his water sparingly. His drinking water was held in a pouch made from camel skin and hung over the wing mirror of his 4x4. As he travelled a small amount of water permeated the camel skin and evaporated giving a cooling effect to the water in the pouch.

Kufra was Habib's favourite place on earth. It was one of Libya's largest oases and three thousand people lived there. The oasis had not changed for a thousand years. Travellers from Africa and traders from Ethiopia used it as a staging post. Some had stayed and the population was a melting pot of several nationalities. The people of Kufra existed in a sort of uneasy calm. The movement of people from Africa through Chad led to a large trade in human trafficking. This brought with it criminal elements, who had little thought for human life. Rival gangs had sprung up, but even these bitter enemies would work to a common purpose, forging temporary alliances to thwart government-led efforts to stop their profitable trade.

CHAPTER EIGHT

The Great Man-Made River was an epic undertaking by anyone's standards. It had long been known that during the Ice Age the Sahara had been under water. The legacy of that time was an underground sea almost the size of the Great Lakes of North America. To tap it, and feed the cities of Libya with precious water, still ranks as one of the greatest engineering and construction feats of modern times.

The people of the desert had watched the newly-arrived foreigners with curiosity as they surveyed the dust-blown wastes with their instruments. These Europeans were the first sign of a scheme that would ultimately cost $21billion and have world banks vying with each other to fund the project. The prize lay unseen two hundred metres below the sand. The oasis was the tantalising proof it was there, if only it could be reached. And it was. The lifeblood of water now flowed throughout the country.

But Kufra had been an oasis for thousands of years and little about it had changed over time. In the customary manner, Habib sought out the leader of the small community. He was met by an elderly man in traditional robes, his face dark brown and wrinkled through his many years under the sun.

"Greetings Habib. Peace be upon you".

"Upon you be peace. It is an honour to meet you again", replied Habib in suitably deferential terms. Ali gestured to a seat beside him.

"Please, take tea with me and tell me why you visit our lonely oasis".

They sat down by a small fire, even though the afternoon was warm. In observance of the Arab custom of measureless generations, Ali filled a metal teapot with cold water and sprinkled in a generous amount of tea leaves. The brew was brought to the boil and after a few minutes the tea was poured into small glasses and handed to the visitor. After traditional pleasantries had been exchanged, the teapot was put to the fire again and mint was added to the brew. Glasses were exchanged by one person to another and a second heavily minted brew poured. The exchange of glasses and drinking from the glass just used by the host was a gesture of confidence and it was essential that the guest drank all that was offered.

He had on occasions performed the ceremony back in Benghazi whenever he had European visitors. He enjoyed seeing their slight reticence at drinking from the glass of their neighbour; a reticence he had taken advantage of in later negotiations. Ali waited until Habib had finished his second glass of mint tea before he asked why he was in Kufra. Habib hesitated and chose his words carefully. This was a crucial moment for him and he needed the support of Ali if his thoughts were to be turned into action.

"Ali", he began, "I need your wisdom. I need to have my mind made clear and I may need your help." Ali looked impassive and took another sip of his mint tea. After a pause Ali said

"Before you tell me your dilemma, let us rest and pray to Allah and we will meet again tomorrow". He immediately appreciated that Ali wanted to take time and probably find out more about him before he was prepared to offer advice. Habib returned to the tent he had erected at the northern end of the oasis. His first instinct was to pray. He turned to Mecca, kneeled and closed his eyes in hope of guidance. What message would Allah send him? Should he embark on this crusade against his fellow Libyans? His prayers lasted for over an hour. Rising from prayer, his resolve was greater than ever. That night he slept better than he had for many months. Perhaps it was the result of the long journey or the return to his roots living in a tent in the heart of the desert. But for Habib it was the blessing of Allah answering his prayers. Now he could clearly see his destiny and why Allah had put him on this earth.

The following day he met again with Ali. This time the meeting was at Ali's office, as it was rather grandly called. The old man held court in a clearing amongst the palm trees, inviting Habib to sit on a seat that left his head lower than Ali's. He had to look up into the lined and sun-beaten face. It was impossible to decide how old Ali was; he looked old but his body appeared strong. His eyes sparkled with life. It would not have surprised him to learn that Ali was in his fifties but he embodied the aura of wisdom and benign leadership of someone who was older.

"Please Habib explain your purpose and I will see if I can help you." said Ali. He didn't hesitate. He had chosen his words well in advance.

"Ali, I am concerned for our great country and the traditions that are close to our hearts. The influence of the West is eating away at our culture, particularly with the young. I feel we need to stop this decline before it is too late. I would like to show our people that there is another way. I have no political ambition. I am not a revolutionary, just a caring Libyan worried about the future".

Ali smiled a false smile. Habib's claim to have no political ambition didn't ring true, but there was some merit in what he said. He viewed the country's troubles in the same way but he had to be cautious. Within the community of Kufra he had enemies who coveted his lofty position. Kufra was about as far away from the centre of Libyan politics as it was possible to be. News from the capital was seen on television and viewed with disdain. Colonel Gaddafi, once seen as the saviour of the country, was now regarded as a pragmatist sacrificing principle for opportunity. His wooing of the West was seen by many as an opportunity to further his own self-interest. He had set up, with great fanfare, the National Government of the country with separate local government for Cyrenaica in the east and Tripoliana in the west, but the truth was that the power was held by a small group based in Tripoli and led by Gaddafi.

Gaddafi was often seen on television living in a Bedouin tent. The reality was that he continued to live the life of a king in his palace with all the accompanying privileges. This was widely known in the country. His conversion to the West had begun in the early years of the present century and was driven by revelations of his complicity in the destruction of the Pan Am flight over Lockerbie. He had offered several suspects to the authorities, confident in the knowledge they could not be found guilty simply because he, Gaddafi, knew they were not guilty. The real terrorists were well concealed inside the Libyan secret service.

The dictator was taken aback when his decoys were found guilty, and sought to make amends. The men's families were taken care of and lived a life of great splendor in Benghazi. He also funded an immediate appeal and finally all but one of the suspects were released for lack of evidence.

But the shift towards Western values unnerved many and disquiet grew in the back streets of the main cities of Tripoli, Benghazi and Tobruk. The slow increase in the number of tourists, whilst financially benefitting a few, was beginning to bring about many of the things Muslims found distasteful in the western way of life. The first McDonalds had opened in Tripoli and a Marriot Hotel had sprung up in Benghazi. Some road signs from and to the airport had English sub-titles. The final straw for some Libyans was the reopening of the American military bases on the outskirts of Tripoli and Benghazi following Colonel Gaddafi's visit to Washington. At his meeting with the President, the status of the US military was high on the agenda. Previous diplomatic meetings and secret service intelligence had identified the growing unrest in Libya and the US diplomatic service had seen an opportunity to increase the American presence in the Middle East.

Colonel Gaddaffi felt increasingly threatened and some of his previously loyal followers were even beginning to question his leadership. The time was right to re-establish the US presence and a deal was struck which gave security to the Colonel but also allowed the small presence of military advisors at a base close to the capital and in Benghazi. Gaddafi went on Libyan television to explain his visit to Washington. He was going to be the great peacemaker of the world; the man to bring East and West and the whole of Africa together in peaceful coexistence. The government-controlled press hailed their leader as a new messiah, but within the souks and suburbs it only fuelled dissent. The announcement of the renewal of the US base was limited to a small paragraph in the national newspaper, but its significance was not lost on the population.

From the American point of view, with oil at $100 a barrel, a foothold in an oil-producing country was of immense strategic benefit. Papers leaked from the Pentagon had suggested that large fields of oil were still unexplored in the middle regions of the country. The unease felt by the middle classes of Libya began to be felt, not only by the religious leaders of the country, but also by the neighbouring states of Egypt, Iraq and Iran. Conflict under the guise of religion had been the order of the day for over a thousand years but the new twist unsettled the fragile equilibrium that had developed over the last few years. Habib had begun to feel the change in the mood of the country and his time in western countries only served to confirm his worst fears.

Where once, criticism of the regime would have been unthinkable, mutterings of discontent began to creep into conversations, even within the civil service. This mood fed Habib's feeling of resentment which first took root in his early years. He could not help but feel a twinge of delight at the recent turn of events.

He started to hold private conversations with many of his compatriots and found that he was not alone in thinking the leader had lost his way. Increasingly others came to him with information and encouragement and slowly a conviction grew that there needed to be a voice raised in protest at the slow erosion of the many Libyan traditions and in particular the Muslim way of life, where state and religion were entwined to such an extent that they were indistinguishable from one another. Habib came to believe he was the natural leader of the voices of opposition.

CHAPTER NINE

He was to be the instrument of God's will. Now he prayed for Allah's guidance on how he should fulfil that destiny. Kufra, this dusty trading station thousands of miles from the centre of government in Tripoli, was a place where preparations could be made. There were men of like mind, who could be trusted. Trade in weapons flourished. Habib isolated himself, spending seven days in the desert in deep thought and prayer.

That he had to act was not in doubt. There was a need to remind the twelve members of the Brothers of Libya of the principles that had taken them to power in 1961. All that was left was to decide how and where.

He returned to Benghazi and attended to his work at the bank. But in the cafes of the city after sundown he heard the same feelings expressed. Something had to be done.

His time in Kufra had not only been spent in contemplation. He had met Aktham El-Rekaby. It had not been an easy meeting. It was widely-known that this was a man whose anger it was best not to incur. His business was people trafficking and the movement of drugs. But Habib knew he was also a man who could make things happen.

At some point in their conversation, Habib had casually invited Aktham to visit him when he was next in Benghazi. But he was surprised when, only two days after his return from Kufra, his unlikely guest arrived on his doorstep. Aktham was a small man with a gentle smile and a diffident manner. It was hard to believe he was the leader of a notorious gang of ruthless men plying their criminal trade. His main prey were migrants from East Africa and the Middle East passing through Kufra on the 'journey of hope' to the coastal Libyan cities. All routes there are under the control of well-organised Libyan-Sudanese gangs. The long and tortuous passage over the desert is made at night in covered trucks. Many are caught and sent back to Kufra, where they have no choice but to pay the traffickers or bribe police officers to start over again.

Unlike his customers, Ahtham had crossed the desert in the latest 4x4, modified with a comfortable bed in the back. With the aid of two drivers, he had made the journey to Benghazi in just eighteen hours. After checking into the Marriott's best suite, he called Habib. He was pleased to hear how surprised Habib was to hear from him so soon.

The meeting was to be at Habib's apartment, a luxury penthouse on top of Benghazi's tallest building. Aktham showered and changed into a European style business suit, his black leather briefcase matched his shining shoes and belt. He was here to do business and wanted to make clear to Habib that he was not just a Bedouin hoping to pocket a few dollars. Taken aback at the speed of events, Habib quickly called two of his closest confidantes, Nabil and Iksan. At his apartment, he hurriedly brought them up to date with his visit to Kufra and his conviction that the Colonel needed a sharp lesson to remind him of his roots. The pair were influential – Nabil, in particular, chief executive of a Middle Eastern oil company, had spent all his life as a city dweller. He had an inherent suspicion of the notorious individuals in Kufra but, like Iksan, he wholeheartedly supported the cause. They were still speculating on the reasons for Aktham's long journey, the door bell rang. The servant showed Aktham into the large living room with its panoramic views of the harbour and downtown Benghazi.

He was surprised to find the two other men waiting for him along with Habib. They eyed each other warily during the required formal introductions and drinking of tea. Aktham, with his western attire, was not what they had expected. He had been in the room only short time but already his presence had created a tension. Aktham took charge.

"My brothers, I have listened to Habib and I and many others have the deepest sympathy with the views that he expressed to me in Kufra. Can I take it that you, Nabil and Iksan, share his views?" Both nodded.

"In that case I have a plan that could further your objectives of bringing our leaders to their senses. It is a plan that will need considerable forethought and will be expensive." He waited for his words to sink in. The three friends looked at each other uncertainly. They were apprehensive and the sinister look in Aktham's eyes made them feel nervous.

He continued. "The plan, although expensive, is simple."

Nabil restrained himself from asking what he meant by the word.

"My plan would be to disrupt the Great Man-Made River project and cause our great cities to return for a short period to the old ways of preserving water and living a more frugal life".

CHAPTER TEN

It was a matter of personal pride to the Colonel that the Great Man-Made River scheme was eventually completed without financial help from the west. His country had triumphantly created the world's biggest irrigation project, despite desperate moments during the last phase in 2008, when it was threatened by collapsing walls. This had merely delayed progress, and finally the water flowed. In the eyes of the people, the Colonel had performed a miracle.

Habib took a sharp intake of breath on hearing the plan. The Great Man-Made River was the very lifeblood of Benghazi and Tripoli and any interruption would cause considerable hardship, particularly for the burgeoning middle classes who had adapted to a new way of life as a result of the plentiful supply of water.

Aktham coldly set out the detail.

"There will be a number of simultaneous explosions at pumping stations at the three main pipeline exits from the drilling platform. I suspect that new pumps could be installed within two weeks and that to our countrymen it would be an inconvenience rather than a disaster. I would guarantee that you and your colleagues would not be associated with the action, unless of course you wished otherwise for reasons of your own."

Aktham looked directly at Habib. He had already guessed that this clever man was seeking much more than a symbolic gesture to the Colonel. Habib looked away in discomfort. Nabil could no longer restrain himself .

"How much is expensive?".

Aktham paused before quietly replying.

"Five million US dollars with $2million up front."

The three men looked at each other; they knew they would have difficulty reaching that figure with their own resources and would have to involve others. There was to be no negotiation. Aktham closed his briefcase and made to leave.

"Let's consider your proposal and we will talk again" said Iksan. At the back of Iksan's mind was the fact that he was the owner of the only major supplier of pumps in the region and his brother ran a security operation that might suddenly be called upon as a result of terrorist action. Aktham spoke directly to Habib.

"I have business in Benghazi for the next three days; let us meet again then".

After Aktham had left, the three men sat down as though relieved of a burden. Habib spoke first.

"I think this is an excellent idea. This is Gaddafi's pet project –he is constantly telling the world how it was his inspiration that gave us the Great Man-Made River. If Benghazi has to cut back on its water usage then that will bring home to everybody how our old ways were developed to survive. It will give the Colonel a shock and no-one will be hurt. But five million dollars – that's a lot of money." They needed friends, friends who had both money and a strong dislike for the Colonel. The idea was fraught with danger, and the more people became involved, the more dangerous it would become. The government had an active secret service and any show of resistance to Gaddafi would be met with a brutal response. In the past several known political activists had disappeared without warning.

CHAPTER ELEVEN

The meeting was held in an anonymous conference room tucked away in the university buildings. According to the official record, the matter under discussion would be a review of the commercial future of the region, with special reference to the Great Man-Made River. Twenty hand-picked men turned up for the meeting. All had been very carefully selected as potential partners. The mood in the room was sombre but Habib was tense with excitement. The right side of his face twitched intermittently. At last he was doing what he felt was his destiny.

He stood before the group, reciting a welcoming prayer, his eye taking stock of the gathering. Most were dressed in traditional Arab costume but there was a sprinkling of European-style suits. Most of the men had facial hair, a beard and a moustache. Habib had always been clean-shaven which accentuated his strong jaw and the determined line of his mouth. The look in his eyes was that of the hunter. So much now rested on his well-rehearsed speech. Western influence was slowly and insidiously wrapping itself around Libya, like the coils of a python. When the moment came, it would strike and the victim would be dead. Heads nodded in agreement and approval. His voice rising in anger, he finished by holding high for all to see a picture of an American flag flying over a military barracks on the outskirts of Tripoli. The audience had become restless and animated and several discussions were taking place among the crowd. Habib let the conversations run for a while before once again calling for their attention. He was in no doubt that the mood provided fertile ground for the plan.

"Brothers, I think we are all agreed that something needs to be done to remind the brotherhood that first and foremost we are Muslims and Arabs. I know you are all men of peace and what I want to propose is a strike that will force Gadaffi to take notice but will hurt no-one." Habib outlined his plan to disable the three main pumping stations of the Great Man-Made River thereby cutting off water supplies to the major cities along the coast. Water drawn from the underground sea was held in great reservoirs and from there was pumped in three directions, to Tripoli, Benghazi and Tobruk. By attacking the stations after the reservoir the major flow of water would be cut off. Hardship would be mainly felt by the middle classes and businesses since many poor Arabs still used the wells and water supply that had been used for thousands of years. The loss of water would force some to return to a more frugal way of life, more in line with tradition.

His speech over, the questions started. Who would destroy the pumps? How would they get past the guards? How would they make it known that the act was not an act of terrorism but a wake-up call to the citizens of Libya?

Habib raised both hands and in a calming gesture asked for quiet.

"First I have to tell you that I have already contacted a person who has the ability to carry out this operation. He has the men and the explosives to carry out the plan – but requires five million US dollars".

Before the shocked gathering could respond, Habib interrupted and said that he would put in the first million US dollars. That would leave only one million needed to launch the attack. The balance of three million would only be paid if the plan was successful. Either of those sums would be shared equally among the twenty members.

Pride as well as belief was now at stake. No-one wanted it to be thought he not afford $50,000 and lose face. As for the rest of the payment was concerned they would deal with that when the time came. Habib silenced the babble of excitement. He called for silence again.

"Brothers, you have shown your passion for this cause, as I knew you would. You have shown you are willing to embark on this great battle in the name of all we hold dear.

"But some of you may wonder, what happens to us and our families if we fail. To you I say this. Only I, Habib Sanussi, will know the name of the one who will strike the blow. That way, no word of betrayal can harm you.

"As for you being discovered through the money you have so nobly pledged... I have a way to safeguard for all of us. There will be financial investment bonds, each for $50,000. That money will appear to go to a regional development fund controlled by my bank".

There was no time to waste. The money needed to be in the bank by the following week. He gave one final rallying call.

"My friends and brothers, you have shown great faith in me and I will not let you down. You have shown the strength of your faith and the love of our beautiful country. You must not talk of this to anyone. If you need to talk to me I will give you a special number to call that will only be used by the members. We will only have one further meeting closer to the time. We must strike decisively to tell the Colonel we are not terrorists but true Libyans with the future of the Libyan people at our heart. We need to return to our true Libyan ways before it is too late".

Already, the sharper business minds in his audience members were already thinking how they could profit from the aftermath of the attack. Tamer, whose business interests included a firm that supplied bottled water, had calculated he would make ten times his $50,000 if he had enough stock. Other minds were also thinking of the ways they would get their money back. The Libyan stock market would fall dramatically and the exchange rate would be hit. After the meeting broke up Habib took aside Nabil and Iksan.

"I must now make contact with Aktham but I do not want you to be in any danger" he told them "I have decided I will meet Aktham alone. You must trust me. I will not see him again in Benghazi, it is too dangerous. The secret police are everywhere, they will have already seen that Aktham is in town and will be watching him closely and monitoring his calls.

"I have decided to meet him in Cairo and I now need to get a message to him that cannot be intercepted. What I want from you, Nabil, is to take that message to him personally. He is staying at the Marriott in room 1208. I want you to appear to be part of room service and deliver this letter to him and him alone.

"He is here until Monday so you should choose your time

carefully. I don't think he leaves his room very often but he likes female company. No-one should see you."

Nabil felt a tingle of excitement pass. The last time that he had done anything clandestine was when he had an affair with a European air-hostess soon after he married. Secret meetings were held in her hotel room and he had become an expert at getting past hotel reception without being seen.

The message for Aktham was simple; it said "I have your money and we will meet in the Mena House Hotel in Cairo on Tuesday afternoon."

Nabil put the message back in the envelope. It had no signature or address and would be meaningless to anyone other than Aktham. Nabil left the meeting and hurried over to his office. He wanted to get the task over as soon as possible and thought for a moment that he could simply slip the note under his room door. But what if he had changed rooms or the butler picked up the note? No, he, Nabil, had personally to hand the note over. The Marriott had an underground car park with a lift to all floors. The lift was programmed to stop at the reception floor and when the doors opened the occupants in the lift could be seen directly from the reception desk. Nabil decided that was his best route and he hurried over to the Marriott. He waited close by until an airport bus arrived at the front door. The bus was full of American tourists. They had started coming in the last year since the visit of the Colonel to Washington. Nabil didn't like them; they were loud and very demanding. They had only a superficial interest in the antiquities of his country. The bus unloaded and Nabil saw his opportunity, he dashed down the ramp to the car park and pressed the ascend button. The lift was stuck on the sixth floor for what seemed an eternity before it descended, stopping at reception, making its way to the car park. Nabil jumped in and pressed the button for the twelfth floor. The lift stopped at reception and as he hoped the area was crowded with the Americans. The girl in reception didn't even look up as she tried to satisfy a huge American who was demanding the best suite in the hotel.

The twelfth floor was thickly carpeted and Nabil walked quietly to room 1208. He tapped on the door and a loud voice that he recognised as Aktham's called out

"Yes who is it?"

Nabil called back "Room Service".

"I haven't ordered Room Service."

Nabil thought quickly. "It's the Sanussi room service, Sir."

Nabil could hear movement and the door opened; Aktham was in his dressing gown, hands in his pockets, no doubt concealing a gun. Aktham quickly recognised Nabil and, after looking both ways down the corridor, closed the door quietly behind them. His hands were out of the pockets now and he looked at the unexpected visitor with a questioning look. Nabil handed over the letter. Aktham read it carefully twice.

"I cannot meet on Tuesday. Tell Habib it will have to be Wednesday and I will look forward to seeing the pyramids again. I do not travel by air as I am easily followed. I will enter Egypt by a road south of Tobruk and I am only coming if he promises me the money."

"He understands that well" explained Nabil.

"Tell him to be careful, the Secret Service is watching me. Last night they even sent a girl to my room pretending to be a hostess, so I pretended to be here to smuggle things. That was of course, after I took advantage of her."

On his way back to his office Nabil called Habib on his private number. It was answered immediately. He relayed the message from Aktham.

"Good, that allows me a further day to get the cash ready." The cash was not a problem. As chief executive of the bank he had access to substantial funds as well as his own money. He called the chief cashier and asked him to have $2,000,000 ready for Monday evening. He gave no explanation to the chief cashier of why he wanted the money but, after all, he was the boss and didn't have to explain himself. The rules of the bank and the government required anyone dealing with more than $50,000 in cash to inform the government on a special form. The cashier didn't dare ask Habib if he had filed the required paperwork. It was more than his job was worth. But the following day, afraid of the consequences if he said nothing, he decided to inform the Deputy Chief Executive of the omission. The Deputy dismissed the matter with a brief wave of his hand.

"He will have forgotten, fill one in for him". The Chief Cashier dutifully followed the instruction and the form was in the hands of the Government on Friday and on the desk of the Secret Service by Sunday.

CHAPTER TWELVE

The early flight had one great advantage. It reached Cairo before the city shook off its slumbers and became the seething, tumultuous place where millions had made their home. And it was all the better to get business dealt with swiftly

Habib had prepared for his trip. It was hard to think of a way of getting through security undetected with two million dollars in hundred dollar bills. Standing in silent contemplation, he peered at his suitcases, his mind testing each possible solution before rejecting it as too risky. Suddenly, his eye was caught by his laptop.

After half an hour with a screwdriver and a pair of pliers, he had finally prised the last of the working parts from the ruined machine. The notes just fitted into the cavity. He was travelling first class so security at Benina International would be cursory at best. But even he was surprised to find himself being casually waved through to the boarding gate without so much as a baggage check.

The taxi entered the chaotic traffic, where drivers sped along with no regard for traffic signals or pedestrians. Cairo was the largest Middle East city with a population of over twenty one million and they all seemed to be on the road to the Mena House hotel. The journey took over an hour and Habib left the taxi with some relief. The hotel stood in the shadow of the three largest pyramids in the city of Giza a few miles from the centre of Cairo. Urban sprawl had meant that the pyramids were now in the centre of a town, a development beyond the imagination of the Pharoahs who had been buried beneath them. Habib checked into a large suite in the old part of the hotel Right on time the phone rang and within minutes there was a gentle knock on the door. He opened it and came face to face with Aktham and another man he did not recognize.

Soon he was studying Aktham's meticulously mapped-out scheme. The other man had remained silent throughout, but stood solemnly behind his boss watching, ready should the need arise.

After they had talked over the plan, there was a momentary silence.

Aktham looked steadily into Habib's eyes.

"There is just one more thing; on the night of the attack I want you with me. I want to be sure that should things go wrong – say, should one of your comrades decide to betray us – then you will suffer, my friend, exactly like me. It will give us the insurance we need. We will give you the necessary training but I believe you have already served in the military forces and are familiar with weapons." Habib didn't hesitate. His thirst for action was growing.

"I will be there, but what about the Secret Service?"

"I will take care of them" said Aktham, coldly. "They have detailed only one man to follow you. They are curious about your two million dollars in cash and that is how I know you have it with you. We must find a reason why you have brought the money in cash to Egypt".

"Perhaps I will arrange for you to have a business meeting tomorrow with a company dealing in the export of

Egyptian antiquities. There is always a demand for the relics of the Pharaohs and cash is the only currency that is used. But tell me, how do they know you are carrying cash? You are the head of a bank. Surely you, of all people, can act without falling under suspicion?" Habib felt a flush of realisation and fear.

If Aktham knew, then so did others – but how? The Chief Cashier would never dare to question his boss. Perhaps the paperwork had somehow fallen into the hands of Gadaffi's agents. His carelessness could cost him his life.

Aktham spoke.

"The money, please."

Habib unhesitatingly handed over the laptop. The money was all new and sealed in transparent envelopes. Aktham didn't stop to count it. He knew that Habib did not dare double cross him. Habib was more of a politician that a soldier, a man who would send others to bear the burden of danger. Habib turned to Aktham's plan.

"Why don't we just blow up the pipeline – there are so many places that are unguarded."

"We can easily blow up the pipeline, my friend," replied Aktham "but it can be repaired in hours. Spares are available at many points along the route and the new welding methods mean that water would be flowing within less than twelve hours. I don't think that would achieve your objective. But what I am not clear about is how you intend getting your message across to the people of Libya."

Habib looked puzzled.

"Surely they will understand that we are thinking of them and sending out a message that we will not stand by and see our country fall into infidel ways."

"My friend," Habib noticed that Aktham was now addressing him in this way, "You will be seen as a terrorist; a man who has disrupted their very quiet life. Unless you are prepared, you will find that you will be vilified rather than praised. You need to be brave and at least be seen as the man who had expressed dissatisfaction with our slow degeneration into Western ways. Think carefully, my friend, because the path you are about to tread is very dangerous. You can stop now and I will take my two million dollars and you can live out your days in peace. But if you give the signal now there is no turning back. You must be ready for what will follow.

"I know your real ambition is much greater than you are saying and you should already be thinking about your next move if you really want to play a major part in the politics of our country. Finally remember you are now a marked man and the Secret Service are close by. We will meet in Kufra two weeks before the intended day and we will have no further contact until then. But you must know that I will be aware of everything you do. And if there is any indication that you have mentioned my name then I will be seeking compensation of a more painful kind administered by my colleague here." The man's face broke into a grin and with that they were gone.

Soon afterwards Habib's phone rang. It was Nabil

"How is the regional development plan progressing?" he asked.

"Wait one moment". He put down the phone and peered out of his room along the dark carpeted hallway. Satisfied, he picked up the receiver.

"We are in a 'go' position" replied Habib, suddenly feeling rather foolish that he had just uttered a cliché befitting a Hollywood movie.

"We need to have a meeting of our members in two weeks time. Please organise one at the university. Our Regional Strategy is about to take a significant step forward."

Habib repacked his case; Sherein the belly dancer would have to wait for another occasion. The Secret Service agent was sitting in the hotel lobby as Habib checked out and called for a taxi. Aktham had given him the address of an Egyptologist of questionable repute.

Still tense after the warnings from Aktham, he noticed a reflection in the taxi window of a small man getting up from his seat in the foyer. Habib instructed his driver to drive slowly in the hope that the agent would not lose him this time. When he reached the office, its formal brass nameplate at odds with the shabby textile workshops that crowded the dusty side street, he was pleased to see a taxi draw up on the opposite side of the road. The Secret Service man had taken the bait.

Inside the airless office, he was introduced to Mr Galtarossa, an Italian running a covert trade in Egyptian antiquities. Export of archaeological treasures had long since been outlawed by the Egyptian government, but a black market trade still flourished. Mr Galtarossa had contacts with a group of people whose houses stood on the sites of the palace and temple of Edfu. The Government were in the process of re-housing them so that the palace could be excavated from under the sand and rubble. But the locals were one step ahead. Many were secretly removing the floors of their houses and digging down into the palace below. Several significant treasures had been unearthed and Mr Galtarossa was an eager customer. There was a ready market for such treasures, which he was able to sell for many times what he paid the finders. Today he had been informed that a certain Mr Al Ben Ali would be calling. Habib introduced himself by that name and went on to tell of his contacts in the USA who were keen to acquire Egyptian treasures. Mr Galtarossa accepted his story readily, sensing handsome profits in prospect. As if to underline his credentials, he went into a long presentation about Egyptology, much to the irritation of Habib, who was in a hurry. His task of misleading the Secret Service over, he took his leave as soon as possible without having betrayed his complete lack of interest in the subject. Back on the street he looked around for a taxi and succeeded in getting a glimpse of his follower. Pleased with his subterfuge, he set off back to the airport turning only to see the Secret Service agent disappear into the offices of Mr Galtarossa. Habib's smile would not have been as broad had he known that the agent had noticed him leaving the Mena House Hotel without his laptop. The Secret Service knew where the cash was hidden. The decoy mission hadn't even got off first base and Habib was already in more danger than he could possibly imagine.

CHAPTER THIRTEEN

"I intend"...Habib announced "to make all the people of Libya aware of our cause. I am going to speak out so that all Libyans have their eyes opened to the way the West is slowly taking our country away from us". Nabil and Iksan sat in silence, absorbing the impact of what he had just said. So this was the real reason Habib had asked them to his apartment, days before the meeting of members.

He had, as expected, told them of his visit to Cairo, although he made no mention of his encounter with the Secret Police. His sudden declaration now took them aback.

The meeting of the members was to be held on the following Sunday. Habib called Nabil and Iksan to his apartment. Habib went over the details of his visit to Cairo and the nature of the plan, leaving out the Secret Service part.

"I must now let my feelings be known. I intend to make a speech at the next Chamber of Commerce meeting that will make clear that I believe our slow drift into Western ways is bad for our country.

"I am telling you this as my good and trusted friends. If we stay or are seen to be friends then there may be consequences that are beyond our control." Nabil and Iksan looked at each other, bemused. They both admired Habib and had great affection for him.

They also thought he was right. Both had daughters and every day they could see the girls pushing at the boundaries of acceptable female Muslim behaviour. Habib explained that, without some statement from him, the attack on the Great Man-Made River would be seen as a random terrorist action and that was why he had to speak out publicly.

After the attack an announcement would be made to Reuters by the Libyan Muslim Front, giving the reason for the action. Suspicion would inevitably fall on him because of the speech he was going to make. He had no choice but to be present during the attack. He would need an alibi. The two men hesitantly agreed.

The meeting of the Chamber of Commerce was set for the first day of August, a month before the anniversary of the revolution. Habib rehearsed his words very carefully. He needed to show his commitment to Libya and his faith in the state. He intended to refer to Gaddafi's Green Book, the equivalent of Mao's Little Red Book and the written embodiment of the dictator's doctrine. The Green Book had been personally written by Colonel Gaddafi in 1975 and outlined his thoughts on democracy. It proposed that democratic rule is best done through popular committees. Colonel Gaddafi describes this approach as a republic ruled by the masses. There are no political parties. Each member of the myriad committees is free to express his opinion of every subject and feed then to the General People's Committee. Over 600 local People's Committees pass information and views to the General Committee. Gaddafi has the power to control the outcome of the process. The Benghazi Local Committee included several members of the Chamber of Commerce and Habib was certain that they would be reporting back to the committee. That meant that in a very short time, Habib's views would be widely known. Word of his intentions had spread, and the speech was eagerly awaited. The ears of the Secret Service missed none of it.

The meeting was held in the vast main Chamber, its walls clad in carved cedar and adorned with messages from the Leader and Guide of the Great Revolution. The room was dominated by a huge crystal chandelier with a speaking platform placed directly beneath it. Habib had dressed carefully for the occasion in his very best pure white traditional abaya. He wanted to be seen as a true Libyan. When the time arrived for him to speak the room was full and a feverish air of anticipation gripped those within. Habib, aware that all eyes were on him, slowly walked to the centre of the stage, smiling and waving to friends and acquaintances. The room became silent. Habib waited for a few seconds before speaking.

"My friends and brothers, peace be upon you. Blessings also be upon the leader of our country, our brother Muammar Gaddafi. May God continue to grant him wisdom."

It was not long before the tone of his address changed. His condemnation of creeping Westernisation, the lack of respect shown by the young and, above all, American military power, was met with murmurs of approval.

They grew louder as Habib became more impassioned. He had the audience with him and he knew it. His fist punched the air with each call to the service of God's will, a gesture echoed by cheers from those listening.

The tumult of noise reached its crescendo. He sat down in centre stage. The light from the chandelier cast a shadow over his face that gave him an almost god-like appearance. He waited for the applause to subside before raising both hands in the air, his palms outstretched.

"We must all do what we can to send our message to our Great Leader and I will lead the way if you want me to". There was a roar of approval; Habib smiled, he felt he was on his way. Even as he sat down the Secret Service was transmitting his speech to Government headquarters and plans were being put in place to remove what was considered to be "an irritation" by Central Office.

CHAPTER FOURTEEN

Over the next few days Habib prepared himself for the defining journey of his life. It would take him to Kufra, and to Aktham.

The elevator doors slid open with a chiming sound and Habib found himself face to face with his deputy Mohammed Aktar, soberly dressed in a navy blue suit.

"Ah Habib, I am pleased to see you. I wanted to wish you well for your period of leave".

Habib thanked him as he stepped into the now empty elevator. As the doors closed, Aktar turned around just in time to be heard.

"And don't worry – I'll look after everything".

Aktar silently rejoiced. He was hoping that Habib would get so involved with politics that he could replace him. He was also furthering his career ambitions by sending a regular dossier of Habib's movements to a certain man introduced by a local official, who had promised him his efforts would be rewarded with the grateful thanks of the Leader himself.

The time arrived for him to journey to Kufra and as planned, he called his two friends. The cover story would be that they would be going into the desert on an Islamic retreat to contemplate and to refresh their religious zeal. In fact, after the first night Habib would journey alone to Kufra and meet Aktham.

The three men set off, at first down the coast travelling west, before turning south into the desert. The track was a well-worn one, due to an endless stream of vehicles taking supplies to the oil rigs. The rough rocky terrain had been levelled by the passage of immense trucks pulling equally immense trailers. The oil rigs were thirty miles or so from the coast. Leaving behind them the bleak steel edifices with their clusters of cabins, the desert track soon became fainter and eventually gave way to a few poles, kilometres apart, acting as guides. The three were making for the tiny oasis of Ledra, a place made up of an ancient mosque and a few buildings left by the Italians. The people of this part of the desert were few and far between and the oasis was mainly a transit point for travellers. They found Ledra without difficulty and set up camp on the outskirts of the oasis. The sight of such lush greenery in the middle of the harsh desert always amazed Habib. He mused on his mission, his reason for being there. Water. Deny it to people and like the fragile desert plants, they perish.

Having set up camp, they made their way to the mosque for evening prayers. Only three other people were to be seen in the cool interior and none gave a second glance to the rather shabby figure, alone and bent in humble submission to his god. As the sun rose the next day, Habib said goodbye to his two friends and set off in his 4x4 across the desert travelling south-west on his way to Kufra.

Nabil and Iksan settled down for a long week ahead. They were prepared to support their friend but both men were beginning to have some apprehension about their own safety. During the next morning the man they had seen alone in the mosque the previous night approached them and exchanged friendly greeting. He introduced himself as a communications officer for the government. Nabil and Iksan knew perfectly well that this was a euphemism for an agent of the Secret Service. To their alarm and astonishment he proceeded to tell them exactly what they had been doing for the last forty-eight hours, who they were and why they were in Ledra. Feelings of panic mounted in the two men, for clearly they were being watched by the most feared instrument of the Gadaffi regime.

"Brothers, you have the chance to leave here free from suspicion but before you do you must tell me what are the intentions of your friend Habib." Nabil and Iksan looked at each other for an answer, but only succeeded in underlining their plight. They had a strong loyalty to Habib but clearly the game was up.

"We have no idea where he has gone" stuttered Nabil, his mind now racing with the potential consequences of this dangerous friendship. Iksan nodded in agreement.

"We came here to contemplate our god and to refresh our souls. We do not know where he has gone or why."

They spoke with little conviction. The agent looked in deep thought, as he held them in his searching gaze. He could question them further or he could believe them. Either way they now knew that the Secret Service was tracking their friend Habib.

"Have you prayed to Allah today?" the agent asked them. Both nodded unable to speak, minds racing, as the certainty of what would come next dawned on them.

The agent shuffled in his abaya as if looking for his wallet. Swiftly bringing the pistol up to shoulder height, he fired directly at Nabil, who reeled backwards, frozen in terror and shock. In an instant, as Nabil awaited the second shot, he saw the pistol drop from the would-be executioner's hand, his gaze pointing sightlessly skywards as he slowly tottered forwards, as if about to break into a run. The dead weight fell onto Nabil with a faint moan. Blood seeped from the back of the agent's white abaya. Iksan looked around, fear written across his face. He could see nothing apart from a small herd of cattle grazing by the water of the oasis in the distance. Not a single human in sight. Nabil struggled to free himself from the limp body, and then, still shaking, began to search himself for the damage the bullet had wrought. A flesh wound on the arm, no more! Iksan pulled the dead agent off Nabil, quickly pressing his thumb on the entry point of the bullet that had so nearly killed his friend. Fortunately it had gone straight through the flesh. It was obvious that the Secret Service agent had been hit just before he pulled the trigger on Nabil. He could not possibly have missed from such short range.

"Let's get out of here fast, I'm okay." urged Nabil in a determined voice. Iksan tore the red and white head dress from the agent and used it as bandages for the wound. He carefully helped his injured friend to their 4x4.

"To hell with our belongings; we need to go, now" and with that the Nissan's wheels spun in the sand, gripped and sent them on their way back to the track and home to Benghazi. In their panic to leave, neither spotted the slight movement in the top of the palm trees nor the man slowly descending, a high velocity rifle slung over his shoulder.

CHAPTER FIFTEEN

The sun was now full in the sky. The small scavenging animals that ventured out in the hours until dawn came had scampered for cover. This was the land where armies clashed in 1941, the European tank crews cursing the searing heat that proved as great an ordeal as the terrors of battle.

Now it was silent except for a cloud of dust from a lone vehicle that ploughed relentlessly on. But Habib too was a creature of the desert. Settled back in his driving seat, he was well-prepared for the long haul to Kufra, with enough water and fuel to last him for days.

He thought about his two friends who by now would have finished morning prayers and would be on their way into the oasis to bargain for fruit and bread. They would have a chaste few days in the desert remembering their roots and refreshing their vows to Allah. Dusk came suddenly and Habib stopped in a small valley of sand dunes. He settled down for the night and fell asleep beneath a clear sky crowded with stars. The moon was full and the 4x4 cast a shadow. Habib lay in the shadow but found it difficult to sleep. Tomorrow he would arrive at Kufra and his training would begin and in two week's time, he would be back in Benghazi with all the consequences of water rationing. How should he react? Should he plan another speech at the Chamber of Commerce? If he was ever to get to the heart of Government now was the time. He drifted off into a deep restful sleep

The following day his mind was brought back to the present as Kufra appeared on the horizon. He could see the remains of the old Italian fort and the adjacent disused aircraft runway. He had arranged to meet Aktham at the old fort and was surprised to see his 4x4 waiting well away from the oasis. Habib stopped so he could see the driver's face. It was Aktham's partner whom he had met in Cairo. A grin and a wave of recognition indicated 'follow me'. The track led around to the south of the oasis away from the land that had been cultivated using giant moving arms that produced a circle of irrigation water. Eventually the vehicle in front stopped by a white painted house on the outskirts of town. Aktham stepped out from under the shadow of a palm tree and greeted Habib with a kiss on each cheek and a hug.

"Greetings, my friend, welcome to my home"

Habib stepped inside. It was dark and cool with carpets on the floor and some utility furniture scattered around the room. Three doors led from the main room and he guessed these must be bedrooms. Aktham settled into an armchair and motioned for his guest to do likewise. Aktham's partner also sat down and was introduced as Mohammed. Habib gave Mohammed a nod of greeting to which he responded with a large grin, showing his white teeth and wrinkling the scar down his left cheek. Habib just couldn't work out how he felt about Mohammed. On first meeting he had been threatening but now seemed almost childlike in his expression. Aktham picked up his confusion and went on to speak of his high hopes for their plan. Mohammed nodded and Habib realised he had yet to hear the man speak.

"We start tomorrow." Aktham spoke in a quiet tone. "We will make sure we all know what we have to do. I will introduce you to my hand-picked assistants and we will see if you are up to speed in using an automatic weapon." Habib started to protest that he had no need of carrying guns but the look on Aktham's face told him he was in no mood for debate on the matter.

"After that we will go over our plans in detail. Our weapons are due in tonight and a light aircraft will land near the fort. The weapons have come from Iraq and they are the most up to-date-Russian equipment, unlike the British who seem to have to make do with antiques."

Having gone over the outline plan, Aktham invited Habib to stay with him. He was shown to a bare room with a single bed in one corner. Water was available and a scrubbed clean shower cubicle could be seen off the bedroom. It was not quite up to the luxurious standard of his apartment in Benghazi but better than sleeping under the stars for a third night.

That evening the three men sat and talked about their lives. Aktham was part Egyptian and had a university education. Mohammed was of Nubian descent and still had the short curly hair typical of men from that region. He had fought as a mercenary in several countries and had met Aktham while serving in the Sudan.

Aktham, although very well-educated, had a difficult time in the Libyan army. In particular he had been treated very badly by American soldiers when he had been working with them during the Middle East crisis. He had been beaten up several times and he confided in Habib that his determination to force the elimination of the Americans from Libyan soil was another reason he had decided to work with him. Mohammed had also had a difficult experience with the US military but all three agreed that individual Americans whom they had met had all been friendly and generous.

"It's the politicians we have to blame", Habib blurted out, before realising that his own greatest ambition was to be a politician leading his country back to its heritage.

That night Habib was restless. He thought about his family and about his cousins, Ridi and Alisha living in Benghazi. Ridi had attended his speech at the Chamber of Commerce and afterwards had warned him of the dangerous path he was taking.

"Be careful, we may live a long way from Tripoli but the Colonel's tentacles are long and sharp." Habib thought about Ridi and Alisha's daughter, Saida, who was in the USA. She was the most beautiful girl he had seen and he regretted not letting her know that before she left for America. He he'd had his opportunity at her leaving party when she took time out to say goodbye to him and gave him a European style kiss on both cheeks. Habib fell asleep thinking perhaps one day if she ever comes back home I will tell her how I feel even if I am older than she is.

CHAPTER SIXTEEN

The Libyan Secret Service agent was due to report back to his divisional headquarters in Benghazi two days ago following his trip into the desert tracking Habib. No word had been received. The division's commander ordered an immediate investigation. It was not long before reports were coming in which revealed Nabil and Iksan were back in Benghazi and that Nabil was being treated in hospital for a serious arm injury. An informant in Kufra had sent a message telling of unusual activity around the area. An aircraft had also been seen landing on the disused airstrip. The informant had seen several men unloading heavy wooden boxes that had been whisked away under close protection. The registration of the plane indicated that it was from Iraq but there was no trace of a flight plan for that day.

The head of security called a special meeting of his most senior colleagues. The last thing he wanted was to have an incident in his territory. Around the table the opinion was clear. If there was indeed some strike being planned then it would be aimed at either the oil pipeline, the water distribution system or the US military bases. The department was put on alert and the army ordered to increase security at the oil wells and the reservoirs. A small contingent of troops was sent to guard the vital points of the Great Man-Made River. The following day the Leader of the Peoples' Revolution would be giving a nationwide broadcast and a public holiday had been declared. The streets would be full. Anything could happen.

Habib woke on the day of the planned raid. He prayed, imploring Allah to speed him on his mission. He was convinced that he was acting in accordance with God's will. His mission was a just one. By reminding the Libyan people of their past he was putting his life at risk in their interests. He donned his combat suit and looked at himself in the mirror, turning to take a side profile. Yes, he looked the part of a Leader of The People. Yes, he could lead the country to its rightful place. Yes, he could do it. Aktham walked into his room without knocking and caught Habib admiring himself.

"Thinking how you will look on the new Libyan currency, are you?" asked Aktham rhetorically and laughed. He had toyed with the idea of telling Habib about what had happened to Nabil and Iksan but decided against it. Tonight he wanted everyone's mind on the task ahead. Aktham's spies had already reported that the guards had been doubled and that several helicopters had been landing supplies at the Great Man-Made River Terminal, one hundred miles north of Kufra. Aktham briefly considered whether Habib might be involved in forewarning the authorities. Had he told his friends about the plan? Had they passed on the information? He put the thought aside and decided not to challenge him. Instead he put his arm on his shoulder.

"Are you nervous, my friend?" It was an unnecessary question. He was sweating and the nervous twitch had returned.

"Tonight I want you to stay by me. The plan is simple.

We enter the three compounds that contain the big sulzer pumps and we place charges around both the inlet and outlet valves. We will also put charges onto the main compressor and the generator. The detonation will be triggered by radio signal from my telephone and all three stations will blow up simultaneously. You and I will immediately start back to Benghazi and you will take your place the following day at the Chamber of Commerce where you will give the speech of your life."

"What about my friends? They may still be in Ledra." asked Habib.

"No they won't. I can assure you they will be in Benghazi cheering you on. More important, when our task is done I want you to think of only one thing. Remember, for your sake, to have the three million dollars ready. And finally, my friend, this mission is dangerous. The Secret Service already has its suspicions and your alibi may be seen through. We should expect some resistance to our work. If we do we must think of the higher cause and do whatever is necessary. Do you understand?"

Habib nodded, dreading the thought that he may have to kill people – good Libyan people – to achieve his dream. He held his gun with the barrel pointing to the ground, hoping he would never have to use it. As daylight turned to dusk, the small convoy of trucks moved out of Kufra towards the three targets. Another group made for the giant reservoir with the aim of creating a diversion by cutting the electricity cables to the main control centre. The timing had to be perfect. After ten miles the groups split and went on their separate ways to the target.

Aktham had chosen to take the centre pump only five miles from the main control centre. He had to allow time for the others to reach their destinations before he could enter the pump compound. They rested for a few minutes. There were five in Aktham's group, all experienced soldiers ready to do whatever was necessary. The dusk turned to night and the two vehicles approached the pumping station as near as they dared without being overheard. They travelled without lights but the moon gave ample light for them to see the pumping station in the distance.

"We walk from here" whispered Aktham.

The team picked up their weapons, all of which had been muffled. The slightest sound travelled a long way across the desert. The team moved silently in single file, Aktham leading with Habib close behind. Habib felt his breathing rate increase and sweat was still pouring down his face even though the evening was cool. As they approached the pumping station two of the team broke away and made their way to the back of the guard house. The two guards were chatting and smoking and enjoying the cool of the evening after a hot day. The raiders were now so near that they could hear their conversation on the night air. The first two team members carefully cut through the wire fence and crawled into the compound, pulling their explosives and weapons with them. They knew exactly where to put the charges. At the same time Aktham and Habib entered the compound from the opposite side. They planned to place their charges directly under the generator that ran the compressor and pump. The plan had allowed that this would take no more than five minutes. But the generator was in direct sight line with the place where the guards were standing. The sound of a phone rang in the guardhouse; both guards sprang to alertness up and went inside. There was a heated conversation between the two men and the caller and Aktham took his opportunity; the diversion was working. He quickly placed his charge onto the generator, checked the detonators and slid back to Habib.

"The charges are in place. We must now leave quickly." As the last word left his mouth banks of security lights around the perimeter of the station blazed into life. The two guards saw them immediately, shouting warnings as they lifted their rifles. But Aktham was quicker. A swift burst of automatic fire and they were cut down. Immediately a group six others appeared from the guardroom, firing wildly. They could make out the two raiders, now scrambling across a moonlit stretch of desert. They were sitting targets. In an instant there was a cascade of gunfire. Habib turned, expecting to see one of the defenders inflict the fatal blow on him. Instead he had a momentary glimpse of a guard falling forwards amid a cloud of dust. Aktham's other team had done their work. They had worked their way behind the guards and unleashed a murderous volley of fire.

In the silence after the last shot rang out, Habib could hear his heart pounding in his ears, his breathing rapid and wheezing. Was what had just happened real or a dream? And then, the realisation. At least eight men are dead because I, Habib Sanussi, made it so. It was only then that he felt the pain in his leg and the stream of warm blood that was staining his combat trousers. The team all reached the vehicles. After the noise of the firearms, the silence was deafening. Aktham looked at his watch; thirty seconds to go. He counted down and then sent the signal through his phone. The response was instantaneous. With a massive rumble and a cloud of debris flung high into the night sky, the charges detonated. The explosions could be heard thirty miles away and the pump compound was ablaze. Nothing would survive, not even the bodies of the guards and soldiers. The three team members quickly reached their 4x4 and were away, going south back to the obscurity of Kufra. Aktham got into his vehicle but realised that Habib, in increasing pain, was stumbling some way behind and holding his leg. Aktham ripped off the trouser leg of the injured man's battledress. A bullet was lodged in his left leg just above the knee and he was bleeding heavily.

Aktham knew what to do. He applied a tourniquet torn from a piece of cloth to stem the blood. But he shook his head gravely.

"This wound is going to require attention, and soon. We need to get you to a hospital before complications set in."

The plan had been to drive the one hundred miles back to Kufra during the night and to disappear in the crowds of immigrants and travellers that populated the oasis. But not now. Aktham turned to face Habib. It was time he learned the reality of their position.

"I have to tell you, my friend, that Nabil and Iksan did not remain in the desert. They returned to Benghazi only hours after you left. They had been followed by the Secret

Service and were about to be shot but one of my team took care of the man who was about to kill them. The Secret Service agent is dead so whatever they told him will remain with him. Unfortunately the shorter, fatter of your friends got a bullet in his arm. They drove off before we could reach them and no doubt they would have to find a hospital. Anyone going into a hospital with a bullet wound will be questioned by the police and we can be sure it will not be long before they are being questioned by the Secret Service."

Habib's sense of dismay was absolute. Not only had his friend been placed in mortal danger but at least eight innocent men had died. Aktham could read Habib's feelings.

"It is too late, my friend, the journey has started. There is no going back."

Suddenly Habib felt faint and very weary. Aktham gently eased him into the back of the vehicle and placed a pillow under his head, still unsure what to do next.

"My cousin is the senior surgeon in Benghazi; he will help and keep our secret" groaned Habib "if we could get to him he will hide us until we can travel." Aktham thought about the nine hundred miles crossing the desert; they would be sitting targets for the security forces. Travelling only at night would take days and could be very dangerous.

"We'll go back to Kufra and I will somehow get a plane to land on the airstrip. We could land on the outskirts of Benghazi at the old military airbase and your cousin could pick you up from there. I will leave from the airport, so make sure my three million dollars are waiting."

With that Aktham slid into the driver's seat and turned south. He drove until early dawn and arrived at Kufra just as the sun was rising. He made Habib comfortable as best he could. A fever had begun to set in and the last thing Aktham wanted was for Habib to die. At least, not until after he had got his money.

Aktham found some of his men in a small coffee shop in the heart of the town. The operation had been almost a complete success; all three of the pumping stations had been destroyed, at the cost of two of their comrades who had died in gun battles with the guards. It was clear the security forces had anticipated trouble and from the strengthened forces that defended the compounds, seventeen soldiers had been killed. The Colonel was already on radio and television denouncing the terrorists and telling the world that they would be hunted day and night until caught. Water rationing was instigated in Benghazi and Tobruk. The American military saw its opportunity by flying in extra troops in what was portayed to the media as an aid effort to the Libyan government in finding the criminals who had perpetrated this crime against the people. The draft of extra units would also ensure 'stability' in the region.

On the morning after the explosion, a letter was found at the offices of the Libyan Peoples Star, the official government newspaper. The letter claimed that responsibility for the attacks lay with the Movement for the Return to Muslim Standards and demanded the removal of Americans from Libyan soil. As it was, the raids had only made the American position stronger. The US base near Benghazi was teeming with activity. Within days the routine stop and search operations were being carried out at check points in the city by a joint force of Arab and American soldiers.

CHAPTER SEVENTEEN

The darkened, smoky interior of the coffee house in Kufra echoed to the murmurs of men growing increasingly restless. All wanted to get their pay-off and go. Aktham calmly reassured them. The final three million dollars was in a Swiss bank and it only required Habib to send a fax to release the funds to an Egyptian bank. But for that to happen, they had to find a way of somehow getting him secretly back to Benghazi where he could authorise the transfer. Aktham's contacts were many and he was a man who could get hold of anything, if the price was right. Soon a light aircraft was on its way from Sudan.

The small group of men waiting by the dusty half mile of desert that passed for an airstrip heard the aircraft before they saw it descending through the heat haze. When it taxied to a halt, Aktham marvelled that the aircraft had got there at all, never mind landed on a makeshift desert runway. The pilot appeared to be half drunk. He was unshaven and already smoking a cigarette as the door opened. He appeared to be European but was so dishevelled that it was difficult to tell.

Habib was gently placed in the rear of the plane and Aktham and Mohammed climbed aboard. The engine had been kept running. and without further comment or ceremony, the pilot threw the cigarette end through his open window and spun around for take-off. The flight path took them due east into Egypt then followed the border north. The flight plan had shown that the plane was flying directly from the Sudan to Benghazi and the quicker they returned to that schedule, the more chance the diversion would not be discovered.

The radio crackled as they approached the old military base airfield south of Benghazi. A voice heavy with interference uttered something inaudible, prompting the pilot to fiddle with the dials. The stricken city of Benghazi could be clearly seen. Habib peered down at it, the city he had deprived of the water it needed to exist and he wondered what suffering his action had caused to the people there.

A few small light aircraft stood forlornly by a rusting old corrugated sheeting hangar. No movement could be seen on the ground. The plane came to a halt, money changed hands and within minutes Habib, Aktham and Mohammed were standing on the potholed tarmac. Habib's fever had abated a little but still he couldn't walk without assistance from both his companions.

Habib used his cellphone to call Mohammed Ridi Sanussi. Although he had not seen him since since his speech at the Chamber of Commerce, he knew Ridi had some sympathy with his views. The phone rang but there was no answer; Habib tried again but still no answer. The three men stood on the tarmac under the shadow of the rusting old hanger.

"We must get you to a doctor" insisted Aktham. The cellphone rang. It was Ridi.

He greeted his cousin warmly. He had always been fond of Habib and watched his rise into the highest circles of the bank with great pride. He knew well of his ambitions in politics.

"I've been hearing that you are out of the country, where are you?"

"I'm actually here in Benghazi with two friends and I need a little help."

"I'll help in any way I can, what can I do?" replied Ridi. Habib held his breath; the pain from his leg was excruciating.

"I need you to come to the old military airfield and pick me and my friends up. Perhaps we can come back to your house and we will tell you why we need help."

Habib took another heavy intake of breath; he felt dizzy and his head was pounding. "I should tell you" continued Habib "that I am under suspicion as far as the Government is concerned and there is danger. They may be watching your house. You must take precautions when you leave to make sure that you are not followed." Ridi hesitated, deeply uncomfortable at what he had just heard. Here was a close member of his family in need but this was far more than just "a little help".

"I'll do my best but where are you?" replied Ridi equivocally.

"The old airport – I've already told you", Habib regretted letting irritation rise in his voice but the pain was now making him feel sick.

"OK, I'll be with you in twenty minutes. I'm driving a black Mercedes 500 and as I arrive at the entrance I will flash my lights twice to show that I am sure I am not being followed and I will wait for you at the main gate". Ridi found himself whispering as he spoke, for no good reason. There was no-one else in the house. Alisha was due to return from an international legal conference at any minute and he had been looking forward to spending a quiet night with his wife.

He switched off all the lights in the house and checked his water tank. Whilst the explosions north of Kufra had forced the rest of the city's population to queue for rationed water supplies, to the Sanussis the interruption was merely an inconvenience. He had, several years ago, installed a thousand gallon tank in the roof space of the house. But elsewhere in Benghazi the effects were being felt. Restaurants had closed, some industries reliant on water were slowly cutting back and the hospital was battling against the ever-increasing risk of infection.

Checking constantly in his rear view mirror for any signs of being followed, Ridi drove slowly to the airfield along backroads. Part of him was still reluctant to become involved at all. If he was caught in Habib's company he would be guilty by association with terrorists. It saddened him to think of the short space of time it had taken for him to be transformed from respected banker in the city to a wanted fugitive. Ridi could not have known quite how desperate Habib's position was. In the short time since he had left for Kufra it had become widely known that he was allied to the terrorists who had gone on to blow up the Great Man-Made River. His acquaintances had taken to denying their friendship with him as word spread. The deputy at the bank had wasted no time in alerting the authorities to an unusual transaction. One of its most senior and respected men had moved several million dollars within the last three weeks. It did not matter that it had been apparently Habib's own money. Within hours the arrests started. The men who had bankrolled the attacks were early targets. Under interrogation some were trying to convince their captors they been duped into thinking they were investing in a major public development project.

Ridi approached the airport from a side road normally only used by commercial vehicles. The road behind him was clear. He turned the corner and drove towards the rusting old hanger. He gave the signal and from out of the shadows emerged three figures all seemingly wrapped together. He made out Habib in the middle with two others holding him up with their arms around his waist and shoulders. All three were in battle dress suited for desert warfare with automatic weapons slug across their shoulders. Ridi had a sinking feeling in his stomach and regretted finding himself in this situation. He shied away from personal involvement in politics and even harboured a quiet admiration for Gadaffi. Life had been good for the Sanussis under his regime, and the leader often supported his hospital and its charities. And yet Habib was family and Ridi had aways admired him for his strength of character and leadership qualities. A leader yes, outspoken yes, but a terrorist? But here he was, armed and in bloodstained combat clothes.

The two men gently placed him in the rear seat of the Mercedes. There was scant time for introductions and all four men got into the car. Ridi drove onto the main road. Here he felt more relaxed, reassured by the sight of other cars. He was just like any other traveller. Unseen behind the gate, two men watched the car leave and turn towards the city. One quickly used his cellphone to relay the news that, yes, the plane had landed, three people had emerged and they were now on their way to the city in a Mercedes 500. The man rapidly quoted the car's registration number that he had written down. Both men smiled at each other. It had been a good day's work – the chief would be pleased.

CHAPTER EIGHTEEN

Private James Toomey came from Albany in upstate New York. An unexceptional high school student, he was seen by his peers as somewhat of an awkward and introverted young man, not comfortable with girls. He spent most of his time pursuing his overriding but solitary passion, reading military history. It came as little surprise to his family when he decided to join the army.

To his undisguised delight, he was accepted by the crack 4th Infantry Regiment, with its distinguished battle history which earned it the nickname The Warriors, and made it the natural choice for deployment to the front line in Afghanistan. The posting pleased him immensely. Like every American, he had felt the shock waves of 9/11. He felt privileged to have the chance of settling the score with those who allied themselves to the perpetrators. Toomey, to his disappointment, was only three days away from leaving on the tour of duty when his Company was reassigned to Libya.

Inside the guardroom a handful of Libyan soldiers were watching football on television while four Americans drank beer, smoked and talked about their sexual conquests. Visits to the local brothel had been banned by the American commanding officer but the warnings about the potential for disease had been lost on the young GIs.

Toomey took no part in the conversation, sitting impassive on the edge of the group, a Budweiser bottle in one hand, a book on the American campaign in Iwo Jima in the other. His comrades viewed him with a mixture of apprehension and curiosity, and knew him as a man of few words.

The drinking had got out of hand. Alcohol was banned in most of the city and the guardroom was one place where the GIs could drink without local constraints. The Libyan soldiers looked on with a mixture of disgust and envy. The GIs, with an average age of twenty-two, were certainly well-equipped in comparison with their newly-found Arab allies. Armed with the latest automatic weapons and communications devices, they cut very different figures from the Libyans, with their old Russian rifles that often malfunctioned or were rendered impotent by bullets occasionally supplied without detonators.

The clerk burst breathless into the room and called to the senior Libyan soldier to answer a call from the National Security Service. The young corporal walked over, rather puzzled to the phone. He, like the clerk, had never heard of the NSS. The chief was in no mood for niceties.

"You are the nearest unit to a location where a known terrorist is believed to be hiding. I want your full strength at the D'Aosta house immediately", he barked.

"Our orders are to be at the roadblock in an hour Sir," he protested.

"This is a matter of the highest national importance and if you do not obey my orders you will suffer for it. Now get down there and let me take care of the roadblock" yelled the Chief.

As he spoke, Sergeant Jim Polizzo, the American sergeant sauntered into the room wondering what the fuss was about. The corporal handed him the phone and the chief slipped into English with ease.

"We have located three men who were involved in the terrorist attack on the Great Man-Made River. They have just arrived in Benghazi and we believe that he is presently at D'Aosta House. They are armed. But there must be no casualties to your unit and the Libyan soldiers you will take with you. It is they who must make the arrests, not you. Is all of that clear?" The sergeant almost saluted; the voice on the other end of the line possessed a degree of authority that he immediately recognised as that of a senior officer. Polizzo responded with a vigorous "Yes, Sir" and put down the phone. He turned to the group of soldiers who had been watching events intently. "Fickey, Bramah, Swindells, Toomey, get your weapons and let's go".

"That's now, Fickey!" he screamed at one GI who was slow to react. He motioned towards the Libyan soldiers.

"OK guys, get your weapons and follow me. We are going a-hunting." The senior Libyan corporal climbed into the American sergeant's jeep and the convoy of three vehicles left the barracks with a squealing of tyres. For the men inside it was a relief to be doing something useful at last, after the inactivity not helped by alcohol, which had fuelled a relaxed undisciplined spirit.

"Hey Toomey", said Bramah, "looks like you're gonna get some action, like you're always reading about in those books".

"Aw, let 'im be John," Swindells cut in. Toomey stared straight ahead and said nothing.

Polizzo stopped the convoy under the shade of high palm trees and climbed out of his Jeep stern-faced. He was unimpressed by the young GIs recently sent out from the USA. He'd seen service in Iraq and Afghanistan and knew how situations could go from being very relaxed to very dangerous in a few seconds. He often had a mental flashback to his days in Iraq when his best friends were blown up by a roadside bomb simply because they dropped their guard.

Polizzo was six feet tall and shaven-headed with tattoos of his active service campaigns on his arms. When angry he was a formidable man and the look on his face alone as he climbed down from his jeep was enough to silence the men. Even the Libyan soldiers stiffened and looked down at their boots. He spoke in a quiet voice, a complete contrast to his demeanour.

"Listen up and get real. This is for real now. This is a mission where I will not accept anything less than professional behaviour." His words were delivered without the usual profanities of soldiers.

"Now check your weapons; ensure that all safety catches are on but that you are ready for trouble. If this guy is a terrorist he will be well-prepared and we must be ready. I don't want any trigger-happy bastards taking out anything that moves. We want to take these men cleanly. You open fire only if I give the order. Clear?" Polizzo glanced at the men gathered around him, looking at each one, directly in their eyes. Nobody was in any doubt who was in charge.

A heavy silence fell amongst the men as they climbed

back into their jeeps. They had about a mile to travel, the last stretch of which was up a long drive lined with king palm trees. They travelled without lights. The only sound that could be heard was the crunch of the jeep wheels on the gravel drive and the barking of the wild dogs that forage around the city outskirts.

The squad left their jeeps halfway down the drive and formed a line with the sergeant leading and the senior Libyan Corporal in the rear. They stepped off the gravel drive and onto the carefully-tended grass. Polizzo was surprised to see this was clearly the home of a wealthy person. There must be some security to overcome. He held his hand up and the line came to a halt. The house was now clearly in sight with most downstairs lights on and one light upstairs. Maybe they are thinking of going to bed. It was already 11pm.

His plan was clear. They would go to the front door with warrant of authority from the Libyan government. Radio messages told them the house was owned by Ridi Sanussi and his wife, Alisha. They had three children and at least one, Saida, was working in the USA.

CHAPTER NINETEEN

Alisha's homecoming had not been quite as she had expected. She found her husband tending to the bullet wound of a relative, with two strange armed men in the house. Still feeling stunned at the story that had unfolded in the past few minutes, she looked on as Ridi cleaned and assessed Habib's wound. It might need surgery. The bullet had left a long gash as it passed through the back of the knee. Without x-rays Ridi couldn't tell if the bones were damaged and hospital was the only choice for a proper diagnosis and treatment. Habib had recovered a little from his fever and after a few painkillers began to feel that he could talk. Aktham and Mohammed had remained silent throughout the car journey from the airport and even now offered only small polite conversation with Ridi and Alisha. In their view it was up to Habib to explain the reasons for their being together. Alisha hurried about getting something for them to eat and the usual cup of tea was served within minutes of their arrival at the house.

"We need shelter for just a few days and I need to get my knee sorted out. I'm sorry to impose on you, my cousin, but I had nowhere else to go." explained Habib, and introduced his two companions. Aktham, for all their travels, still looked clean and smart. His polished voice and well mannered ways seemed out of sync with his battledress. The automatic rifle was still slung over his shoulder. Mohammed gave a small smile when he was introduced but didn't speak; his eyes were watching the windows. He felt vulnerable and he frequently crept towards the door and peered outside.

Ridi read his mind; "The whole area is covered by alarms. We have television surveillance and alarms on all the doors and windows."

Mohammed was not convinced and took a place to one side of the main window where he could get a good look down the long gravel drive. He didn't have long to wait. An alarm sounded, security lights came on and the soldiers at the front of the house could clearly be seen on the grass by the gravel drive. The GI sergeant stepped from the shadows, his semi-automatic at the ready. His men had already slipped into the shadows and were making their way around the back of the house. Ridi stiffened at the sight of the American soldier walking up his drive, gun at the ready, making for the front door. Ridi quietly signalled for Habib and his friends to get under cover. Alisha quickly ushered them into a back room and through a door into the garage. They could not risk these men being found in their house. If they could only get them out of here quickly, they might stand a chance. Hurriedly, she gave them the keys to the car and showed them how the automatic garage doors operated. With the soldiers attention diverted they could escape down the drive. Just pray that the jeeps were not blocking the way.

"We need to move. The authorities know we are here and who you are. We are putting the lives of the Sanussis in danger. We must go and go now." Aktham's voice had changed. He was in no mood to hear dissent. Habib limped towards the garage and lay down in the back seat of the car. Aktham took the driver's seat and got ready to start the car.

The sergeant and Ridi faced each other through the door's glass panel. He smiled reassuringly at the doctor, who slowly and cautiously went to open it. The moment of calm was short-lived. They both froze as another alarm sounded, followed seconds later by a crash. At the side of the house, Bramah and Fickey had tried a door, triggering the siren. In panic, they reacted by breaking the door down with their rifle butts. Fearing ambush from the shadows, both men opened fire as the shattered door fell open, spraying the interior with bullets, and bringing down a cloud of plaster dust.

Both Ridi and Polizzo froze at the sound of gunfire only yards away inside the house. Ridi, gripped by terror, turned away from the door and fled, calling Alisha to run, run for the stable yard, anywhere away from the shooting. The sergeant shouted after him.

"Mr Sanussi, no! Please stay where you are!"

Barely able to see through the dust, Bramah momentarily glimpsed figures running for the back door, but had no time to level his rifle. "Targets heading for rear stable yard. Stop the bastards, now!" he yelled down the radio.

Toomey was covering the stable yard. His training had all been to prepare him for this moment, and he shouldered his weapon. As the door thumped open, he fired two rounds at the white clad figure running towards him. The man fell, mortally wounded. A scream, and seconds later another figure, the second terrorist, was framed in the door. The muzzle of his rifle spat flame as he unleashed four shots. Alisha Sanussi was dead before she hit the ground.

The three other GIs heard the shots and were on the scene in seconds, just in time to hear the car roar away over the garden wall. They found Toomey, his gun by his side, pointing towards the ground, staring open-mouthed at the two blood-spattered bodies by the doorway.

"Hallelujah Toomey, you got 'em. Scratch two terrorists" whooped Fickey. Seconds later Polizzo was on the scene. He looked aghast at what he saw.

"Oh you assholes...you trigger-happy stupid assholes. You've just killed the wrong people. I said no shooting".

Toomey continued to stare at the bodies, unable to speak as the realisation of what he had just done slowly sank in.

"You've probably fucked up the whole American plan for this country. How we going to explain that we've just shot two of the most important people in the country and let the real scumbags get away?"

In fury, he drew back his fist, ready to punch Toomey. Swindells restrained him. But his anger was uncontrollable. "What we gonna do? What we gonna do, huh, smart guy?" he screamed at Toomey.

When he finally relaxed and began to calm down, Swindells released his grip. Thinking fast, he weighed up their predicament in silence for a full minute, then spoke.

"OK, now neither me nor any of you want to get busted by a court martial., right? 'Cos that's what's gonna happen if we tell what went down here. You wanna do time and be remembered as the soldiers who screwed up a whole theatre of operation? Then go right ahead, it's your ass on the line.

"And it's not just Toomey who's gonna be all over CNN News. They're going to ask about who started shooting first". He looked at Braham and Fickey. "We'll all get busted, and big time.

"So I'm gonna file my report to the CO. Only it's gonna say we were covering everywhere but the stable yard. And those three terrorists must have shot these two to stop 'em talking. When we got here, this is how we found 'em. So that's how I'm filing my report. And if anyone asks you, you say that's how it was. Ok?"

The men looked from one to another, each nodding his head. Toomey's expression remained unchanged. All eyes were on him. They heard the approaching sirens of the Libyan police. Finally he too nodded his head.

CHAPTER TWENTY

"You can get up now".

Aktham spoke quietly and calmly to the two figures lying prone on the rear seat of the car. Aktham used his cellphone. "I need a plane and I need it now" he insisted, his voice controlled but firm. The response on the phone appeared ambivalent.

"I need it now. Find one." With that he pressed the end button and, not speaking, concentrated on his driving. He had decided he was going back into the city where the traffic was still busy. It would be the best way to avoid the checkpoints which by now would be on full alert.

Aktham's cellphone rang and he answered, listened but did not speak before ending the call. He swung the car around in a screeching u-turn and drove at high speed back to the old airport. The street lights finished and the long straight dark road was lit only by the car's headlights. There was little traffic and no sign of a checkpoint. The car bounced over the rubble and stone-strewn road that led to the airport. The three men hadn't spoken, all lost in their thoughts of what would happen next. The airstrip was deserted. No plane on the tarmac. Aktham lowered the car window. In the distance he could hear the drone of an aircraft engine. He turned and spoke.

"Mohammed, help Habib to the end of the runway. I'm going to get rid of the car. If anything happens, don't wait for me."

With that he drove off. The two men stood in the dark, Habib supporting himself with his arm around Mohammed's shoulder. The pain was easing. The plane was now very close and the strip was illuminated by the lights of the Mercedes parked at the end of the runway. The plane drifted in. It was the four-seater they had arrived in only a few hours earlier. One of Aktham's friends had managed to contact the pilot before it had left Libyan airspace and had persuaded him he had enough fuel to return and pick them up. The plane came to a sudden halt close to Habib and Mohammed. The door shot open, the engine still running at high revs. They scrambled in and seconds later Aktham appeared, breathless from running down the airstrip. He jumped in and straight away the plane was taxiing and turning to face the direction it had landed. There was no time to go to the far end of the runway to take advantage of the slight wind. The engine roared and seconds later they were airborne.

Habib leaned back against his seat, eyes closed. Two months ago he was a leading figure in the Libyan banking sector and now he was a fugitive with a damaged knee. He suspected, from the volley of shots they had heard as they fled, that two of his family members had been harmed or worse. A wave of bitterness swept over him. His hatred of all things American rose up within him. There were now to be no half-measures, no symbolic gestures. He would now seek to destroy the American presence in his country by any means possible. Sleep didn't come easily but, overcome by weariness, he fell into a deep sleep and he dreamed of entering Tripoli an acknowledged leader with cheering crowds and the green flag of Libya flying over his new headquarters. All Aktham could think about was how he was going to get his money.

PART THREE

CHAPTER TWENTY-ONE

Life was looking good for Saida Sanussi. These past few months had been the happiest of her life. Her work on hurricanes had established her as a world authority in her field and won recognition in the media and academic circles alike. But above all, her love for John had made her feel complete.

Mercifully, she was not pregnant after the brief overwhelming passion had overcome her beliefs and conscience.

It had been the one time she lost control. They understood that their bond was now deeper, and it could not happen again. Not, that is, until they were married.

Although they had yet to announce it to the world, they had decided to spend the rest of their lives together. Their love could overcome anything.

Indeed, plans were already in hand and John's mother had to be restrained from unilaterally arranging the wedding of the year in Dallas. Of course there would be at least two weddings and possibly a third in Benghazi. They would have a ceremony in the grounds of the Willliams' house and there would be services according to both Christian and Muslim rites.

It would be more than just a wedding. The status of the families decreed that it would be a symbol of healing and reconciliation between conflicting faiths, a message of hope to the world at large.

Saida's mother and father were already booked on flights

and there had been much discussion of the importance of rituals. The Islamic way of marriage still required the groom to give a dowry to his wife and the wedding was viewed more as a legal contract than a religious ceremony. The bride's father had to sign the contract in front of two witnesses on the night before the wedding and in more traditional Islamic weddings the celebrations didn't take place until after the marriage had been consummated. For Saida none of these rituals mattered, she just wanted to be with John.

She smiled again as she thought of John studying Islamic Law and finding out that he could have four wives. Saida had to inform him that few men ever took up this option and, in his case, it would be life threatening if he even thought about it. Saida and John laughed together about many of the things that could arise from their different religious backgrounds.

John had been spending increasing amounts of time away from Miami. His star was rising in the bureau and his advice was being regularly sort by senior officials in Washington. His latest trip had taken him to the House of Representatives for a meeting on climate change. He was due back today and Saida had promised to meet him at Miami International Airport that afternoon. The thought warmed her as she slowly awoke, relieved that it was a Saturday and so no need to hurry to get ready. It was going to be another beautiful day in Miami and the weather from there to Washington was set fair. The plane would be on time and they would have that delicious moment when they first caught sight of each other and waved and kissed as if they had been apart for months, not just four days.

She let out a sigh and a yawn as she rolled to the edge of the bed and sat up. She planned her morning: she would have a shower, get dressed in her new casual jeans and t-shirt, have a light breakfast and go shopping for food for dinner that night. She was dining at John's apartment and knew that he, like most bachelors, would have a refrigerator that was empty but for a few bottles of beer. Perhaps tonight they would have a typical Libyan meal of lamb and vegetables, accompanied by couscous bil-Khodra, a combination of tomatoes, carrots, jalapeno and garbanzo beans topped up with a small amount of chilli pepper. John no doubt would want a glass of red wine with dinner and dessert would have to be something sweet to suit his American tastebuds. Saida sat on the edge of the bed and took off her cotton nightdress, throwing it back on the bed. She was completely naked and as she stood up just as the phone rang.

It was her elder brother Abadallah. That he should call at this time alarmed her. That something was seriously wrong was confirmed by the tone of his voice. She would never forget the words.

"Saida, my dear sister..." There was a short silence, his mouth unable to speak the words.

"Mother and father are dead. They were killed by terrorists in their home last night. You must come home immediately. We are having the funeral tomorrow afternoon, we need you here."

No. It was a mistake, a dream. Not her parents.

She felt immobilised, rooted to the spot, unable to speak. Silent tears started to run down Saida's face as she listened to her brother. She asked few questions, what was there to ask? They were dead, shot by terrorists but for what reason? Abadallah waited to gauge Saida's response but all he could hear was her breathing.

"I must go now; I have many things to do. Let me know when you are coming." Saida put the phone down and slumped on the bed. Slowly she uttered a moan which gradually gave way to a scream of anguish. Tears flooded down her face. She sobbed and looked again at the telephone. How could her world be shattered in such a few seconds?

Her mind raced. Burials in the Middle East take place almost immediately after death. In this case perhaps it may be delayed while the police investigate the murders. She desperately wanted to tell someone but there was no-one. John would be already at the airport.

Saida found herself pushing clothes into a suitcase. The direct flight to Tripoli was from Atlanta with Delta Airlines. She had to get to Atlanta. No time for checking reservations, she would take her chance. She pulled on the clothes that she had intended to wear to meet John. She closed the suitcase only half packed. If she needed something she would buy it, she reasoned. No time for notes or explanations. Throwing her baggage in the car, she began a journey that would bring dark clouds over countless lives.

The Delta terminal was jammed full of passengers. Saturday was a popular day for holiday travel. She had left her car in the Dolphin Car Park 2 and had the presence of mind to leave the ticket in the car. She would get John to pick it up later. In spite of her distress Saida's logical mind remembered to write down the parking bay and floor number so that she could let John know where the car was parked.

The big display screen showed the next flight to Atlanta was at 11.35am and it was already 10.30. She ran to the check in desk; there was still a long queue. There were only three people at the ticket counter. She stood in line fretting hardly able to contain herself as an old lady continued to harangue the ticket clerk. Five minutes passed, the woman still asking questions. Suddenly another counter clerk opened up. Saida ran forward jumping ahead of the man next in line.

"A single ticket to Atlanta, please, and a second ticket to Tripoli, Libya". The clerk looked up at the dishevelled and clearly stressed woman in front of him before scanning his computer screen.

"I can get you on the 11.35 to Atlanta but it's standby only on the Tripoli flight."

"I'll take anything you've got, first class if necessary."

"There are no seats at all on the Tripoli flight and you will have to take your chances".

The clerk printed her ticket but, before giving them to her, made a discreet mark on the top left hand side of the boarding pass. As he handed her tickets another rush of anxiety gripped her. Passport, where was her passport? Being Muslim Saida had got into the habit of carrying her passport with her. She searched her handbag; there it was and yes, it was up to date. A sigh of relief escaped her. As she walked up to security she glanced at herself in a mirror. Her hair was tangled and unbrushed; her eyes were the eyes of someone who had been crying for a long time. She looked a mess and she quickly ran her hand through her hair. At security she kicked off her shoes, removed the belt from her jeans and passed through the scanner. The official on the other side asked her to step aside and she was given a body search by a young female aide. As Saida stepped forward to retrieve her shoes another older woman dressed in an official-looking uniform asked her to follow. Saida protested she needed to catch the 11.35 and she now had only twenty minutes. The official was unrelenting.

"Please come to my office, there are questions we would like to ask you."

As if the day had not been so nightmarish already, now there was another ordeal to ensure. All her documents were examined by two separate armed security officers and Saida was questioned in detail about herself and her reasons for travel. She looked at her watch – 11.20, she had no chance of catching the Atlanta flight now.

"Okay, you may go" said the official to her relief.

Grabbing her bag, Saida ran to Gate 21. As she ran along the corridor to the gates she could see people still at the check in podium. Her heart was pounding and she arrived to see the plane had been delayed by twenty minutes; she was ok. She sat down and tears once more streamed down her face. The anxiety, stress and emotions overwhelmed her. People close by looked at the slender Arab-looking woman sobbing and thought she must be leaving her family behind. In truth she was leaving behind the only man she had ever loved and it would be many months before she saw him again in very different circumstances.

She dried her tears and took control of her emotions. For all her slender size, Saida was made of steel. Her unhappiness was slowly giving way to her determination and inner strength. She promised herself that would be the last time she was going to cry. Her only priority was to be on the 6pm flight to Tripoli even if it meant trying to bribe other passengers to sell her a seat. The Atlanta flight was called and it took off thirty minutes late. The captain's smooth voice came over the speaker system apologising for the delay but favourable weather conditions meant that they would arrive in Atlanta only ten minutes late. For the first time Saida relaxed and tried to think about the last four hours. She lifted her head with a start. John would be landing in Miami in thirty minutes expecting to see her. He would be searching the crowds for her face, calling her cell phone and her apartment. He would worried and puzzled. She was the most reliable woman he knew; he would fear the worst. Saida reached for the phone located in the back of the seat in front of her. The phone worked with a credit card and Saida used her American Express to slide through the side of the phone. She punched in John's cellphone number and waited. It rang but no answer. She tried to leave a message but lost the line. She sat back and felt the waves of grief turn to sleep. The captain's voice woke her with a start. Arrival in Atlanta in twenty minutes. There were four hours until the flight left and the check-in desk was unmanned. At last she had time to call John.

He recognised the caller ID and spoke first.

"Where are you? Are you ok?"

The anxiety in his voice was clear; he had been trying to contact her for two hours and was now at her apartment. The state of the room had told him something was very seriously wrong. He had searched for a note or anything that would give him a clue and had seen one of her suitcases had gone.

"Don't worry; I'm in Atlanta airport on my way to Tripoli if I'm lucky."

Calmly, she told him the entire story of her dreadful morning. He found it hard to credit that she held herself together but then he always admired her as a woman of great strength. He offered to join her in Benghazi as soon as possible.

"No" replied Saida "there is no point. I will attend the funeral and make some enquires about the future then I will come home. There will be the estate to sort out between myself and my two brothers. There is an Islamic tradition that I must visit the graves on the 40th day after death then hopefully I will return. I think we will have to delay the wedding as my family will be in mourning for a while." Saida looked up and saw the check-in desk opening up,

"I must go, John, I love you. I will call you from Tripoli when I land tomorrow, that's if I get on the plane."

With that she pressed the off button and ran to the podium. The Delta agent was shifting paper behind the desk; he didn't look up although Saida coughed without effect. Eventually she could wait no longer.

"Excuse me, please can I talk to you?"

The man gave her a discouraging look but didn't speak. Saida explained how she was on stand-by and how desperate she was for a seat whatever the cost. The agent kept his eyes fixed on the papers in front of him.

"Look at the screen", he added curtly, pointing to a large television screen above the seating area. It gave details of the seating and a list of all the names of the people on standby. Saida was second on the list. She turned back to the agent

"Are there any First Class seats available?"

"It's called Business Elite and they are all gone" he replied. Other people were gathering around the podium and the agent turned his attention to an old man waving a boarding card and asking for a change of seat. Saida looked around feeling desperate. There was nothing left to do but wait; she sat patiently as near as she could to the podium. Suddenly the miserable agent walked across to her and without speaking gave her a boarding pass. She called thanks to his back as he walked away. So he really had been listening.

The flight was called on time and Saida walked down the sky way to her seat in Business Elite. It had a lay-flat bed and soon after the plane had left Atlanta, Saida stretched out and fell asleep, mentally exhausted. The flight was thirteen hours and Saida woke just in time to have breakfast. Much as she disliked airline food she was so hungry that she ate everything before her. The man in the next seat offered her his bread rolls as a way of opening up a conversation; ten hours of the flight had passed without any words between them. Saida had no desire to talk to a stranger and even less to talk about her problems. That didn't deter him from his monologue. Although in civilian clothes, he was a major in the US Army's military police. Apparently he had been stationed in Tripoli for one year and was returning from a ten day leave. He clearly wanted to have a conversation with Saida. He spoke of his concern with the build-up of terrorist activities particularly in the east of the country. He was anxious for the security of the US military base and recently GIs had been banned from spending late evenings in downtown Tripoli for fear of violence.

There had been a series of explosions that had disabled the Great Man-Made River Project and he hinted that a gang led by a rogue senior business figure from Benghazi were thought to be responsible.

Saida excused herself from the conversation and used the airline phone to call her brother. He answered the phone in a hushed tone; he was about to go into the mosque to pray to Allah and make preparations for the funeral.

"It's at two o'clock today" he whispered "I'll send a private aircraft to pick you up from Tripoli. Just go to the business jet section and you will be shown where to go."

Saida heard the phone go dead and her mind started to think about the next few hours. She said goodbye at the airport to the American Major without mentioning that she knew all about terrorists. Some of them had just destroyed her life.

CHAPTER TWENTY-TWO

The private jet was waiting for her at the runway. It was 8.30am and she was still in her jeans and t-shirt. The only clothes suitable for a funeral were at the D'Aosta house and she had no desire to go there until the police had finished their investigation. She called Abadallah's wife, Fatima, who was a similar size to Saida and would have some suitable clothes.

Her brother was waiting with a limousine at Benghazi. As they embraced, Abdallah was overcome and the sobs shook his body. But Saida remained tearless. She had cried herself to the point where there were no tears left. Maybe it would be different at the funeral.

The car took them to Abadallah's home and before long Saida was donning her black dress and head scarf. As she dressed, atavistic feelings became strong in her. She was an Arab again. The USA seemed far away and even her thoughts of John very distant, as if they belonged to a past time.

It is the Islamic belief that forty days before death , a leaf on which the name of the person who is to die falls from the tree beneath the throne of God. Izra'il, the angel of death, then visits the dying person, paving the way for them to enter either heaven or hell. When death is imminent the body is placed on its right side and the first testimony – 'there is no God but Allah' – is whispered in the ear. None of this had been possible for Saida's parents and it was therefore necessary for a special service to be held.

The bodies of Ridi and Alisha were brought from the funeral parlour where they had been carefully wrapped in clothes. As decreed by custom, they had been washed and cleansed, Ridi by his sons and Alisha by Fatima. During the cleansing process Fatima took special care to clean Alisha's wounds. Alisha was a beautiful woman and the attack on her had not affected her facial good looks but there were vicious wounds where bullets had torn into her. She removed Alisha's jewellery. When the time was right she would give it to Saida. The bodies were placed, not in the coffins normally used in the West, but on open tiers carried by relatives of the family. The women walked behind. At some funerals women were occasionally hired to actually cry and wail but no they would have no need of them for this occasion. The Sanussis were one of the most popular families in the city and hundreds of mourners turned up. The funeral procession reached the gates of the cemetery and only the men moved forward. The wailing and crying abated and Saida followed the cortege several steps behind. The bodies were carried by male members of the family and as they stopped by the grave side Saida whispered to Fatima

"Where is Habib? He truly loved Ridi and Alisha." Fatima replied in a hushed tone.

"I will tell you when the two days mourning are over. We need to explain to you what has been happening here since you left home."

The Imam had now reached his position to say the final ritual before the bodies were placed in a deep burial chamber with shelves on either side. The head of Ridi was placed towards Mecca as the Imam looked on. Alisha's body was placed so that it rested alongside her husband, but further away from the Imam.

The priest recited the Salat ul Janazeh, the prayer for the dead, three time, first with his hands raised high above his head, the second time he was joined by the mourners and the third a silent prayer for all Muslims. With the bodies in the grave each mourner threw three handfuls of soil into the grave carefully avoiding the bodies and saying a silent prayer before departing. Saida threw her three handfuls of earth into the grave and walked away. She had not shed a single tear all day and her overwhelming feeling was of anger. How could terrorists strike down two wonderful people and what were they doing in the D'Aosta house anyway? Her mother and father had no enemies, certainly none as a result of politics, in which neither of them was active. They supported Colonel Gaddafi but also genuinely embracing benevolent ideas to all mankind. They had rejoiced at the news of Saida's impending marriage to an American and a non-believer.

The inner core of the family made its way back to the home of Abadallah and Fatima. The mourning would last for forty days after death. The sombre mood of the house was relieved only by the pleasure with which the other members of the family greeted Saida. Many had not seen her for five years and commented on how mature she seemed compared to the nervous young woman to whom they had said farewell at the Berenici Hotel. Saida, still puzzled over Habib's non-attendance at the funeral, waited until she was alone with Fatima before she broached the subject again. Fatima was reluctant to speak about it, which only made her even more curious.

Two days later Abadallah and Fatima invited Saida to their house. They told her of Habib's increasingly outspoken condemnation of the direction the country was taking and it seemed the arrival of American soldiers in Tripoli and Benghazi had been the last straw for him. Habib had appeared to be neglecting his work at the Bank, and had taken to going on frequent trips out of the city. They were not sure where he was but they knew that at one point he had been to Kufra. Abadallah waited for the news to sink in before coming to what he had to tell her next.

"I am sorry to have to tell you, Saida, but the authorities are certain the terrorists who shot our mother and father were led by Habib."

Saida was quiet for a moment, her eyes widening in amazement. She stood up angrily, her voice raised.

"It's not true! I know it cannot be true. Habib loved my mother and father! They were close friends. How can you let people say these things?" She turned and glared at Abadallah.

"Surely you don't think that it's true?"

He looked back at her, holding her resentful gaze. He knew his sister well but had not seen this defiant look before, combined with an anger of a kind that was not appropriate for a woman to display towards a man.

"What would you have us do? Habib is in hiding, he has not come forward to defend himself. All of the television news bulletins show pictures of him. The Chief of Police says they have witnesses that confirm he was there and there are finger prints that show at least three people had entered the house. The rear door had been broken down."

Saida looked down for a moment then with a look of defiance she stood up.

"It is not true and I am going to prove it's not true no matter how long it takes or how much money I have to spend. The police have finished with the D'Aosta home and I am going to move back there and then I'm going to find Habib."

Her brother understood how she felt. He also found it hard to believe that Habib had shot his mother and father or even let others do it. What was the purpose? It certainly didn't help the terrorist cause, whatever that was. It had angered the local population and there was even talk of the Americans using it as an excuse to set up a further camp in Benghazi to help fight terrorists. But the facts seemed clear. They had wildly speculated that Habib might have been held hostage. After all the Sanussis were one of the wealthiest families in Libya. Saida embraced her brother and his wife and said her farewells.They could find her at D'Aosta house if they needed anything and in the meantime she would find out the truth about Habib.

CHAPTER TWENTY-THREE

The D'Aosta house was as she remembered it; tall and elegant with a dark cool interior in contrast to the hot sun. The police had removed their barriers and the house looked remarkably untouched. The entrance hall was clean with no sign of the shooting. The back door had been repaired. All trace of the attack had been removed even down to the painting of the wall that was pock-marked with bullet strikes. Strange, thought Saida, a concern for such detail was not the normal behaviour of the Benghazi police force, although the chief of police was a family friend. Saida checked through the house. Nothing had been disturbed. Her emotions nearly overcame her when she entered her parents' bedroom but her newly-found inner strength stopped her short of crying. That night she lay in her old bed and thought of all the happy memories she had of this room and this house. Nothing would ever be the same; it was now a house of unhappiness. Saida let her mind range over the things she would do over the next few days. She would go to Habib's apartment where she knew the janitor well and getting in wouldn't be a problem. Then she would go to the bank and see what his assistant had to say. She racked her brain for the names of Habib's close friends and eventually remembered Nabil and Iksan. They, if anybody, would know where Habib was. Yes, she would check with them tomorrow. Suddenly she remembered John. Was it only three days since she left the USA? She hadn't called him and he would be worried.

It was now 11pm in Benghazi; 4pm in Miami. She called John's number at the bureau. His secretary Amanda answered. John was out of town at a meeting in Boston. He would be on the early evening flight back to Miami later that day. Amanda suggested that Saida should call him in an hour's time when he would be at the airport.

"Fine. Please tell John I've called just in case I miss him later. And tell him I'm OK".

Saida undressed and climbed into bed. She decided to read for an hour and then call John. Stretched out on the bed, she flicked through the Benghazi newspaper. A short paragraph mentioned the funeral and referred to the obituaries that had appeared the previous day. Still clutching the newspaper, she drifted off to sleep, exhausted. When she awoke the lights were still on but dawn was breaking. She had missed her phone call and decided to try again later that day before falling back into a fitful sleep until a loud knocking on the front door woke her up. The caller was none other than the Chief of Police. His driver waited in the sombre black official police car outside the front door. Saida donned her dressing gown which reached the floor covering all her body, leaving only her hands and face visible. The Police Chief removed his hat as he entered the house.

"My respects Miss Sanussi. We, like you grieve for your honoured parents and share in your sadness. They will be remembered as great Libyan patriots". His speech had clearly been rehearsed and his excessive formality sounded awkward.

She invited him in. After some small talk over a cup

of coffee, she decided it was time to get to the reason for the visit.

"Miss Sanussi, it is hard for me to tell you this, but I cannot fail in my duty. All the evidence points to your cousin, Habib Sanussi and two others breaking into the house and killing your parents. The security forces went to the house as quickly as they could but it was done. They saw that the men had stolen your father's car. It is little comfort, but I can assure you their pain was not prolonged. They died quickly.

"I see. Which security forces were the first to arrive?"

"It was the southern area detachment, the duty sergeant and two soldiers together with four American soldiers. They drove here to try to protect your parents when it was learned the terrorists had occupied the house".

He paused, took a sip of coffee and thought before he spoke. Clearly there was something else on his mind.

"Tell me, Miss Sanussi, have you heard from any of the family's servants since you have been here? As far as we are aware, only Laila the cook was in the building at the time, and she was asleep in her room in the servants' quarters. We have been trying to trace the others in the hope they might be able to give us more information about the killers. But it seems they are in such fear of Habib and his gang that they have gone into hiding".

Saida shook her head.

"If you do happen to hear from any of them"... He reached into his top pocket for a card. "Please call me as it might help us catch these murderous dogs more quickly. And tell them we will protect them from any threats by terrorists".

After the Police Chief left, Saida's mind began to turn over what she had learned. For some reason she was feeling uneasy about the explanations she had been given. It was hard to imagine Habib breaking into D'Aosta House. And he had the greatest admiration and love for Ridi and Alisha. Surely he would never lead assassins to their home.

It also troubled her that the house had been cleansed of any trace of the incident. On the other hand, Habib had disappeared and had been giving impassioned speeches about a return to Arab ways. She was certain he would have been unhappy with the presence of American soldiers in Libya and she had always felt that he believed he had a greater destiny than that of a banker.

Saida dressed in her more traditional clothes and made a note to call John at 7am US time, 2pm Libyan time and then drove to Habib's apartment. The janitor was all deference and smiles and didn't hesitate to take Saida up to the fourteenth floor. He opened the door for her and recounted how the police had already searched the apartment and removed some items in cardboard boxes but he wasn't sure what was in them. The janitor left and Saida closed the door behind him. It was a beautiful apartment tastefully furnished. She didn't know what she was looking for and simply walked around looking from time to time at the splendid view of the harbour. She saw the many photographs of her family scattered around the room. Saida left with no other clues and now more than ever convinced that she had yet to hear the whole truth.

Perhaps she would find out more when, as arranged, she met Nabil and Iksan at a small café close to the harbour.

She arrived early and sat with a coffee musing over the last twenty four hours. A woman in full traditional dress brushed past her, spilling her coffee. She looked up in surprise. The street was not busy and there was plenty of space to pass. Barely had she turned to remonstrate with the woman than she had gone. Saida looked at the stain of dark brown liquid on the paper tablecloth. It was then she noticed a folded note on the table. She waited until the cafe owner had wiped up the mess and returned inside, then opened the note.

Please come to the old Post Office in Friendship Street tomorrow night after prayers if you want to know the truth about what happened to your parents. Please come alone. Ensure you are not being watched. My life depends on your discretion. Trust me. I swear before Allah this is no trick.

It was unsigned.

She folded the note and placed it in her bag just as Nabil arrived. She was surprised to see his arm in a sling. Iksan followed minutes later. Nabil bent a little closer to Saida.

"We must be brief. We are probably being watched".

"I don't understand. We are old friends, meeting again. What is wrong with that", she asked, puzzled.

"Let me tell you about Habib and then you will understand my fear." He went on to recall the meetings at the Chamber of Commerce and Habib's visit to Kufra. He told how, whilst trying to set up an alibi for Habib, he had been shot by a Secret Service agent who had then been killed by an unknown gunman just as the agent was taking aim at his head. Since then he had had little contact with Habib but knew from police questioning that Habib was a wanted man. The explosions at the water pumping stations had caused great hardship in the cities and towns. Water was being rationed and, contrary to Habib's plan, the attack was being looked on, even by the poorest Libyan, as an unacceptable act of terrorism.

"Please, before you go, tell me how I can reach Habib," Saida implored.

"He could be anywhere, probably out of the country," replied Nabil. Or he might have returned to Kufra, where a man can more easily disappear", he said. "And now we must go".

They looked around the street to see if they were being observed then went their separate ways.

Saida was left alone with her thoughts. It looked as if the unthinkable had really happened. A member of the family had murdered her parents. If that was so, she would first be sure beyond doubt. Then she would have revenge.

She looked at her watch; the bank would be closing for two hours at 1:00pm. That would be a good time for her to see Habib's deputy, Mohammed Ajid. She called and received the reply she wanted. He would be delighted to see her at 1:30pm. When Saida arrived she was ushered into a large office with panoramic views of the city. She recognised it as Habib's office.

So they have decided he is a killer and wiped away every trace of him, replacing him with this irritating little man.

Ajid was all smiles, transfixed by the sight of this

stunningly beautiful woman of great intelligence. How he would like to have her as his wife instead of the rather large lady who was the mother of their three children.

He explained that for the last three months, Habib had not been his usual self. He had gone missing on several occasions and had drawn $2million from his own personal account. He had not explained his actions to anyone at the bank and in fact had not reported his bank withdrawals in line with government currency rules. The cashier had no option but to report the matter and as there was no explanation forthcoming from Habib. The bank, with great sadness, had taken a decision to remove him from his position.

His bank accounts had been frozen but not before a further $3million in cash had been withdrawn from the development bond account. Saida couldn't help but feel that the deputy was quite content with the turn of events despite all his protestations of concern. Ajid was now the chief executive officer of one of the most powerful banks in Libya.

CHAPTER TWENTY-FOUR

The phone rang ten times before a drowsy voice answered.

"Hello, it's me". John was instantly alert, sitting up in bed.

"I was just dreaming about you. How are you? When are you coming home? What about our wedding?"

"Slow down!" said Saida "First of all, I love you and I'm missing you but there are things here that I need to sort out. How are you?" John could hardly contain his excitement.

"I've been asked to join the Government Climate Change Committee as a permanent member and we will be reporting directly to the Senate. The President is a liberal and I think for once someone in the White House believes we are changing the climate. It means I will be in Washington an awful lot but I'm sure that I can arrange for you to be with me. I think I might even get to meet the President."

Their conversation continued back and forth in the excited, playful way that lovers talk when they are apart. Eventually tiredness brought an end to their conversation but they vowed to call each other every day no matter what the time.

Saida put the phone down, laid back in her chair hands above her head. She stretched and shrugged her shoulders. What should she do now? Her mind had been completely distracted by her call with John but the harsh, gnawing reality of her parents' death would not go away. She was officially still in mourning but the thought of spending the rest of the day doing nothing didn't appeal to her. There was much to do in the house and both her mother's and father's clothes needed to be cleared. She wandered down to the bedroom and looked in her mother's wardrobe. The dress that Alisha had worn on the night of Saida's leaving party was hung neatly along with a glittering row of designer clothes. Her mother always took advantage of her trips to Europe and the USA to buy the latest fashion. Saida opened her mother's jewellery safe; the three string pearl choker necklace was still there with its antique diamond fastener as were the gold and diamond rings she had collected over the years.

She gave little thought to the money she was about to receive in the wills, which were to be read the following day. Wealth meant very little to her, perhaps because she had never been poor. Of greater importance was that in twenty more days she would be going back to the USA and life would return to normal. That night Saida lay in bed and her mind drifted back to D'Aosta House. Abdallah and Fatima should have it, to keep it in the family like an heirloom, preserving her family memories for the next generation.

She had to find Habib. There had to be an end to this, one way or another. If he was indeed the killer everyone said he was, he would surely not hesitate to kill her too. Even in their childhood days, she knew Habib's feelings for her extended beyond those of a cousin, recalling an occasion when she was only thirteen and Habib had tried to put his hands on her. They had been out riding. He had helped her down from her horse and his hands had slipped up her dress and in between her legs. There had been other occasions when he had made clear his desire for her but to Saida he was family. Saida's girlfriends all thought that Habib was wonderful. His handsome good looks, his easy manner and man of the world demeanour made for an extremely attractive man and no doubt, unbeknown to Saida, he had seduced more than one of them.

CHAPTER TWENTY-FIVE

Saida and her brothers gathered at the lawyer's office at the appointed time. There was family business to attend to despite the events of the previous day, which had left her shocked, torn between the different stories, not knowing who to believe.

Neither she nor her brothers had a clear idea how much money her parents had. She knew that she had never wanted for anything and that both her father and her mother worked for fulfilment rather than for money. Tradition dictated that men were entitled to a greater share of inheritances than women. But Saida's mother had always believed in a more equal role for women in Islamic society.

Saida didn't even know if there was a will. The family lawyer had simply called to ask her to attend a meeting with her two brothers. The offices were in an old building in downtown Benghazi. The senior partner Mr Parvezi had been a family friend and the family lawyer for three generations. He knew them all well and greeted Saida warmly.

When Saida arrived her two brothers and her sister-in-law were already seated around a large table in a room surrounded by hundreds of books on shelves. Tea was served. The old lawyer coughed as a way of starting the meeting and carefully laid out several papers on the table. His clerk deposited several boxes behind him on the window ledge and then left. The lawyer coughed again and in an official tone read out the agenda.

"We are here to read the last will and testament of Mohammed Ridi Sanussi and Alisha Sanussi. The wills were drawn up not anticipating that they would die together but the law states that, in circumstances where both parents die together and there is no clear way of determining who died first, it is to be assumed that the man died first. In this case it is not possible to decide who died first therefore the will that has the appropriate legal standing is that of Alisha Sanussi.

"However I can tell you this issue has made no difference to the terms of the settlement as both parents had decided that everything should be divided equally between their three children. There are some additional bequests to the hospital but the majority of the legacy has been left to you, their children".

The lawyer stopped as if to let this news sink in before going on to the terms.

Alisha had left some of her jewellery to Fatima.

There were bonds, shares, property and cash. In a matter-of-fact manner, he announced that the total worth of the estate amounted to roughly 1,000 million dinar, equivalent to US$100 million.

"There is of course the short term problem of the major reduction in value of the currency as a result of the recent terrorist activity but most of your shares are in Europe and the United States and the property is in Switzerland." The old lawyer leaned back in his chair. It was not every day he was called on to impart such news and he was gratified at the stunned looks on the faces of his clients. He could see Abadallah mentally dividing a thousand million dinar by three. Whatever the answer, it was a fortune.

"The question I face is how to divide the portfolio and I suggest the three of you should look at the list of assets and try to come to an agreement on the best and most efficient way to divide them up."

The trio agreed. Theirs was a close relationship and money would not come between them. The family stood up to go, thanking Mr Parvezi and assuring him he would remain the family lawyer. Saida drove back to the house confused and rather lonely. She would definitely call John when she got home. It would be very early in the morning but he wouldn't mind.

The family business was dealt with. She would now be free to return to the USA and to John. But one thing would keep her there, and that was the search for the truth.

No-one you ask in Benghazi can tell you for sure why Friendship Street gets its name. There are various theories, ranging from an old myth that it was traditionally a place of peace where no fighting was allowed through to a modern notion that it was merely a popular spot to meet.

Whatever the reason, in reality, it was just another dusty street off an unremarkable avenue near the city centre.

Saida walked apprehensively down it as the lights on the pavement cafes came on and front men came out to try and persuade passers-by to come in and sample the menu.

On one of its quieter sections was the old Post Office, now disused and boarded up. She slowed her pace, looking all around the mysterious messenger. There was no-one in sight. So as not to draw attention to herself, she didn't stop and wait, but walked a few hundred yards down the street before returning, then retracing her steps again. After ten minutes of this, only the occasional passer-by had ventured past. It was getting darker. This was a cruel hoax.

As she walked past a narrow, darkened alley, a pair of hands lunged out, stifling her scream with one hand and pulling her into the alley. She closed her eyes in terror expecting for the metallic ring of a knife being drawn, the sudden blow, the mortal pain. None came. Instead, a hushed voice hissed a warning.

"Miss Saida, it is me, Jasmin. Please do not cry out or we will be discovered. It is Jasmin. I am here to help". She released her grip on Saida's mouth.

Saida recognised her as the stable girl from her parents' house. The two had been firm friends before she left to study at MIT.

"Jasmin, what is happening?"

"Miss Saida, there is danger everywhere. I fear for my life. They have been looking for me. If they knew what I had seen, they would surely kill me..."

"What you had seen? What do you mean?" whispered Saida, confused.

"Miss Saida, I saw them. I saw them kill your parents".

"Kill them. Who?"

"I was working in the stable when they came, shouting and pointing guns. I hid behind a stable door and they did not see me, but I saw them..."

"Who? Who did you see?" said Saida urgently, her voice rising.

"Please Miss Saida, be quiet or they will find us". She paused, her expression darkening.

"It was the Americans Miss Saida. The Americans killed your parents. They shot them as they left the house, unarmed and running in fear. The soldiers were drunk. I heard them talking afterwards, and they all decided to blame it on Habib and his men. The police must have gone along with it".

"It can't be"... stuttered Saida.

"I am telling the truth. I have risked much to find you, so that you should know. I saw it all".

"Americans – drunk on alcohol? No". She fought with disbelief.

"Miss Saida, it is as it happened. There is one more thing. The others spoke to the man who fired the shots. I heard them. They spoke to him by his name. It was Tumi".

CHAPTER TWENTY-SIX

The only clue to Habib's whereabouts was that he had visited Kufra at least twice in the last two months. The small desert town was a long way from Benghazi and a dangerous place to be, especially for a lone woman. She wondered whether she dare do it. Certainly if she told her brothers they would forbid her from going but they seemed prepared to accept the circumstances of their parents' death and had not shown any desire to question the authorities any further.

There was no way that she could catch a plane to Kufra for as far as she knew the old military airfield there was unusable. She had enough money to hire a plane but that would require a flight plan which would mean that she could be tracked wherever she went. Her only course of action was to drive and the following day she bought a new Toyota Landcruiser fitted out for desert travel. She decided to say little to her family, only that she was making the most of her short stay in Libya to remind herself of the happy carefree days she had enjoyed with her father chasing gazelles in the desert. Satellite navigation and satellite telephones made travelling much easier than in the days of sun, compasses and the stars.

Saida checked the weather. It was still months before the notorious ghibli winds blew from the south creating ferocious sandstorms which brought everything to a halt. The weather would be hot in the day and cold at night. She hadn't thought about the weather for several days and she decided to look up the Miami temperature on the internet. It was 78⁰F with clear skies. February was a perfect month in Florida and for a moment she felt homesick for the US. How strange to feel homesick for another country. She called John but he was away so she sent an email to his personal address rather than embarrass his secretary with her love letters at the office. Saida spent the afternoon and early evening preparing the Landcruiser for her journey. She needed at least seventy gallons of petrol and twenty litres of water, all of which was easily stored in the rear of the vehicle. The rear seats turned into a bed and she had decided that she would sleep in the car rather than in the sand. With all that fuel on board if anything went wrong the cruiser would explode but that was highly unlikely and at least in the car she would be away from the scorpions and the cold night air. She had decided to leave before dawn and to travel west then south along the main highway towards Tripoli. The coastline west of Benghazi took a sharp southward turn and so offered a faster route into the desert. She slept badly the night before she left and decided to write a letter to her elder brother about her misgivings and how she intended to find Habib. She left the letter in the kitchen. As she couldn't sleep, she would hit the road about 4am. She dressed in a military-style camouflage suit with a white headscarf, looking anything but the young girl who had left seven years before to go to the USA. She set off down the drive on her way to Kufra, a journey she prayed would lead her to the truth.

As Saida made her way down the drive from the house two pairs of eyes watched her go. They made no attempt to follow her; the homing device they had attached to the car would do that. The sergeant turned to his fellow GI and looked satisfied. He wondered whether this was someone determined to discover the truth of her parents' death or just a young woman lost in a sea of emotions and confusion. Time would tell but he was not going to let anything come back on him and his men. He had already dealt with the military chief whose appetite for young girls made him vulnerable to blackmail and the Libyan soldiers were left in no doubt that they too would go down with Americans if the story got out. Now that the funeral was over no-one need ever know anything different. The only exceptions were considered to be terrorists who would be shot on sight.

After two hours driving west Saida turned southwards off the metalled road into the desert. The track was well worn and easy to follow even though the terrain was very rocky. The Landcruiser bumped and jarred over the rough stony ground and occasionally a rock would scrape part of the chassis. Saida knew to avoid the larger outcrops which could easily crack the sump and cause the engine to lose its oil. The petrol cans clattered together in their holding straps. She had been driving for four hours and the last thirty miles had taken her an hour. The rough land slowly gave way to solid hard sand and speeds of sixty miles an hour were now possible. The desert was so smooth and free from obstacles that she could cover the miles quickly. Her travel plan was to head south for about five hundred miles and then turn south east. That way she would miss the sea of sand with its huge escarpment and treacherous surface. The soft sand was almost impossible to traverse and it was easy to get stuck down to the hub caps in the blink of an eye. Even with sand tracks to fit under the wheels she would find it impossible to get out by herself.

The hard sand was perfect for fast driving and Saida covered two hundred miles on the first day. That night she lay in the back of the cab looking out at the cloudless night sky. A sky with no light pollution and thousands of shining stars. She saw several shooting stars as meteorites hit the earth's atmosphere. In the west they made a wish when they saw a shooting star and she made her wish. She wished that she would find the true story of her parents' deaths and later thought that she should have wished for John. Perhaps she could make another wish tomorrow night. She slept soundly and by break of dawn was already on the way following her satellite navigation computer. She had set the latitude and longitude points so that when she reached the point of turning south east the warning light would alert her. She hoped to get to that point by midday on the second day. Driving in this part of the desert was like being in an enormous saucer of sand. There were no landmarks or hills of any kind. Only the sun could be used as a guide and inexperienced travellers often found themselves following the sun and in doing so making a large arc to the west.

Saida's navigation system bleeped. She had reached the point of her change in direction. She had driven for five hours and not seen a living thing. She stopped the vehicle and stripped off her stifling clothes, pouring water over her

head and feeling the tepid water run over her body with
relief. Refreshed, she started out again knowing she would
be within striking distance of Kufra the following day.

By the third day there were signs of tracks made by other
vehicles. She was nearing her destination. She had no
plans other than to book into a small boarding house
referred to in an old travel magazine that she had found,
if it still existed. Suddenly on the horizon she could see
palm trees and the tower of a mosque and almost
involuntarily checked how she looked in the mirror behind
the car's sun visor. Her hair was tousled and uncombed.
She donned her head scarf and pulled it across her mouth
and nose leaving only her dark brown eyes visible. Within
minutes she reached Kufra and was surprised that the
dusty track that was the main street was so busy.
Vehicles, camels and donkeys all seemed to be on the
street. Pedestrians criss-crossed and there was the
occasional shout of hostility when a truck failed to slow
down to let them across. The people were of a variety of
races; Arabs, Nubians, central Africans and she thought
she saw the occasional European face. She parked the car
at a market stall being looked after by a woman. Saida
asked her about accommodation but her dialect was so
different from that of the city that she had difficulty
understanding her reply. A voice behind her interrupted
the conversation. It was a small well-dressed Arab who
spoke with an impeccable accent.

"Madame if you are looking for accommodation let me
help. There is a small but clean villa on the outskirts of
town that has accommodation suitable for a young woman

on her own."

Saida turned to look at the man; he spoke with a cultured accent and was immaculately dressed. She had been in Kufra only fifteen minutes and here was a man trying to help her.

"Let me explain; my name is Aktham-el-Salida and, forgive me, I know you are Saida Sanussi."

Saida couldn't believe her ears. How could it be possible that someone should know her. The first signs of fear gripped her but she quickly took control of herself. Keeping her face almost totally covered, she looked straight into Aktham's eyes which in turn stared back.

"Please tell me how you know my name if indeed it is my name" she asked.

"Let us not talk here Miss Sanussi; let me buy you a coffee and I will explain.

She hesitatingly followed Aktham across the street to a small café. All the outside tables were empty and he carefully chose the table that was the farthest from the old man standing by the door waiting for customers. Aktham waited until the coffee had been served before politely asking Saida if he could use her first name. It was a question she hadn't heard for some time. In the USA people used first names as a matter of course and she had got into the habit even with the most senior director of the Weather Bureau. She gave a small nod of her head. Aktham had planned to tell her about the last few weeks in a gentle and roundabout way. But now he recognised a strong, purposeful woman. How else could she have travelled one thousand miles of desert on her own.

"Saida, let me be direct with you. You are here to find Habib and to find the truth about your parents' deaths. I will help you but first I have to warn you that you are in danger. Your movements are being followed by the US military and they are hoping you will lead them to Habib."

Saida was puzzled, "I haven't told anyone where I am going. My family think that I am travelling west to Tripoli. I have not spoken a single word about my journey."

"It is not too difficult", replied Aktham "they, that is the police and the military, have been watching you ever since you entered the country. It started when you sat next to a military policeman on your flight to Tripoli. You hardly spoke to him but he made a note. You did not know that he had been sent by the army headquarters to investigate your parents' death."

Saida's puzzled look encouraged Aktham to explain further;

"Your family have all accepted the fact that your mother and father were killed by terrorists. Only you have questioned the police version of events and they have very good reason to be concerned about your questioning but that is for later. First we must lay a false trail. We must detach the tracker from your vehicle and I will arrange for it to be attached to one of the vehicles that are going to Chad."

Saida hesitated; she had been in Kufra for less than an hour and already she felt that she was not in control of her destiny. Aktham noticed her reluctance to leave the café and reassured her she was with friends and that he would lead her to Habib. She followed him to the

Landcruiser. Although only four days old, it already had the look of a vehicle that had travelled many miles. Aktham stopped at the back of the vehicle and knelt down, feeling under the wheel arch until he eventually pulled out a small magnetic device. Saida was still suspicious; had he had the device in his hand before he knelt down? He handed her the tracker. She had seen them before and was surprised to see it was of a type made in the USA. Suddenly she felt tired and a little overwhelmed. She looked Aktham in the eye;

"Ok I believe you. Show me to this accommodation you are talking about."

Aktham walked across the road and gave the tracker device to a young man. After a few words, he hurried away towards an area where six or seven huge lorries were parked.

CHAPTER TWENTY-SEVEN

"We will take your vehicle, if that is ok" said Aktham,
"I will drive if you wish." Saida was in no mind to let him
drive her anywhere. At least in her own vehicle she felt she
had some control. Her handgun was under the driver's
seat and she could easily reach it by pretending that she
was adjusting the seat. If there was an emergency she
knew she wouldn't hesitate to use it. The main street was
less busy now. The heat of the day had driven most people
indoors waiting until the sun had started to sink into the
west. Swirls of dust blew down the road making Saida
thankful for the scarf she still had drawn across her face.
The heat was oppressive and Saida remembered that
understanding the weather was her profession. The
weather in Kufra was certainly easy to predict. It was
always clear skies and hot in the day unless an occasional
low pressure system kicked up a strong wind from the
tropics of Africa.

Aktham directed her through a variety of narrow alleys
until they reached the outskirts of the town. The houses
were made of a mud based material and painted white.
The windows were no more that open slits in the walls
minimising the heat inside. They came to a detached
building surrounded by palm trees. By the standard of
other houses nearby it was large and even looked cared
for. As they approached, the door opened and out came
Habib. He was dressed in traditional Arab costume and
looked as handsome as ever. She remembered his tall

stature and shaven face but it was more lined than when she had last seen him five years ago. Habib stepped forward and opened the Landcruiser door for her.

"Welcome to Kufra, my cousin; how good it is to see you." Saida still felt nervous. If Habib had killed her parents then it would be of no consequence for him to kill her. But it just didn't make sense, although she wished she could get to her gun in her car. There was no chance of that. It would have to wait. She would know in the next few minutes what was in store for her.

Habib led her through the large wooden door into a dark room with leather furniture set around the room in front of a large television set. Several doors led off the main room and Saida could see an unmade bed in one room where the door was slightly open. The house had all the smells of desert living; a spicy aromatic smell that came from use in cooking and washing. A woman came from what appeared to be a kitchen, her shufti shawl close over her face. Habib turned to Saida,

"My cousin", he said uneasily, giving a gesture of greeting. "Can we get you anything, water perhaps or coffee? Madea will prepare lunch for us shortly."

Saida declined; at least so far so good there was no threat in Habib's voice.

"We have a room here if you would care to stay with us. Are you intending a short visit?" he asked with a little curiosity creeping into his voice. Aktham had come into the room carrying her bag with the change of clothes.

"You will perhaps want to refresh yourself and afterwards over lunch we can talk" Almost as an afterthought Aktham broke in.

"By the way you may feel safer with this." He took out her handgun from his abaya and handed it to her handle first. She took it without comment and slid it into her camouflage suit trousers. It appeared that nothing escaped Mr Aktham, she thought as he ushered her to a side room. The room had a pleasant look with a small wash basin in one corner and a single bed in another. Saida looked at herself in the mirror on the wall above the sink. Suddenly she thought of John. They had only spoken twice since she had left the USA and she felt almost as if she had entered a new world with America a distant past.

She washed and changed into her second outfit. It was military style with trousers and a blouse, akin to a battledress top. Her hair was in need of washing but that could wait. She decided to leave off her headscarf and her hair fell down to her shoulders. That was how John liked it although at work she always wore it tied back in a ponytail. She realised how much she was missing her work and the material things that went with it. She also missed the generosity and kindness of her friends and work companions. As she was about to leave the room she remembered her hand gun. She checked it. The bullets were still in place. When Aktham had handed her the gun he had risked that she wouldn't use it on him. That gave her a little confidence. Nevertheless she put it back in her pocket just in case.

When Saida re-entered the living room the table had been laid for three people. A simple meal of salad and fruit had been prepared. Habib and Aktham were not in the room. She went to the door and could hear hushed voices outside. When she opened the door both men stopped talking and looked towards her and smiled. Habib stretched out his arm and gently guided her back into the house. She sat between the two men and for a while they chatted about generalities until Habib looked at Saida and started to tell her about the last three months. He began to talk about his beliefs about foreign influence in Libya. The final straw for him had been the arrival of American troops in Tripoli and Benghazi. He explained his role in trying to bring a dramatic message to his fellow countrymen and how it had backfired. The Great Man-Made River was still out of commission and as a result was causing hardship to many people and achieved nothing. Habib left nothing out of the detail and showed Saida his leg wound. He waited for Saida to take in his explanation and wanted her to appreciate and hopefully agree with his views. Neither Saida nor Aktham spoke. Habib went on:

"I was wounded, needed a doctor, a surgeon, and I thought of your father. Aktham organised a plane that got me to Benghazi. Your father picked us up at the old airport and we went to D'Aosta House. Your mother was home and they made us welcome. I am not sure that your father approved of my actions; the water shortage at the hospital had caused serious hardship at first. But he was my friend and so was your mother. Before he could finish treating me the door bell rang. It was an American sergeant and two Libyan soldiers. Aktham and I were hiding in a corner near the garage when we hear shooting. It was coming from where the American soldiers were waiting. Saida, it was the Americans who killed your father and mother".

Saida's face was an impenetrable mask. There was no sign of a tear as she stared into the distance.

Habib continued.

"Saida, I beg for your forgiveness. I have destroyed the lives of the two people in the world I most admire. Perhaps I've also destroyed the lives of you and your brothers all in the name of the quest to bring our country to its senses. Now I am a hunted criminal and had it not been for Aktham I would be dead and perhaps that's what you would wish."

Saida's anger was not directed at Habib; it was the thought of those drunken Americans breaking into their home and killing people as if they were in some ridiculous western or gangland film. Saida turned to Aktham,

"Is it true?" she asked.

"Yes, every word, I swear on the Koran."

Aktham had come to like and admire Habib and shared his dislike of the American presence in their country. They had become great friends and Aktham claimed that the money was no longer his prime consideration.

Turning her back on the men, she left the room saying nothing. It all seemed to fit. What Jasmin had told her... the police chief searching for the servants... and now Habib. Had the authorities really helped cover up murder? She would have proof.

Habib had expected Saida to use either her words or worse as weapons upon discovering that it was him who led the Americans there. It was all caused by his vanity, his wish to be a leader, his misguided pursuit of a just cause. All he didn't do was pull the trigger. But his actions had put his beloved family in the firing line. He held his head in his hands. He could not expect forgiveness from Saida. He would have to seek it from Allah.

CHAPTER TWENTY-EIGHT

In the Southern section guardhouse, the external line rang insistently. Private Swindells, his feet on the desk, a Jack Daniels in his hand, answered.

"Hello hello, it's the Southern Show. And herrrrreeeesss Johnny!" he shouted, taking another sip. It was not the usual call from the supply section. Instead, there was a woman's voice, a young American woman's voice, sounding seductive, giggling at his introduction.

"You're funny" she laughed. "And how are you today?"

Swindells swiftly drew his feet from the table and sat upright, nearly spilling the whisky in his haste and surprise. His face broke into a lecherous smile.

"Well hello baby" he drawled. "I'm fine, real fine, all the better for hearing from you".

She giggled again.

"And to what do I owe this...uh...pleasure? Is it me you're wanting? You know, you sure have a cute little laugh".

"Ooh, you sound cute too. But I'm sorry to say it's Private Toomey I'm looking for".

"James Toomey?" spluttered Swindells.

"Why yes. I'm the girl he left at home. And he was my special boy who I treated sooo good", she purred.

"He left you?" flirted Swindells. "Come see me babe, there's no way I'm gonna leave you".

"Now behave yourself Sir" she said in mock rebuke. "Jim Toomey is my hero. He's out there in the firing line. Why only last time we spoke, he told me he got himself two terrorists.

Shot 'em both. They won't be doing no bombing again".

Swindells guffawed drunkenly.

"He told you what?" he said incredulously, between laughs. "You gotta be kidding. Them weren't no terrorists. No way. Jimmy Boy got the wrong target and shot two towel-heads. Rich ones right enough, but towel-heads just the same". He was convulsed with laughter.

"No no babe. Jimmy, he's been tellin' you tall tales. The real terrorists, they got away. He plugged them targets all right, got 'em clean, but he plugged a couple a couple of fat rich tent-renting scumbags. They're ten for a dime out here, but boy, did it bring down some shitstorm. We're all supposed to say nothing about it, so don't go letting on to Jimmy Toomey that you've found him out. Now me, I could tell you 'bout some real action if it's a hero you're needing...hello?"

The line had gone dead. Puzzled, Swindells put the phone down. The other three men of the section filed in.

"Hey Toomey" said Swindells, twisting his head round at the tall figure. "You never told us you got a girlfriend".

Toomey's expression did not change.

"I don't" he replied.

In her room in Kufra, Saida Sanussi stared straight ahead and gripped her cell phone, her hand shaking as rage overcame her. Americans had often complimented her on how good her southern accent was.

CHAPTER TWENTY-NINE

"I now stand before you and swear my allegiance to the cause of removing America from our soil."

Habib and Aktham stared in amazement at the woman who had made her life in America, caught unawares at the formal way she declared her intentions. Saida had let them know that, female or not, she was their equal. And she was a Libyan.

During the long evening Aktham revealed more of his background. He was from a poor Egyptian family that had been persecuted by the authorities for their beliefs. As a young man he had been taken away from his parents and managed to survive on his wits. He was self-educated but had studied the habits and mannerisms of the upper and middle classes and had found that adopting their ways had opened doors to him that otherwise would have stayed firmly closed. He realised that, like most countries, the quest for money drove all levels of society and it had not been long before he had become a successful go-between distributing illegal weapons and moving illegal immigrants. He had made his base in Kufra as it was one area to which the Libyan authorities turned a blind eye – mainly because they received significant amounts of money from criminal gangs. Aktham, for all his illegal activities, wanted more than anything to be a respected and recognised citizen. To date, the authorities had not linked Aktham to Habib. The frequent news bulletins that showed photographs only of Habib, mentioned the presence of two other terrorists, but as yet they were unnamed. The conversation lapsed for a moment before Saida returned to the business in hand.

"I came to find you, Habib, to discover the truth about my mother and father. I now know the truth. They were murdered. Murdered by Americans, who are in this country to further their own interests and take our oil. They laughed about it and then covered it up with lies. Well, they will soon not be laughing so loud. You have stood up and said that this country needs to be rid of the Americans. I now have no desire to return to America. In the name of our family, I will fight with you for your cause. My one condition is that I am treated as an equal."

Saida felt strange, uttering words she never believed would ever pass her lips.

"We already see you as an equal" replied Habib "but there is nothing to join; we are not a freedom-fighting group, we have no identity and no-one to fight with us". Aktham can call on mercenaries that will do as he asks if he pays them. Other than that there are only our ideals. What can we do? We have considered the options and none seem to work."

Aktham joined in.

"We have considered a raid on the American camp in Benghazi. We could easily launch a rocket attack on their base. Their security is not without flaws. I already have people working inside their camp as cleaners and drivers. We have thought this through and looked at the achievements of other attacks in Iraq and Afghanistan. All that happens is that reinforcements are sent and the garrison is built up. The Government will use it as an excuse to invite more US units to the country so we have ruled out any action in Libya. We have thought about an action in the USA but the lesson of 9/11 is clear – that any strikes there are used as an excuse for the Americans to unleash their aggression as they see fit. Look how Bush used 9/11 to invade Iraq when in fact Sadam Hussein hated Al Queida and was a good ally against Iran."

The three of them continued to range around the possibilities for some effective action that would protect the country from Westernisation, including the removal of Colonel Gaddafi. Even this suggestion was not viable. The likely successor to Gaddafi was his son who had been groomed for the job over many years, and was even more enamoured of western ways than his father.

They retired to bed. Saida sat in her small room and reflected on the momentous twelve hours in Kufra. She thought of John. It was now impossible to build a life in a place which had shown that it would allow nothing, even the lives of innocent people, to stand in the way of its greed. She put John out of her mind and undressed in the dark. The bed was hard but better than the back of the Landcruiser. She could see the clear sky through the narrow window and watched as a shooting star sped across the horizon. She made a wish, turned over and fell into a deep sleep.

Her dreams were vivid, and strange.

She was alone, and being hunted through a desert landscape by something unseen and terrifying. It was gaining on her. Breathless, she ran faster in an effort to get away. She could hear the pounding of the creature's paws on the sand and its rhythmic panting.

It had rained, and patches of the desert were covered by flowers. A lone butterfly rose from one of the flowers. Suddenly there was a deep, deafening rattling sound as millions of wings beat in unison. The air was filled clouds of butterflies, with yet more rising up in dense swarms. They were angry at the intrusion and pursued the creature as it turned and fled. She felt redeemed, cleansed, vindicated. Standing in the desert with her eyes closed, her hair was tossed by the wind created by the myriad wings.

She was woken by the sound of the early morning call to prayer. It was barely light and Saida cleansed herself before praying to Allah. The night before, as was the custom, she had prayed alone.

The morning sun hit the horizon and within a short time the full sun was in the sky. Watching the sun rise and set always made Saida realise how short a life was. She sat in the small chair in her bedroom and turned over the discussion of the previous evening. Aktham was right; attacks on the US military and the occasional terrorist act on the mainland only served to strengthen the American retaliation. After all three thousand people had died in the 9/11 attacks, half who were non-Americans, and as a result at least one hundred thousand Iraqis and four thousand American soldiers had died. The monetary crisis of 2008 had reduced the American spend on defence and it was likely that a national crisis would reduce it further. A thought struck Saida. Hurricane Zoe had caused $5 billion of damage; Even though she had saved many lives, the storm surge damage, particularly to property was enormous. If Allah should decree it was battered by regular hurricanes, it might have to use all of its resources at home, including military support.

The dream had stayed with her all morning. She could not get the image of that butterfly out of her mind. Ah yes, the butterfly...she was reminded of her days with the great Professor Lorenz. She smiled to herself. What was it he so famously said? The beating of a butterfly's wing in Brazil could cause...she suddenly felt as if a lightning bolt had hit her as the thought struck home.

Saida paced around the room, hands on her head, eyes closed, perturbed by the notion that now couldn't be dislodged. Like an unruly crowd vigorously arguing among itself, the thoughts race around her head in unstoppable circuits, going around, and around again.

"No surely, it couldn't be done. Impossible... but they have had some success with rain-making...the water temperature would have to be just right... but what would create such a downdraught...?"

She was deafened by the noise in her head and at the same time exhilarated. Saida opened her door and walked into the desert. Finding a quiet spot on the reverse slope of a low dune, she sat down in search of clear thinking.

She remained there, motionless, for two hours. It was at least theoretically possible. Most hurricanes started from the West African coast. A storm crossing the African coast could easily pick up strength from the warm ocean. The reality was that the storm that initiated a hurricane started, not on the African coast, but inland where desert and land covered in lush tropical vegetation met. The combination of the hot desert air and the moisture of the vegetation came together to produce a rising column of air which, when meeting the colder atmosphere, created a small rain shower and a mini depression. Depending on the local conditions the rainstorm just petered out or occasionally was the start of a more serious storm that eventually could become a hurricane. Saida's mind reacted to her excitement; what if she could devise a way of starting a small storm? Lorenz had hinted at the possibility in his later work.

Of all people, The US military had done it using a fighter jet and in fact the US Nuclear Regulatory Commission in Washington had spent millions researching the origins of tornados. If she could create a series of devastating hurricanes to hit the east coast of America, the financial consequences would be enormous and the need for help from the military could lead to a reduction of the American army worldwide.

Saida found Habib and Aktham in the main sitting room, watching the Al-Jazeera television station; there had been another attack on the US embassy in Syria and the familiar scenes of Syrians burning the stars and stripes were being shown.

"How could Gaddafi be so blind as to think these people are his friends?"said Habib, at which both men nodded sagely without attempting to answer the question.

The table was laid for breakfast but there was no sign of Madea, the housekeeper. Maybe she was more than a housekeeper to Aktham, although she had hardly spoken to any of them and had eaten alone in the kitchen.

Habib turned to Saida.

"Did you sleep well?" while looking her up and down in a manner that made her feel uncomfortable. She didn't answer his question and instead sat down and poured herself a strong cup of coffee.

"I have been thinking about our dilemma and I may know of a way".

Both turned their eyes away from the screen.

If I say this in the wrong way they'll think I'm mad. If I get it right, they'll probably think I'm mad anyway, she reasoned.

"We must find a way of causing the Americans to have greater need for their military to be at home rather than here. As we said last night to attack them does not work. What we have to hope for is a natural disaster of such significance that they have to withdraw their troops to help at home."

Habib interrupted.

"We have prayed to Allah many times for him to strike at the infidels but it is a big rich country and even the occasional earthquake has not made any difference."

Saida waited for a moment then introduced her idea.

"What if we could create a national disaster, several national disasters more significant than ever before?" She continued. "You are aware that I have been working in Florida for the National Hurricane Centre. You won't know that it was me who predicted the exact landfall of the last major hurricane to hit the coast. I am a world expert in hurricanes; just imagine hurricane after hurricane hitting the coast of America. Just imagine the weather maps with a series of high intensity storms battering the major cities."

Saida realized she was getting carried away with her excitement for the project and she slowed down.

"The most experienced weather people in the USA with an understanding of tornadoes are Howard Bluestein and Thomas Grazulis. They both concluded that tornadoes could be started artificially if conditions were right and in fact they used a military jet to produce a vortex in the Arizona Desert. The research programme we funded by the Nuclear Regulatory Commission – after all, a tornado packs the power of an atomic bomb. If it is possible to start a tornado then I think that if I get the conditions right we could develop a hurricane. What is needed is a continuously rotating updraft of air. I think that I can work out the necessary mathematics to be able with your help to generate a series of hurricanes that would strike the east coast of the USA. They will cause such devastation that the cost and the restoration work would require all the manpower and resources they could muster and we and maybe the rest of the world would for a time be free from their aggression."

Saida stopped; she was breathing heavily and felt she had overplayed her hand. Habib and Aktham remained silent for a while absorbing what she had said. Saida couldn't wait for the silence to break and started again.

"There would be no need of weapons. This would be the power of God, delivering blow after blow, punishing America for its infidel sins".

To her surprise Habib seemed enthused.

"Do you really think it could work? If what you say is true..."

Aktham was more sceptical.

"Let us not get too far in thinking about the result. Let us first ask if this can be accomplished. What would we need and where would we have to be? How much would it all cost? How many men?"

Habib held his hands up to Aktham in a gesture that said slow down, stop.

"If we think the plan has any chance of working let us work slowly through the details. Where do we start?" he asked Saida.

"I need a powerful computer to work out all the possible factors and try to find all the parameters that will be necessary to act as the trigger for a vortex. Then I will need to have access to world weather conditions; even weather conditions in the Pacific affect the jet stream and I will have to have the best information possible. I have already thought that my starting point would be the University of Benghazi. The professor of mathematics knows me well and I'm sure he would let me use his department's computers. They are powerful, though not as powerful as the ones I had in Florida. but I will find a way. I'm sure he won't mind helping out. He knows that I have always had a dream of making it rain in Libya and that's why I studied mathematics and meteorology. The type of programmes that I will be running will lend credence to that explanation. If I don't succeed in finding the correct formula then I will get a message to you somehow."

"We must be careful to use only my men to make contact. Do not under any circumstances try to make direct contact; it could mean death for all of us." Saida looked at Aktham. "Do I understand that you are supporting the idea?"

"Habib and I need to talk first. I am willing to go along with your crazy idea at least up to the point you think you have all the answers, and then we'll address it again. Please prepare for your long journey back to Benghazi. I will have your vehicle made ready but before you go I will need some help from you."

"Anything" replied Saida, now filled with a sense of purpose she hadn't felt since her work on Hurricane Zoe.

Aktham looked at her young enthusiastic face knowing she didn't realise what he had in mind. He continued.

"As you know Habib hasn't left this house since arriving and no one knows he is here. More importantly, no one knows of my connection with Habib and that's how it must stay. I've recently been informed that two Secret Service men have arrived in Kufra and have disappeared. They are looking for you and maybe, just maybe, they have met someone who saw me with you when you arrived. I would like to find them and what I want you to do is walk down the main street as if out for a stroll. If they are still in town they will start to follow you and I will be watching. When you have walked as far as the market, just beyond on the left is a narrow alley. Walk down there until you come to a junction. Stand at the junction as if you are looking for directions. You have nothing to fear, these men merely want to question you and anyway I will be close by all the time. I just want to identify them."

Saida dressed in her camouflage suit and wound her head scarf across her face and around the back of her head. Habib, who had been standing in the background, looked longingly. She really was a beautiful woman and he hadn't had the pleasure of a woman's body for some time. He moved into the shadows of the house as the door opened and the bright light streamed in. A waft of hot dusty air blew into the room and Saida quickly stepped outside and hurriedly closed the door

She had never been a decoy before, and the thrill of setting a trap gave her a tingle of excitement. The main street was about a quarter of a mile away and she made her way down an avenue of palm trees. The incessant barking of the wild dogs was the only noise breaking the silence but as she approached the main road she began to hear voices. As she turned the corner she could see the market stalls already set up, their owners sorting through the vegetables and meat. America had given Saida a taste of good hygiene and she felt repulsed as she looked at the hundreds of flies surrounding the meat hanging freely from the wooden rafters of the stalls. She set off down the centre of the road. There was very little traffic and the camels and donkeys seemed to be the only means of transport. She looked around, didn't see anybody and decided to have a cup of coffee at the coffee house where Aktham had first taken her just two days ago.

Afterwards, she resumed her walk past the market, turned left down the narrow alley and soon came to the junction that Aktham had described. Aktham had not told her where to go from there and she looked left and right before realising that two men were standing near to her. It was if they had materialised from the very air. She had no idea she had been followed. The men looked menacing but one smiled and asked

"Are you Saida Sanussi?"

Before she could reply, a bullet hole appeared in the man's forehead, his eyes almost popping out as he slowly fell backwards. The other man turned as if to use Saida as a shield but a second later he lay dead at her feet. She resisted screaming, though she was splattered with blood. It was even on her hands which she wiped furiously on her camouflage suit as if trying to expunge the memory of the last two minutes from her mind. A small cart pulled by a donkey passed and she heard a whisper,

"Get on".

Without a second's hesitation, she sat up by the driver. The donkey and cart could hardly get through the narrow lane and she looked back. Both bodies had disappeared. The man driving the donkey and cart was Aktham; he turned and gave her a grin. She couldn't believe that someone who had just killed two people could possibly be so calm but in the smile she saw a malevolence and enjoyment that she had not previously noticed in the Aktham she had seen before. She shuddered. It was a smile she would see again but in different circumstances.

CHAPTER THIRTY

Saida began her long lonely journey back to Benghazi. She had plenty of time to think about the last few weeks. Her investigation was adding to her dislike of America and all Americans. The thought of living with John in Washington, once a dream was now becoming a nightmare. She could never go back.

The long journey passed uneventfully and a tired Saida arrived home. The lights were on in the house and in the staff quarters. She stopped the Land cruiser at the bottom of the drive. She felt for her handgun under the seat. It was there and she checked that bullets were in the chamber before slipping quietly out of the car and silently making her way up the drive. The staff quarters were next to the garage and she approached them by walking over the grass, avoiding the gravel drive. She tip-toed the final few feet and very carefully peeked through the window. A powerful looking young man sat on the sofa, his feet resting on the coffee table. He was watching television. A soccer game was in full flow and the man leaned forward in anticipation as the national team launched an attack. Saida slowly turned the handle on the door, gun in hand. The door creaked and the man leapt up and took cover behind the sofa. Saida called out.

"I have a gun, show yourself."

The man gradually put his two hands above the sofa and finally the top of his head appeared. His face was frightened and his eyes darted from side to side.

"Who in the name of Allah are you? Saida asked,

The man stood up and took a pace away from the sofa and moved towards Saida. She waved the gun motioning him to sit down.

"I am Mustapha Ben-Aflick and I am your bodyguard. I thought it would be tomorrow morning before you arrived. You must have driven partly at night to get here so soon. Please forgive me for taking liberties with your home."

His voice softened and he became more subservient.

"I have been sent here to protect you and to help you in your quest. I have prepared the house for you and I would be happy to make you a meal."

Saida still had her gun pointing at the man's head and she slowly let it move down until it was pointing at the floor.

"Please, Miss Sanussi; let me show you how I have prepared your home".

He moved towards her and she immediately raised her gun but stepped to one side and followed him out of the staff quarters to the front door. He obviously had a key, how she had no idea. The burglar alarm system was not switched on and Mustapha opened the door and let her walk in before him. The first thing she noticed was the beautiful flowers on the table in the hall. The house smelled clean and everywhere was spotless. The marble floors shone better than she could ever remember. This man really has been working hard.

"Can I prepare you some food?" he asked. "Perhaps you would like to shower first and when you are ready I will leave a tray of food in the drawing room. The water is intermittent but I think it is on at the present time. The report on the television says that water supplies will be back to normal by the weekend."

Saida started to relax; if the man was about to attack her he would have done it in a different way.

"I will have a shower and, thank you, I am hungry. If you can make me some food I will be grateful."

Mustapha gave her a smile and went into the kitchen. The upper floor was as immaculate as the ground floor and there were flowers in her room. She showered with the gun inside the shower cubicle wrapped in a shower cap. She felt very vulnerable in the large marble shower room and very quickly washed and dried. She put on an old kaftan dress and went downstairs. Her dinner was laid out for her but Mustapha was nowhere in sight. Saida ate her meal with gusto; if this was Aktham's idea of a bodyguard she was very happy with it.

Saida slept well that night, but even so, she kept her gun under her pillow. The following morning she lay awake and, for a while, felt good but slowly her mind started thinking of her parents and the many happy hours she had spent with them and her brothers. A feeling of sadness then depression overcame her which eventually turned to anger. She jumped out of bed, washed quickly and put on her traditional Arab dress. It was a dress she had worn when attending university and the feel of the cotton against her skin felt good after days of wearing a camouflage suit. Saida's mind once more became occupied with her plan. She must get to the Benghazi University and see her old mentor from the Mathematics Department She decided it would be best if she telephoned him first and she looked at her watch – 7.30am; he would be there by now.

Professor Ahmed Al-Ardawi was about to leave his office when he heard the phone ringing. He retraced his steps and looked at the caller identity number showing on the phone. He didn't recall the number and moved to ignore it but curiosity overcame his need to be elsewhere. It was Saida; he remembered her well, the best mathematical brain he had encountered in all his years at university. He regretted not being able to persuade her to study at the University of Benghazi but realised he was no match for Edward Lorenz at MIT. Saida asked if she could see him and they made arrangements to meet later that day at the university.

Saida put down the phone feeling better for doing something, something that would be part of her process of revenge. She didn't feel there was any risk to the university in her actions and all she wanted to do was to start her work. Mustapha had laid out her breakfast and as she passed through the living room she caught a glimpse of him cleaning her car.

I rather like having a bodyguard she thought to herself, and smiled for the first time that day. After breakfast she sat down at her father's desk and wrote a list of all the aspects of computation she would need for her work. The list was comprehensive and perhaps too much for the university. At least with her new found wealth she could purchase the best equipment and donate it to the Computing Department of the university.

Thinking of money, her mind turned to her brothers.

Abdallah would be at work by now so she telephoned his office. He was short with her at first. The whole family had been worried and no one had received a call from her. Gently she reassured him and told him she had to get away and mourn by herself and that she had not bothered looking for Habib. She told Abdallah she was back now and was planning to immerse herself in weather research at the university.

"I thought you would be going back to the States" enquired Abdallah, "I thought you were going to marry an American."

His voice sounded puzzled He knew his parents had even bought airline tickets in anticipation of the wedding and there had been much talk in the family of the need for a second, traditional Muslim wedding in Benghazi.

"I shall not be going back to America and I am not getting married and the way I feel I will never get married."

Abdallah was curious, "Why, what happened?"

"Nothing" replied Saida in a voice that didn't encourage any further discussion. Abdallah changed the subject.

"Our lawyer needs to see you, not least because he needs to know your bank account numbers. He is recommending we turn at least fifty per cent of the assets into cash and leave the rest in assets in Switzerland."

Saida acknowledged her brother's superior knowledge of the financial markets but thought to herself she would rather have American dollars than Libyan dinar in spite of my dislike of all things American. As she put down the telephone she could see that Mustapha had changed into a more traditional dress and was waiting by the car.

As she moved past the front window Mustapha looked up and waved. He walked to the front door and opened it for her and she explained to him that she had an appointment at the university.

"I will drive you" he immediately replied and before long they were on their way into the city. Conversation was very limited. Mustapha seemed absorbed with looking around, checking his rear-view mirror and generally being on alert. Saida felt safe in her own city and was not sure she needed protection but Mustapha was adamant. His instructions were clear. She must be protected at all times.

At the university Saida was greeted like royalty. Her reputation and achievements were well known to staff and students alike. She was greeted at the door by Professor Ardawi and taken to the Department of Computer Science. Professor Ardawi insisted they visit a lecture theatre where a class was in progress. The Professor introduced Saida to a ripple of applause from the students. She felt touched that in her home country her reception meant more than the plaudits she had received in Miami. These were her people; civilised, god-fearing and family-orientated.

Eventually the Professor took her back to his room and over a cup of coffee, Saida explained that she was deeply interested in rain-making. But to understand all the necessary parameters she needed exceptional computing power of the type that was used by the university. If necessary she was prepared to buy extra equipment and donate it to the department. Professor Ardawi explained that they had recently upgraded the computing set up of the whole university but it would be necessary for her to use it mainly in the evenings and at night.

"That won't be a problem" she said. It would suit her to be working when there were no prying eyes. Her cover story was very credible and for some aspects of her work she might even enlist the aid of students.

As Mustapha drove her home her mind started to draw up a list of the things she needed to know, not least to find the best point close to the west coast of Africa that could be her starting point for the great mission. Her knowledge of the West African coast was limited and that evening she pored over maps and weather charts. Her knowledge told her that the base must be where desert and green forest came together. In most instances there was a gradual change in vegetation as the coast drew nearer, but the ideal was somewhere where the change was abrupt.

Over the following days and weeks she worked day and night. Students clamoured to help her but progress was slow and disjointed and at times the students felt the wrath of her impatience. Mustapha followed Saida wherever she went, never complaining about the long waits in the university. His way was that of servant and master. Whenever Saida asked him questions about his background, he always gave vague answers. But he guarded her as if his life depended on it, and perhaps it did. On one occasion Saida had seen Mustapha with his shirt off working in the garden. He had a strong lean muscular body and she felt a momentary urge to touch him but as she watched he glanced up and the mean look in his eyes reminded her that he was in the pay of Aktham who had, within the last few weeks, shot at least two men in cold blood.

After an exhausting three months Saida at last began to make some headway. She was confident of much of her work but the exact location for the base camp eluded her. The Sahara Desert almost reached the sea in Southern Morocco but the land from the desert to the coast had little vegetation. The southern part of Mauritania had a much more fertile coastline and the lush vegetation extended fifty miles inland before reaching the Western Desert, but the terrain was poorly documented. Her few conversations with Habib had been short and to the point. Habib insisted he needed to know what equipment would be required and how many men. He was taken aback when Saida requested a large helicopter preferably a military version with fixed blades, in addition to an executive jet. Much to Saida's amazement Aktham replied that both helicopter and jet were available at a reasonable cost, but would take a little time to organise.

Finally there came the message the men had waited for. She now had the formula for creating the hurricane – at least in theory – and had decided that the most suitable base for her experiment would be in Mauritania. The capital Nouakchott was on the coast towards the south of the country. It had an airport but she believed her trials need to be conducted further south and about sixty miles inland. She had identified the small town of Mbout as having all the requirements of a regular tropical rainfall within a few miles of the desert together with a large lake. Mbout was close to the border with Senegal and the relationship between the two countries was tense. It would be necessary for Aktham to ensure all the diplomatic channels were in place especially if they were to use a military-style helicopter.

CHAPTER THIRTY-ONE

The two men pondered the strange turn of fate that had left them in a position they could never have imagined possible. Habib, only a matter of months ago, had aspired to be the new leader of the country, bringing it spiritual renewal on a tide of popular support, Aktham had taken on a well-paid but risky piece of business and had allowed himself to be drawn into a conspiracy to attack America in the name of Libya. And here they were, both hunted men, reliant on a woman, a woman driven by a thirst for personal revenge, to launch the completely untried weapon that would fulfil their destiny.

Aktham reassured himself that at least there would be money-making possibilities for him in the scheme somewhere. For his part, Habib reasoned that this time, the Libyan people would be in no doubt. This would be more than a symbolic gesture. They would be attacking the real enemy, in a way it, for all its power, money and military might, could do nothing to stop.

Aktham had done business in Mauritania before, thanks to his role in funnelling a stream of illegal immigrants, anxious to get into Italy or France, towards their destination. He knew it to be a very poor country, torn by internal strife and bitter tribal rivalry. For a short time a democratic government ruled the country but was toppled in 2008 by an army coup led by General Mohammed Ould Abdel Aziz. Aziz had benefited from Aktham's generosity on more than one occasion.

Habib called Saida. They could see to it that she had everything she needed, including a private jet and pilot. Saida would have to organize all the technical equipment such as computers and weather-monitoring instrumentation. The helicopter presented a little more of a problem. A large military machine flying over North Africa would cause alarm in Algeria and Morocco. Aktham would have to make arrangements with the Mauritanian militia.

The private jet would collect Saida and Mustapha at Benghazi airport in ten days time. Habib and Aktham would make their own way to Mbout, probably via Chad. Mbout had an airport of sorts with a runway three thousand feet long, just enough to get the Gulfstream IV down safely. They would worry about take-off when the time came.

On the evening before she left, Saida had a farewell dinner with her family. They had readily accepted her story that she was doing field trials to create rain clouds. They had no idea who she would be working with and the location of her work seemed very unclear.

Mustapha drove Saida to the dinner, but declined the family's offer to join them, as usual waiting patiently outside. Over dinner there was speculation about Habib's whereabouts. The police and army were looking for him and his associates but had made little progress. There was talk of the American armed forces joining in the search. The family still couldn't believe that Habib had been responsible for the murders but the Chief of Police had presented them with his evidence and it all seemed convincing. Saida said little. The truth would have to wait until another day.

The following day was hot and dusty. The ghibli wind was blowing from the south and a fine dust stung the eyes and coated everything in its path. The south wind always brought with it an intolerance and irritability in people. The airport officials were no different, inspecting every piece of luggage and arguing among themselves. Papers had to be signed and every step was exhaustively protracted. The Gulfstream had landed at 7am but it was 11am before Saida and Mustapha were allowed onto the tarmac. A middle-aged, distinguished Englishman walked down the aircraft steps to greet them. His uniform was sweat-stained and there were buttons missing.

"Welcome aboard" he said with a huge grin, his hand extended forwards.

Saida smiled and took his hand very lightly. Mustapha, hands full of luggage, just nodded in acknowledgement and stepped onto the plane. Saida followed him. As she walked up the steps she turned and caught the pilot admiring her rear He looked away, embarrassed. She was wary of Brian Huxford, but Mustapha made clear that he was Saida's bodyguard by standing between them.

Huxford introduced himself. An ex-RAF pilot, he had been working for the UN in Sudan and then for the military junta and for a while had ferried the army generals to their secret villas in Switzerland and Spain. On one occasion, having left his passengers in Zurich, he had heard news that the Sudan military coup had been overturned and, fearing trouble, had landed in Libya. He used the turn of events to take ownership of the jet and now occasionally chartered the plane to Aktham. It had been a lucrative business with no questions asked and now Aktham had promised him a generous sum for some work in Mauritania.

Taking his place in the cockpit, he announced they would fly in five minutes. Within seconds the engines started and the plane taxied down the runway. The blowing sand covered much of the runway lights and became a storm as the twin Rolls-Royce engines developed maximum thrust as the plane powered skywards.

The Gulfstream had a flying range of 4872 miles, more than adequate to get to Mbout. With its cruising height of 45,000 feet, it was capable of escaping the worst of any weather turbulence. Saida settled into the leather armchair and looked out of the window. There was nothing but sand and barren land. Their flight would take them across Algeria then turning south west into Mauritania, a journey of 2,600 miles. The journey was set to take over five hours. Saida considered the events of the last few months. How her life had changed; no mother or father, no fiancé, more money than she ever dreamed of and above all else a burning hatred of all things American. She thought about Habib and Aktham who had already reached Mbout and a feeling of unease troubled her. Could she trust them? She already knew that Aktham was a cold-blooded killer and yet she was about to unleash a plan that could spell death for untold numbers of people. She banished that thought from her mind; she was following her destiny, perhaps saving the lives of many of her countrymen who would otherwise die under American oppression. Although she could not admit it, she was taking satisfaction from the thought of the power she would wield if her work succeeded.

Her introspection stopped as the cabin door opened and Brian peered around the door.

"There's coffee and some Danish in the galley at the back and you'll probably find some salmon in the fridge. If you make coffee I'll have one," he called out before disappearing behind the door.

Mustapha opened his eyes. Saida noticed how he gripped his seat arms and it surprised her that a man such as him would be afraid of flying.

"I'll get the coffee" she said, "would you like one?"
Mustapha nodded as if unable to speak.

Saida made three cups of coffee and served a traditional strong black brew to Mustapha. Saida knocked on the cockpit door and walked in. Brian turned his head, grinned and pointed to the co-pilot's seat. Saida sat down; it was the first time she had sat with the pilot and she marveled at the array of dials and switches.

The terrain outside was still desert broken by the occasional mountain range. They had crossed the border with Morocco and Brian was engrossed in a conversation with ground control. Apparently his flight plan had not been received by the authorities and there was a danger of the Moroccans scrambling their fighter attack squadron. After much heated conversation it emerged that it was the plane's designation letters that had not been recognized. The simple answer was that Brian, in flagrant defiance of the rulebook, had changed them so that the authorities in Sudan and at the UN couldn't trace the plane.

Travelling over Mauritania presented no such problem. The country was in such chaos that little, if any, monitoring of flights was carried out by the authorities. Saida returned to her seat in the rear of the plane. Mustapha had relaxed.

"Let me make you something to eat" he offered, carefully standing up for the first time, convinced that sudden movements by him would upset the plane's balance.

He moved to the galley and made the best of the food that was there. His courage left him when Saida asked him to take a sandwich through to Brian; looking through the windscreen of the plane was just too much.

Mbout's airstrip was deserted except for the battered Range Rover waiting by the corrugated hangar that doubled as a departure lounge. Two scheduled flights a week went into Nouakchott and an occasional light aircraft on crop spraying duty would land for fuel and supplies. The runway was cracked tarmac with the occasional weed growing through. Habib and Aktham sat together in the vehicle watching the distant storm slowly grow and move closer from the south. The lightning lit up the dark cumulus clouds which stretched high into the sky. With any luck the plane, approaching from the north, should arrive before the storm reached the airfield. Two locals stood idly by with nothing better to do than hang around and let the day drift by. The part-time airport manager came striding out of the hangar, buttoning up his uniform jacket as he walked. His was an all-encompassing role.

He doubled as air traffic control, baggage handler and ticket clerk. The aircraft was on its landing flight path. It would land from the north-west into the prevailing wind. The plane suddenly became visible as it turned and the wing lights could be seen against the dark background of the thunderclouds. Within minutes the jet screamed overhead and landed with a tremendous roar of the engines as they went into reverse thrust. The whole of the inside of the jet seemed to rattle as it slowly shuddered to a halt. For the last twenty minutes of the flight they had caught the edge of the storm and even after they had come to a halt Mustapha sat white-faced clinging to his seat.

Habib and Aktham were waiting. They greeted Saida warmly. Mustapha, his confidence restored, emerged from the plane. He stepped down and gave the two men the traditional Arab embrace. Within minutes a battered lorry arrived to collect Saida's equipment, arousing her fears highly delicate instruments she had brought. Aktham took charge, ordering the labourers to take care. They made an exaggerated display of gently loading the wooden boxes into the back of the truck, knowing that the state of the road to the camp site twenty miles away meant they might as well have thrown the crates into the back of the lorry.

The small convoy moved off. Brian seemed to know Aktham very well and they talked about past adventures. Habib spoke rarely. He asked after the family and Saida told him of events in Benghazi. The murders were still mentioned in the newspapers and on television and Habib was being portrayed as an evil terrorist out for his own ends. She noticed how he seemed to have aged considerably over the past few months. The fervour which had shone through in Kufra didn't show in his voice as he talked in a passionless manner about the details of the campsite and of the plans for the next few days.

The terrain was hilly with dense undergrowth. The afternoon rains had left the leaves shining in the early evening sunlight. Pools of water filled the hollows along the road way and hot air caused the humidity to rise such that everyone was uncomfortable. Saida had opted to wear her camouflage suit with a wide leather belt decorated with studs. She wore boots and her trouser legs were tucked into the socks. Hot weather didn't bother Saida but the humidity left her feeling breathless.

The small convoy arrived at the camp site, a cluster of tents and a wooden construction marked WC. A stream flowed nearby, clearly running down to the lake they had passed on the way to the camp site. Cooking facilities were already in place and two men dressed in soldier-like uniforms busied themselves around the place. In one corner the largest tent stood beside a generator and the labourers were now unloading the crates into the tent. There even appeared to be something approaching a shower. Saida got out of the Land Rover and stretched. It had been a long day and the day light was beginning to fade. The noises from the jungle became louder and the fireflies were out in their hundreds. Fortunately, the area was untroubled by mosquitoes but the ants, cockroaches and scorpions made up for their absence.

Aktham showed Saida to her tent. It had a metal framed bed in one corner and a makeshift dressing table in another. There was even a small mirror on the dressing table. Aktham and Habib's tents were on the other side of the compound and Brian and Mustapha were sharing another. It appeared that the labourers would be sleeping rough while not on guard duty. Saida sat on the edge of the bed. She felt tired and edgy and a feeling of insecurity invaded her. Not one single person in the world knew where she was apart from the people she was with. She regretted her decision not to leave that note for her brothers just in case something happened to her and vowed that at the first opportunity she would somehow let them know what she was doing and why. They had a right to know the truth about their parents' death.

The tent was lit by a single bare bulb which flickered occasionally, spluttering then burning brightly for a few seconds. The light cast shadows on the tent walls and Saida imagined that her silhouette could be seen from the outside. She would have to be careful when undressing not to have the light on. Mustapha had supervised the preparation of a meal and the four men and Saida sat around a wood fire and ate rice spiced with a curry of vegetables. The conversation was subdued, each one deep in his own thoughts. The shadows cast by the fire accentuated everyone's features and Habib with his dark eyes, hooked nose and high cheek bones had the look of a desert hawk. Aktham, sitting bedside him, looked small and insignificant. So much for appearances. He was a man capable of untold acts of violence. Brian had lost his cheerful look and stared down at his plate in serious contemplation, carefully picking the last grains of rice from his tin plate. Saida noticed his hands; they were small and graceful with long fingers, the opposite of his stocky body and broad shoulders. Aktham broke the silence,

"Saida, what are the things we need to do tomorrow?" She looked across the fire at the four men. She had spent many hours thinking about this day and was very clear in her mind what was needed.

"Firstly I need to set up my instrumentation and computer links. That should be relatively simple providing nothing was broken in transit but what is most important is that I view the geography of the area. I need to find the perfect position to start our experiments. I'm looking for a gentle slope down to the lake where the lake is wide and lying in a south-east to north-west direction. The vegetation should be dense but close to the hot sand of the desert. Scrub land won't do. I need to measure the water temperature of the lake and find how variable it is. I've brought an infra red camera so that I can be sure where the temperature gradients are. To do this I'm going to need the helicopter to survey as much of the lakeside as I can."

Aktham interrupted her.

"There is only one small problem with the helicopter. I have located one at the army base at Kaedi. It is a Lynx and I believe it has the fixed rotor blades that you wanted. The helicopter was left by the old military. But when they fled, they took all their experienced people with them. The helicopter has no pilot so we have to find one." Everyone looked towards Brian, who raised his hands as if to defend himself.

"I don't know how to fly a helicopter. I've only flown one once and that was a small Alouette."

His protests fell on deaf ears and Habib and Aktham continued to look across the fire at him. Eventually he gave in.

"OK I'll have a look but if I'm in any doubt then I'm out."

That agreed, Saida continued with her list of actions. She suddenly felt in charge and a renewed spark of excitement started to grow within her until her tiredness caught up and she returned to her tent to turn in for the night. Habib and Aktham remained by the fire talking in whispers and Saida wondered what they were plotting. She had a feeling that somehow there was a hidden agenda. Recently there had been less talk about freeing Libya from the Americans and so far she had not been asked for any money. She prepared for bed in the dark and retrieved her hand gun from her baggage. As she climbed into bed she resisted putting the gun under the pillow. Instead it lay on the bed with her right hand resting on it.

Next morning Saida woke to the sound of a vehicle starting. It was already daylight; she had slept well and felt refreshed. She could see a shadow outside her tent and called out.

"Who's there?"

"It's me, Mustapha. I have some hot water for you and I will bring your breakfast soon."

She could see him place the bowl outside the tent flap which was securely fastened with a heavy internal zip. She quickly washed and dressed and joined Habib and Mustapha for a cup of coffee and an assortment of crude breads. Aktham and Brian had already left for the military base at Kaedi, a two hour drive away and Saida busied herself opening crates and setting up her computer network and instrumentation. The computer link to Benghazi University was by satellite and only available at restricted times. By a stroke of luck the equipment had travelled well and for a few hours she was able to send test signals and pick up the weather satellites. She carefully made adjustments and to her surprise the USA weather channel emerged from the haze on the screen. She watched, fascinated. How well she remembered it from her other life, the one she had left behind. There was the lead meteorologist Paul Goodloe, talking about the latest storm in the Caribbean. He told how it would not trouble the USA. It continued to be a very quiet season for hurricanes. Suddenly the programme switched to the National Weather Bureau.

"Let me bring in John Williams, the Head of the Storm Unit."

Saida's heart missed a beat. There was John, looking handsome and completely self-assured as usual, agreeing with the meteorologist that all the indications were in favour of another quiet year. She turned the computer off and hurried from the tent feeling confused and angry. Doubts crowded her mind. Habib waved to her from across the campsite and she gave a perfunctory wave back as he strolled across in her direction.

"Are you happy with your equipment? Is it working?" he asked.

"It's fine," responded Saida.

Habib seemed to be in a gentle and calm mood and a little of her misgivings eased away.

"I think I've found the place you need. Shall we go and investigate down by the lake?"

Saida nodded in agreement but inside she could feel the tension of being alone with Habib.

The two of them began to make their way through the thick vegetation down to the lake side. The jungle growth resisted his machete and the quarter of a mile distance proved slow going. Saida fell or stumbled on several occasions. Habib helped her up and held her hand as they broke their way through the vines and shrubs. She realised this was the first time she had been alone with Habib since she was thirteen and a touch of apprehension again gripped her. But Habib was fixed on his task and eventually they reached the lakeside. She looked back up the slope and could see the smoke from the campfire rising in the distance. That would help them to find their way back.

The lake was smooth and sparkling clear. It looked inviting enough for a swim, but the fear of crocodiles and snakes quickly dismissed the idea from her mind. She unpacked her thermometer and carefully measured the surface temperature. It was 98°F. That was ideal. The humidity at that temperature was so high that the air was laden with moisture. As she collected her instruments Habib suddenly stood upright; he was listening to a sound in the distance and eventually they could both hear the rapid scything of a helicopter engine. They looked at each other and let out a shout of joy, hugging each other for a moment before Habib stepped away with an apologetic look on his face.

"Let's get back and see what they have brought us."

Saida's heart was beating a little faster and for a moment she wondered if she did have feelings for Habib. The two of them scrambled up the gentle slope, Saida following him as he broke branches and trod down the vicious thorny plants. There seemed to be no evidence of the path they had made on the way down and by the time they reached the campsite their clothes were torn and they were out of breath.

The helicopter, sombre in its green and brown camouflage, appeared over the horizon and was soon hovering unsteadily overhead. The clearing close to the camp was surrounded by tall trees and the descent was slow and nervy. Eventually it came down to earth with a sickening bump and a rather shaken Brian emerged from the cockpit. The blades of the helicopter slowly came to rest and the twin jets died away with almost a sigh of relief.

"Aktham is driving the truck back," Brian called out to them, mopping his brow as he ducked under the blades.

In spite of his cheerful smile the journey had been fraught with difficulty and many scary moments. They gathered around the fire and Brian, in his most dramatic style, described the journey from Kaedi. There had been no problem in getting permission to take the Lynx. Aktham had already agreed terms with the camp commander and the guards. The problems came when he sat in the cockpit. He had no idea how to start the engines. He searched in vain for a button or a key, but he was baffled until one of the guards came across. Although the guard couldn't fly the helicopter, he had been delegated to occasionally run the engines. He pointed out to Brian the three switches that were needed to turn on the Rolls-Royce Gem engines and within minutes the engines fired. Brian knew that the engine warm up-period was crucial. Turbine discs had been known to burst into fragments due to over-anxious airmen trying to get airborne too early. After much experimenting and near disasters, Brian managed to get the helicopter to lift off the ground and adopt a forward movement. Hovering proved much more of a challenge and after five attempts he gave up. He tried landing but had no sense of his height above ground and on two occasions had hit the tarmac with such force that the undercarriage bars almost bent.

Aktham had looked on with admiration. The journey to Kaedi had been full of protests from Brian but Aktham kept reminding him of the potential financial rewards of his deal and the pilot finally shrugged his shoulders.

"What have I got to lose – only my life!" he mused.

There was no doubt that Brian was pleased with himself and he accepted the praise from the others with feigned modesty. He was now looking forward to another flight and laid out the maps he had acquired from the base. The lake was in fact a reservoir with a large dam at the northwest end. The river forming the dam was a tributary that eventually ran into the river Niger. Saida and Brian were studying the map in detail when Aktham arrived back, his

truck loaded with aviation fuel. He greeted Brian with a
hug and retold the details of Brian's first attempts at take
off. It was Aktham who persuaded him to persist and to
Brian's credit he had got back on board and started again.
The whole of the military garrison had turned out to watch
and he felt like a rodeo cowboy who got on the back of
bulls and kept getting thrown off only to climb back on
again. He lost control more than once but slowly began to
master the levers and foot pedals. Eventually he felt
confident enough to do a victory circuit around the
garrison. The watching troops dispersed, disappointed
they hadn't seen a crash.

They believed they had found the best match to Saida's
parameters. Nevertheless she decided she needed to
understand the terrain better and persuaded Brian to take
her on a flight around the lake. The distance was well over
one hundred miles and there was little to be seen but
dense vegetation and the occasional small boat used for
fishing. Brian took the opportunity during their flight to
ask Saida why she was so intent on this mission. To him
here was a woman who had everything, intelligence,
money, good looks and a nice personality and, as Brian
looked at her, he thought for the first time in a very long
time that he was in need of a woman's company.
Saida, irritated, deflected his questions. She seemed more
intent looking at the terrain and occasionally checking
water temperatures using her infrared camera than
making small talk. They lapsed into silence. His mind
turned to Aktham and his promise that his life would
change as a result of this venture and he wondered if he

could trust him.

On their return Saida sat beside her two computer screens and brought the direction finder to bear on the satellite dish. Now they had decided on the starting point, all that was needed were the right weather conditions. The combination would need to be a northwest dry hot breeze blowing after a heavy thundershower that had raised humidity to almost 100 per cent. The helicopter would hover fifty feet above the ground causing a massive down draught. The moisture-laden air would be forced down into the ground and deflected back up again in a swirling vortex. The anti-clockwise movement of the air would, if they were lucky, be caught by the north-west wind and carried out over the lake where the hot moist air would feed more kinetic energy into the whirlwind as it pushed across the fifty miles of open water. Saida realised that as it hit the shore line it would lose momentum but with only another fifty miles to the sea there was every possibility that the growing storm would have the energy to keep going. Once at sea it would be unstoppable. That was the theory at least. Saida's biggest worry was the strength of the downdraught. She had to be prepared with another plan if it proved inadequate to the task, and set about working into the early hours of the morning checking statistics, reading world weather maps and applying her own detailed mathematical formulae. The jet stream over the USA was favourably positioned to the south on the western seaboard and well north at the east coast. Any storm hitting the USA in the next week or so would not be pushed away from the country back into the

Atlantic but was more likely to be dragged inshore by the surrounding low pressure. The more she examined her data the more she began to realise that the next few days would be the opportune time to launch her experiment. The north-easterly was already blowing from the Sahara Desert and the thunderclouds were forecast to return over the following week. The wind tended to die down in the late evening. There was a critical time when the humidity was high and the wind was still strong. This occurred towards five in the afternoon and they would have to be ready for that precise moment.

Saida waited until all had gathered around a makeshift table that evening before announcing that tomorrow at five pm would be the moment. The excitement grew and the conversation went on long into the might. Soon after the day dawned, she started checking all her data once more. Brian flew her over the lake again. Temperature gradients from land to water were measured and the upper air temperature was monitored from the helicopter. The conditions couldn't be better. All that was needed was for the afternoon thunderstorms to roll up from the south. But she was uncertain about the length of time the helicopter needed to hover and at what height. Saida was not an expert in airflow dynamics but her best estimate was fifty feet. The precise spot for the hover was chosen with great care. The ground had to be level to give an even reflection of the downdraught so that the air rose up from the ground in a conical spiral. Everything was quickly in place.

From the vantage point of a small featureless hill near the camp, the five looked southwards for the early signs of the afternoon storms. The first dark clouds appeared at two o'clock and swiftly moved north. Lightning streaked the dark sky and the sound of thunder rolled around the adjacent hills. Momentum was gathering. Their long wait was near its end and they suddenly found themselves rushing to make preparations. Aktham had decided to ride with Brian while Habib offered to measure the force of the downdraught, which meant him standing immediately below the helicopter. Saida watched and waited and, with everyone in their places, conversation ceased and a tense silence took over. Five months in the planning and now was the moment of truth.

The rain had been heavy. The air was so humid that rivers of perspiration ran down Saida's face and back. She looked up; the storm was about to pass, now was the moment. She signalled to Brian who took off in a southerly direction and came back with the wind from the south-west. The hover point had been marked and levelled and Habib stood in the centre of the circle with his instruments to measure airflow, humidity and temperature. The Lynx manoeuvred into place and gently descended towards the appointed height. The downdraught was almost blowing Habib off his feet and his abaya flapped helplessly in the blast of air. The time for the hover had been set for ten minutes. But to all of them it seemed an eternity. On Saida's signal Brian slowed the engines and gently descended to the ground. Habib quickly moved the instrumentation and ducked his head as the rotor blades came closer. Saida rushed back to the hill and scanned the air for signs. She had seen the swirling air rush skywards and elements of debris had soared to several hundred feet. There were no signs of any cloud movement. For all she could tell, it was as if the experiment had not even taken place. She tried to imagine what she had expected to see. Perhaps it was a daydream after all to expect to see a swirling mass of air proceed down to the lake.

That evening conversation was subdued. Saida went over all her data. Everything pointed to the fact that conditions today had been perfect. They should try again the next day. The favourable atmospheric conditions seemed set to last for three days so there could be at least two more attempts. But the next two days followed the same pattern. On the third evening the mood was subdued. Saida had turned her thoughts to how the vortex could be increased in strength. After Brian had finished his regular tipple of whisky she turned to him

"We need to get a stronger reflection of air from the ground. I want you to get closer to earth."

"Fine", he answered passively. He looked at Aktham.

"This had better be worth it," he muttered.

Saida returned to her computers to check on the jet stream over the United States. Tuning into the Weather Channel had become a relatively simple matter and the familiar face of Jim Cantari was soon delivering the weather pattern over the USA. It was unseasonably hot on the Eastern seaboard. The jet stream had retreated north and New York and Boston were baking in temperatures in the eighties. When the forecaster turned to Florida, Saida had a moment of sad reflection. Was it only a few months ago that her life was so perfect? She sighed and weariness overcame her. Two more days and she would call it all off. The television presenter turned to the Storm Watch segment and a map of the Atlantic including the coast of Africa flashed up on the screen. Suddenly Saida was wide awake listening carefully. The presenter pointed out three small tropical storms off the coast of Africa and was reassuring his viewers that the storms at present seemed small but that they would be watched very carefully. The three storms were further north than usual and very close together and could merge into a larger tropical storm that could become a hurricane.

Saida let out a scream and the men, who had been sitting around the camp fire gossiping about their past escapades, jumped up and ran to Saida's tent. She put a finger to her lips and pointed at the screen. But the presenter had moved on and was now talking about bush fires in California. Saida could hardly speak for excitement,

"We did it! All three tests worked and the storms are already in the Atlantic!" Brian picked up Saida in his arms and hugged her in a little dance around the floor while Habib and Aktham smiled at each other.

"Now just let's see what devastation we can bring to the American infidel," Habib said triumphantly.

Saida left the communication computer running and they all sat around in the operations tent until an hour later when the Storm Watch segment returned to the television channel. The picture was as before and the presenter made a passing remark about how far north the storms were compared to the usual path close to the equator. Saida knew that it would take at least fifteen days for the storms to cross the Atlantic. Her next step would be to try and predict the landfall. Her first guess was that it would be a direct hit on Maryland and then on to Washington. Habib and Aktham moved away from the campfire and Saida could hear them talking in hushed tones. They looked serious but both were turned away from her. The only words she caught were,

"We should do it now", and with that they moved into Aktham's tent.

PART FOUR

CHAPTER THIRTY-TWO

John got to the office early. Even so several members of his team were already hard at work and the large open-plan room was lit up with the flickering computer screens. His plan was to finalise his report on global warming for his boss as soon as possible. It was meant to be a presentation of cold fact and analysis, but John was finding it increasingly hard not to spell out his own view to the Board. The previous bureau Director, Billie Wallace, was well known for his views on global warming, which had considerable influence on Government policy. Billie had now retired and John's position on the Climate Change Committee had been strengthened. The change of President had brought with it a new attitude towards the environment. Nevertheless it was still a formidable task to persuade others, particularly politicians, that there was a problem.

John viewed all the papers on his desk and inwardly groaned. Where to start? His PA interrupted his chain of thought by bringing him a cup of coffee and a print-out of his more important emails. He was receiving over two hundred and fifty a day and needed help just to keep on top of his communications. Instead of settling down to work John stood up, coffee cup in hand, and looked out of the window. The university campus was quiet as many students were on the fall break. He watched a dark-haired young woman walk across the pristine lawns. For a fraction of a second he thought it was Saida and his heart filled with momentary joy. The woman looked up and he saw it was the new assistant in the data collection department. John had not heard from Saida for over three months and even her family didn't seem to know where she was. He had come to accept that for reasons he couldn't understand Saida was deliberately cutting off contact and with a sense of overwhelming sadness he realised it was over between them. The storm tracking office was at the far end of the corridor and although John wouldn't admit it to himself, he wandered down there from time to time just to remember the times they had spent together. The new Head of the Storm Tracking Section was a fresh-faced young Canadian, Jack Parenteau. When John entered the office he immediately stood up respectfully.

"Are you prepared for the new season?" John asked, knowing full well that he had been working night and day to meet the demands of the job.

Jack looked down for a moment before explaining that he was still struggling with the mathematical methodology that Saida had developed. Whatever approach he tried, it was impossible to get a fix on the landfall of storms crossing the Atlantic. John looked at the three screens. Two were full of complex calculations and a third showed the current Atlantic storm positions. The three new storms that were now two hundred and fifty miles off the African coast were growing in intensity. It was the first time that John had realised they were in line and so close together and even more worryingly they were a hundred miles north of the usual starting point. John spoke quickly,

"We need to watch those very carefully. Keep me in regular touch."

He stood, hand on his chin, looking at the monitor and didn't move for fully two minutes. He then turned on his heels and quickly made his way down the corridor.

Back in his office he knew he had no alternative but to buckle down and get his report done. A well-presented report would do wonders for his promotion prospects and the position of the National Deputy Director was due to become available in the next few months. John managed to assemble his thoughts and began the long process of condensing the information into an accessible format. He knew that the politicians would only read the executive summary and take from it only that information that fitted with their predetermined views. Even those who believed in global warming found little comfort in the figures for the last three years, which had shown a reducing global temperature. John's mind kept drifting back to the weather chart he had seen in Jack's office and eventually he switched on his own computer that could monitor the world's weather in real time. The three storms were moving slowly and wind speeds were still low. Perhaps they would blow themselves out. The storms were a long way north of where would be expected so maybe they'd just vanish. John felt reassured and returned to his report to the Climate Change Committee.

He finished the draft by ten o'clock in the evening and immediately emailed it to the committee secretary. The office was deserted and only a few lights were on. The security guard put his head around John's office door and asked him if he would be long. As he stuffed papers into his briefcase the computer registered a new email. It was from the committee secretary informing him that a Senate Committee Hearing had been called for a review of the Government's position on climate change. The hearing was to be in five days and the chairman wanted a personal briefing from John in Washington as soon as possible. The secretary had added a note saying "this means tomorrow". John put down his briefcase and searched the internet for flights to Washington. United left at 10.30am, arriving in Dulles Airport at 1pm. He emailed back saying he would be in the chairman's office by 2pm the next day. The security guard came by again and John reassured him that, this time, he really was going home. When he reached his car he sat for a moment, thinking, as he had done a thousand times in the past weeks, about Saida. He knew her mother and father had been murdered and that she had spent a short time in Benghazi; he had even managed to talk to her brother but since then had no success in finding her whereabouts. Perhaps her brother was protecting her but they genuinely seemed as puzzled as he was as to where she had gone. Even the local chief of police had joined in the search but to no avail. Apparently she had left the country with a young man that no one knew. John came to his own conclusion and tried to pretend it was for the best.

CHAPTER THIRTY-THREE

The roads were deserted as John made his way to his apartment in Coral Gables. It was an impressive home extending to 5,000 square feet, with views of the sea and to the north, the pristine white beaches of Miami Beach. The apartment had its own elevator shared with just one neighbour whom he had never seen. As he fumbled to get his keys into the door lock the door opened. Jennifer gave John a big smile and a hug which he returned with limited enthusiasm. He had met again with Jennifer a few weeks after Saida had left. They spent a pleasant evening together and, on the rebound, John had asked Jennifer back to his apartment and she had been there ever since. There had been no conversation about marriage or babies and they both strenuously avoided mentioning Miami Beach or the Fontainebleau Hotel. John was already regretting asking Jennifer to move in. But at least she had kept on her old apartment.

John's father was deeply troubled by Saida's disappearance. He had taken her to his heart and had spent several evenings at the Cattlemen's Club regaling his friends about Islam and how Muslims, like most people on earth, only wanted to live in peace and be allowed to follow their own traditions. He argued the extremists were in a very small minority but aggressive action, such as the war in Iraq, only served to harden attitudes of the ordinary people against the USA and create more terrorists in its wake. When sceptics spoke of her sudden return to Libya, he combatively asked what they would do if their parents had been shot by terrorists.

"You look bushed, John, let me get you something to eat and we'll go to bed" said Jennifer.

"I have to go to Washington for two days. I need to pack but at least the flight isn't until 10.30am".

He headed to the bedroom without looking back. Jennifer already knew she should never have come back. As much as she loved John, she sensed that he had not got over Saida. She kissed him gently as she slipped into bed but received no response. John turned on his side with his back to her and appeared to fall asleep immediately. But his mind would not rest. The forthcoming presentation played on his mind. Eventually he had no option but to slip quietly out of bed and return to his study to redraft his work. Jennifer feigned sleep and lay on her back planning the next day. She would wait until John had left and then she would pack and return to her own apartment. At 2am John returned to bed and realising she was still awake, apologised for having to work so hard and promised to make up for it on his return. Her resolution to move out weakened. One loving word from John dispelled a hundred of his acts of discouragement. They fell asleep huddled, both full of their own doubts and insecurities.

Jennifer dropped John off at Miami International. She watched him go with a heart that was troubled but full of love. He turned as he headed inside the terminal, blowing Jennifer a kiss and giving her a broad smile. She really didn't want to lose him even if he had been moody and distant for the last few weeks. A policeman waved her on and she slowly drove down the exit ramp. As she did she reached across for her handbag and with her one free hand fumbled through the contents of the bag until her fingers touched a small packet of tablets. She wound down the window and threw the packet into the nearest verge. The ants could benefit from her contraceptive pills because now she had no need of them.

John threw his raincoat over his shoulder and was amused by the irony of his position. Here he was, about to lecture the country's decision makers on climate and he didn't know what weather to expect in Washington. Autumn could be cold but he guessed with the jet stream very far to the north and an anticyclone approaching from the mid-west it should be dry and warm. He settled into his seat and started reviewing the presentation. He stared at the words uncomprehendingly, his mind drifting. He knew his relationship with Jennifer was going nowhere and he was beginning to realise that nothing would fill the void created when Saida deserted him. And desert him she had. He just had to accept it. He contemplated following her to Libya but if she wanted him she would have made some communication. Surely she must know that he had made contact with her family. He could not, would not, rest until he had spoken to her again.

The flight attendant's voice came over the speaker and brought John's mind to the present. The plane landed ten minutes early and within a short time the bureau car was taking him downtown to the meeting room. The bureau sent a black Lincoln town car with magnolia upholstery. This one smelled new, reminding him how the office in

Washington, full of its own importance, accorded itself lavish treatment. The office in Miami had to make do with a five-year-old SUV.

The normal meeting room was part of a government building not far from the White House but on this occasion he was taken to a Georgian-style house in a leafy suburb of Washington. Security was tight and after a detailed personal inspection he was shown to an imposing room panelled in walnut. A polished boardroom table was surrounded with large armchair seats. Oil paintings of past presidents peered down from the walls and the thick carpets dulled the sound of the voices. The chairman, Red Russian was already seated and stood up to greet John with an outstretched hand and a big smile. Red's first name was Redwood but Russian was his real family name, thanks to a clerical error more than a century ago. It appeared that when his grandparents arrived at Ellis Island after emigrating from Russia, none of the officials could understand them so their name had simply been put on the register as Russian, and it had stuck. Over the years the family had become very successful, firstly in real estate then the law and Red had studied at Princeton. His unusual name meant that everyone he met remembered him. It also coincided with his political views so that even at university he became the leader of the left-wing faction of the Democratic Party. Nevertheless he was proudly American and was as anti-communist as he was anti-conservative. Red was not only the first member of the family to become a lawyer but also a politician and a member of Congress.

All the seats in the meeting room were taken and it appeared that all twenty five members of the committee had turned up. The membership of the committee was made up of politicians, academics and a sprinkling of business leaders. The secretariat was run by civil servants and the secretary motioned John to sit next to him. Formalities were dealt with by Red, who then turned to John.

"Ladies and gentlemen, as you know the new President is committed to reassessing the climate and the consequences for America and the world. You all know John Williams Junior and the key issue at today's meeting is to receive his report of the Weather Bureau's considered view of what is happening in our world today. You are all aware that on Friday I have to report to a Senate Committee reviewing our policies and it is essential that I have your full and considered views before then."

John opened his laptop and switched it to his PowerPoint presentation. The projector screen lit up with his name and job title. At the press of a button the screen changed to the title of the report – 'Factual Evidence Relating to the World Climate'. John began,

"Mr Chairman, ladies and gentlemen. You are all aware of the many conflicting opinions that exist across the world regarding the changing nature of the climate. Today I am not going to try to convince you one way or another. I will try very hard to confine myself to facts and let you decide. There are in reality two questions. One, is the climate changing? And the second is, if so is it the result of man's activities? The answer to the first question is easy. It is 'yes', the world's climate has always changed; one has only to think of the Ice Age that gripped the world all those millions of years ago. But what is happening now? The answer is complicated and judgmental. The use of satellites to measure land and sea temperatures has given us a vital tool but at the same time vast amounts of data to interpret."

John moved his slides on to a graph of temperatures around the world and how they differ from the average, some hotter, some colder.

"We at the bureau have used complex mathematical computations and have concluded that global temperatures have fallen in the last four years after a rise in the previous six and the current prediction is that the global temperature will be unchanged at the end of the decade compared with the beginning."

Some conversation broke out around the table and Red had to call the meeting to order. John started again this time showing that sea levels had barely changed over the last ten years and once more the more right-wing members of the committee began to voice their opinions. When the room quietened, John put up his next two slides showing the ice caps at the North and South Poles comparing the position ten years ago with the position today. The photographs clearly showed the reduction in the ice pack particularly at the North Pole which in John's view, had to be a sign of warming. John presented several more facts including the work of a world-leading Swedish professor, Bjorn Lomborg, who also agreed that there was evidence of slight global warming. John let the conversation continue around the table for a short time before continuing.

"You will see that the evidence is contradictory and no matter how clever the analyses the results are the same – that it is not possible to be certain that global warming is taking place. There are many people, academics and politicians, who have taken a very positive stance one way or the other. Just look at Al Gore and his film, The Inconvenient Truth. He received a Nobel Prize for his work but many of the presentational facts are questionable. You are all aware that a whole industry and academic stream has been built around the premise that the world is getting warmer and it gets harder to persuade people in entrenched positions to have an open mind. Therefore, ladies and gentlemen, the answer to the first question –is the world getting warmer – is simply that we, and by that I mean everybody, don't know.

"Turning to the second question – is mankind changing the climate – then in all probability, yes, but not by very much. Returning to Professor Lomborg... in his opinion if all the Kyoto Agreements were put in place it would only reduce global temperatures by 0.0075 degrees centigrade by the year 2100. But what I would like to show you now is a photograph of the world taken from the latest space walk. You will notice the very thin blue layer around the earth. That, ladies and gentlemen, is our atmosphere. You will see it does not ascend very far from the earth's surface and that is all that protects us from being fried alive."

John sat down and several arguments broke out around the table. Red once more called the meeting to order,

"Ladies and gentlemen, do you have any questions or comments to make to John?"

The first hand shot up. It was a governor of a mid-west state:

"I'm very disappointed to think of all that money we spend on the bureau and all you can come up with is a handful of contradictory charts. Is that the best you can do?"

The arguments raged around the room and Red temporarily lost order until he stood up, all six foot four of him, and banged on the table for order.

"You have heard the facts. They are contradictory and when statements are made one way or another then you know that however positive some academic or politicians seem to be, they are ignoring the alternative evidence. We know that there is now a whole business that has grown up around the global warming theory involving academics, business and government who have a vested interest in using the fear of global warming for their own financial ends."

Red called for one final question and an attractive young woman who had not spoken raised her hand. She stood up to ask her question and John noticed her trim figure and blonde hair and blue eyes.

"My name is Amelia Spencer. Could Mr Williams please tell us what his personal view is and what action we should take, if any?" She asked the question as if reading it from a written paper and in a very businesslike tone. John waited for her to sit down before answering,

"I am here today to give the official view of the bureau and I have tried to give you facts rather than opinions.

Totally off the record and definitely not to be associated with the Weather Bureau my view is that there is a relatively small rise in global temperatures and that there is an even smaller possibility that the activities of mankind are contributing to it. On the other hand as we don't know, I think it would be sensible to take measures to reduce our carbon emissions. I strongly feel that the political approach of trying to get people out of cars or asking countries like China and India to reduce their emissions is totally the wrong way to go about it and actions like the Kyoto Agreement are, in my view, doomed to failure. I think we as a nation should see the problem as a real opportunity. If I was the President, rather than trying to get individuals to reduce their carbon footprint and conserve energy, I would have a major initiative to develop the alternative to oil and coal. As a Texan boy I know that will sound like heresy to my friends and family, but I know we need a co-ordinated major effort ensuring university researchers work together across the whole country and that businesses are encouraged to co-operate in new developments. We could be world leaders in new forms of energy. We lead the world in aerospace, in defence equipment and in computers. I think we should make sure we lead the world in all the new forms of energy. The government should act in a way that uses the current situation to bring about a focused drive with everyone co-operating."

John suddenly realised that he was speaking with great emotion, his voice raised and his hand gesticulating. He stopped himself and grinned,

"I mustn't get carried away. Please remember the facts that I've presented."

Red called the meeting to a halt and the committee members gathered in small groups talking about John and his presentation. Occasionally a voice would be raised and fingers pointed. Red caught John's eye and beckoned him over.

"I want you to accompany me to the Congressional Hearing on Friday. You can sit immediately behind me and if I get stuck you can help me out."

Red didn't give John a chance to reply and as he walked away called over his shoulder,

"I'll see you an hour before the Hearing starts in the main hall of the chamber."

John had planned to be on the early evening plane back to Miami and he stood looking at Red's large back as he marched from the room. Pointless trying to get out of it especially as Red would simply ring up the Director of the bureau and anyway it would be interesting to go to Government House and attend a hearing, something he had only seen on television. As he watched Red disappearing down the corridor the attractive woman who had asked the last question came across and put out her hand.

"Congratulations on a very even-handed presentation" she said as she shook John's hand with a firm handshake,

"I have to say I don't agree with you. To me the evidence of the disappearing ice caps is all I need. I'm Amelia Spencer by the way and I'm a Professor of Nuclear Physics and Engineering at Buffalo University. This is my first meeting and I hope they are all as good."

John smiled and held her hand perhaps a little too long before congratulating her on her question.

"Best question all afternoon," John heard himself saying for no good reason.

As they walked from the building they passed a small coffee shop. They both looked at each other and laughed. They both had the same thought and within minutes they were drinking coffees together. Amelia was visiting Washington for two days to attend the meeting and then the following day at the Pentagon to discuss some military application that she was working on but was not allowed to discuss. It wasn't long before John had asked her to dinner. She readily accepted.

He had chosen a boutique French restaurant just off Pennsylvania Avenue. It was above his expense allowance but he decided he would make up the difference. Amelia arrived at the restaurant looking very elegant. She had changed into a classic black dress and a simple gold necklace with matching earrings. As she walked across the restaurant to their table heads turned to look. Amelia walked with the upright stance of a model in a way that was full of confidence in her own good looks. John felt rather shabby; he still wore the same clothes that he had worn for the meeting but at least he had managed to shower and shave. For a pre-dinner drink Amelia asked to see the wine list which she studied at length before ordering a glass of Duckhorn Viognier. John settled for a Jack Daniels on the rocks. Conversation for the first few minutes centred on the meeting and their views on their fellow members, especially Red Russian. Amelia hadn't taken to Red and suspected that his opinions, like most politicians, would change to suit the circumstances and the audience. Before long they were exchanging details of their personal lives. Amelia was divorced with no children; her ex-husband had left her for another woman some years earlier and since then she had concentrated on her career. Her work had given her the opportunity to travel widely and he found her conversation both interesting and at times provocative. As John looked at her across the table he mentally tried to guess her age and under the make-up were a few lines and wrinkles. She was probably older than he first thought, at least ten years his senior. They both ordered foie gras followed by duck breast and cherries, and John cast his eye down the wine list looking for a suitable wine. Before he could decide Amelia suggested a South African Chenin Blanc for the appetiser course followed by a Spanish Rioja with the duck. After two bottles of wine and a cocktail, John was glad he was within walking distance of his hotel. Amelia ate her food slowly but with obvious pleasure and the wine seemed to go down with great ease. As she ate John smiled as he remembered an article in Nature he had read on the plane about obesity. Apparently MIT had carried out research to ascertain if eating quickly caused obesity and in doing the research they asked three hundred people not only about their eating habits but also about their sex lives. The outcome had been that people fell into four groups; those who ate slowly but with enjoyment, those who ate slowly with no apparent pleasure and similarly with fast eaters some ate with relish and others ate quickly without even noticing what they were eating. The research had shown a direct correlation between their eating habits and their sexual performance and, if the research was anything to go by, Amelia would be awesome in bed. The meal was over and coffee was being served as John's mind turned to wondering if he should make a move on her. He wasn't a fan of one-night stands but Amelia was very attractive and hotel rooms could be very lonely. The conversation over dinner had been flirtatious and at other times serious. He had established that she had a regular partner in Buffalo for whom she appeared to have a great deal of affection. The coffee drinking was coming to an end and the waiter had presented the bill but John's dilemma was swiftly brought to a conclusion. Amelia put down her coffee cup and looked straight at John,

"Would you like to take me to my room, the hotel is just across the road? I'm sure we could get a nightcap or something there." John hesitated only for a second.

"Sure let's go'" and with that he stood up and held his hand out to Amelia and helped her on with her coat.

The walk to the hotel seemed to take an eternity and they hardly spoke. John took her arm and escorted her up the marble steps into the foyer. Amelia already had her room key and they stepped into the lift together and went to the sixth floor. John took the opportunity to gently kiss Amelia on the forehead to which she responded with a full-on passionate kiss on his lips. Once inside Amelia's room she didn't hesitate; in almost one movement her dress dropped to the floor and without looking she kicked it to one side.

John admired her beautiful figure, enhanced by elegant red underwear. She still had her high heel shoes on and she was wearing stockings. His body reacted instantly and he realised that he still had on his jacket and tie. His sudden urge had made his trousers very uncomfortable and he started to take off his jacket. Amelia stopped him and began to gently undress him, first his jacket then his tie. For a moment she struggled with the buttons on his shirt but stopped him when he made a move to help. "We must do this slowly," she whispered and gently opened his shirt to reveal his well-toned body. It was her turn to admire and as John put his hands on her shoulders he could feel a slight tremble. He still hadn't moved and as Amelia removed his belt he suddenly had the thought that he could end up just dressed in his shoes and socks. He moved away from her and kicked off his shoes and removed his socks in almost one movement. Amelia had stood back to watch but then returned to undressing him, pulling down the zip and letting his trousers fall to the floor. It was taking all of John's control not to grab hold of Amelia and throw her on the bed but she was determined not to rush. At last he stood naked in front of her, his penis firmly erect. He moved to hold her but she stepped back leaving her hand gently stroking him. John felt as if he would burst. He was on the verge of a climax and he hadn't even touched her. Amelia stepped back again and slowly removed her bra, her breasts were not large but firm and her nipples were as erect as his penis. He moved towards her and this time she put her arms around his neck so that he could feel the full contact of her breasts on his chest. He picked her up and laid her down on the bed. For a while Amelia tormented him but there came a moment when John could not hold back any longer. With his strong arms he pinned her to the bed and proceeded to make passionate love to her. Amelia groaned with pleasure and John was soon past his climax. As he rolled over she was breathing heavily, beads of perspiration on her forehead and her top lip. She smiled at him and looked down at his manhood, which was already showing signs of relaxation.

"Is that it?" she grinned at John "or do you think you could be up for dessert?"

"You are going to have to give me five minutes then we will see."

That evening they made love three times before John staggered back to his hotel. As he was leaving her he began to say something about seeing her again but she put her finger to his lips,

"Shh, don't spoil everything, let's just live for tonight."

CHAPTER THIRTY-FOUR

John didn't sleep well. He arrived back in his own hotel room at four in the morning. His night of lovemaking had taken its toll and as he looked into the shaving mirror he could see the redness in his eyes and the lines around his mouth. He took a cold shower and felt better. It was 8am and the hearing didn't start until 10.30. There would be time to have a brisk walk and then some breakfast. He looked at the phone and thought he really should ring Jennifer but with the guilt of the previous night still hanging over him he decided to leave it until after the hearing then he would have something to talk to her about without her asking what he had done the previous evening. John suddenly remembered he was meeting Red an hour before the hearing. A momentary panic seized him but he realised he still had plenty of time if he cut out the walk and had a light breakfast. As he was leaving his hotel room the phone rang; he hesitated wondering whether to answer it. It may be Red with new instructions. He picked up the phone. It was Amelia.

"Hi, how are you feeling?" she asked. Her voice was bright and breezy

"I called to make sure you were awake and not missing your meeting. You seemed a little tired when you left."

"I'm fine" John replied putting a brightness into his voice "Absolutely fine. It was a great evening."

Amelia interrupted him,

"I also wanted to know if you will be coming to the next

climate change committee. Perhaps we could book into the same hotel."

John looked at his watch,

"Sure, I'll get back to you a couple of weeks before the meeting. I've got to go now, don't want to keep Red waiting." Amelia finished the call and was gone.

John rushed breakfast; just a quick cup of coffee and a Danish. He checked himself in the lobby mirror, straightened his tie, picked up his briefcase and started the twenty minutes walk. The Government hearing was in a Senate Chamber and the investigating senators sat on a high dais with the chairman in the centre looking down on the interviewees. The hearings were conducted under oath and John had a recollection, like millions of other Americans, of Oliver North in his uniform, ramrod-straight, giving evidence about the Iran Contra affair. John already knew where the Senate Chamber was and took the steps of the large stone stairway to the main entrance two at a time. The first person he saw was Red who was holding court with a number of reporters. As John passed he called out and the reporter and television cameras turned towards John.

"This is one of the foremost experts on climate in the world" Red announced to all within hearing distance "and he will be supporting me today."

The reporter turned to John who smiled and dodged a couple of questions before following Red into the Chamber. It wasn't as big as he had expected and already several of the senators were standing together possibly discussing the proceedings or, more likely last night's football.

Red went over the document that John had presented. In spite of his brusque manner he had managed to absorb almost all of the facts that John had provided. Red was the main witness as Chairman of the Climate Change Committee. John, sitting immediately behind Red, listened to every word intently and was a little surprised when he praised John for his part in the work. The chairman hesitated for a moment then whispered in the vice-chairman's ear. He turned back to Red.

"If Mr Williams is so well-informed let's hear from him directly. Is he here?" Red turned and pointed towards John.

"Please come forward, Mr Williams, and take a seat next to Congressman Russian. John felt an attack of nerves. He knew his subject but this was different. He needed to be word-perfect. These were legal proceedings, matters of state.

He was asked to give his personal thoughts on climate change. He repeated pretty much the same facts he had given the previous day to the Climate Change Committee including his impassioned plea for the Government to see this as a business opportunity. All that was needed was the will to make all the parties work together. Senator Walton of Louisiana was not impressed. The global warming nonsense was one more attempt by foreigners to undermine the United States, although which foreigners he didn't specify. He also thought the idea of everyone sharing ideas for the benefit of the American people was just another form of socialism creeping into the country. He quoted James Taylor, Senior Fellow of Environment Policy at Heartland Institute in Chicago, who had declared that there was not one single fact to support global warming. The hearing adjourned at 12 noon. Red took John to one side.

"I'd like you to stay for the rest of the day and perhaps we could have dinner together, that's if you are not previously committed."

Red looked straight at John, a knowing smile on his face.

"No, I'm not committed at all, be happy to join you."

In reality John had planned to catch the early evening plane back to Miami but was still feeling guilty about his night with Amelia. Perhaps one more night away and he could face Jennifer without it showing.

The hearing went on until 5. Red sent John a message saying he would meet him at the Ritz Carlton at 7.30. Several other members of Red's committee turned up but not Amelia. He called Jennifer but she was not at home so he sent her a text message letting her know he was delayed and would be home midday Friday. But he fell asleep that night thinking only of Saida.

CHAPTER THIRTY-FIVE

John woke to the sound of the telephone. He hadn't asked for an early morning call. Perhaps it was Jennifer. He answered the phone sleepily and the voice of a woman asked if she was speaking to Mr John Williams Junior.

"Yes" he replied "and who, may I ask, are you?"

The caller ignored his question and asked,

"Are you alone?"

His irritation built up.

"As a matter of fact I am but what the hell has it got to do with you?"

"Mr Williams, I am calling from the private office of the President of the United States and he would like to speak to you."

John jumped out of bed. Was this a scam? Then a voice came on the phone that was instantly recognisable as President. Unwittingly, John found himself standing to attention.

"Mr Williams, forgive me for calling at this early hour. I understand you gave an excellent presentation at the hearing yesterday. Congratulations. We are already giving some thought to your suggestions. However I am calling you on another matter and I would appreciate it if you could come to the White House this morning at nine. Come to the West entrance and there will be someone there to meet you. I would also appreciate it if you did not mention your visit to anyone, not even your girlfriend."

"You have my complete reassurance Mr President,"

John tried to hide the slight waver in his voice then he heard the phone click as the President hung up. John's mind was in turmoil. The President wanted to speak to him, but why? On matters of bureau policy and strategy there were more important people than he in the service.

It was 7.35, time for a shower and shave. He needed a clean shirt preferably white. He called the concierge who calmly asked what size he needed. Sixteen-inch neck and 33-inch sleeve. the shirt would be with him in fifteen minutes.

"Oh and not a button-down" John called as the clerk put the phone down.

The clean shirt appeared at 8, perhaps leaving time for a cup of coffee and then a brisk ten minute walk to the White House. Yeah, it's just another morning, he thought, and I'm calling on the President. What do I say? "Hi Mr President, how you doing? And what can I do for you today?"

He walked down Pennsylvania Avenue, still half expecting this to be a hoax, and looked for the West entrance. It was one of the less imposing entrances and as he approached he looked at his watch – 8:40. Best kill five minutes then appear at the security barrier.

The guards greeted him as if they knew him and of course they already had photographs and his details on a screen in front of them. John was surprised how quickly he was through. No body-search or identification, though he passed through more than one surveillance device without being aware. As he walked through a large mahogany door he was confronted by a young woman dressed in a smart black business suit. Her dark brown hair was taken behind her ears, revealing expensive-looking pearl earrings. She smiled politely and asked him to follow her down a long carpeted corridor past several offices. At the end of the corridor they turned right to a noticeably hushed area. The young woman showed him into a small comfortably-furnished room with two large chairs and a sofa. A tray with coffee cups was on a small table. The young woman pointed to an easy chair.

"The President will be with you shortly" she said and quietly closed the door as she left.

There were only two coffee cups. Could it be possible he was about to have a one to one with the President of the United States? Before he could muse any further a second door opened and in walked the President, hand outstretched to shake John's. The President invited John to sit down in one of the easy chairs so that they were slightly at an angle to each other.

The President looked older close up and there was the first sign of grey hair around his temples.

"Mr Williams, what I am about to say to you is highly secret. Only five people know the substance of what I am about to tell you and that includes you and me. Have you seen the weather charts in the last two days?"

The President didn't wait for an answer but continued,

"Three hurricane force storms are in mid-Atlantic and heading for our coastline. If the storms continue to build up they could have a serious effect on Washington and the country.

"I know you predicted the land fall of Hurricane Zoe

with great accuracy and we need to do the same with these new storms."

John went to speak but the President held his hand up.

"I am sure that you and your staff are already working out the details as accurately as you can. None of this is why I have asked you here. This country has received a ransom note for two hundred million dollars from persons unknown who claim that they have created these hurricanes and more will be started in the near future if I, by which I mean the United States of America, do not accede to their request. My question to you John, is – is it possible?"

John waited a few seconds before answering.

"Well, Sir, it is highly unlikely. The conditions needed to create the initial spiral are not too difficult but the next stage is much more demanding. There needs to be just the right humidity, wind strength and sea temperature."

The President interrupted.

"Didn't some professor talk about the flapping of a butterfly's wings in South America could create a tornado in Texas or something like that?"

"You are correct, Mr President, that was Professor Lorenz, one of our greatest meteorologists, but he is now in his nineties."

"Mr Williams, I am going to level with you. We, the United States, have already produced, started or whatever you care to call it, several tornadoes in the Nevada Desert. The work is highly secret and is being developed under the banner of the Nuclear Energy programmes. The lead academic is probably known to you. She is Amelia Spencer, and I'm sure your work is known to her".

So that's what Amelia is doing at the Pentagon. Before John could let the coincidence sink in the President continued by asking who could be behind his development. John took a deep breath .There was only one person he knew who had the mathematical skill, the computer programming knowledge and a detailed appreciation of meteorology to even start to put together an experiment to create storms and that was Saida. John decided to keep his thoughts to himself, at least for the time being.

"John, let's talk about these storms that are only three days away, where will they make landfall?"

John felt himself shaking inside; he hadn't even looked at the weather forecast over the last two days. Before John could answer the President got him off the hook,

"Perhaps you could call your office and give me the latest update. I seem to recall that when Zoe went through you predicted the exact location and the height of the storm surge. I think I even called your chief to offer my congratulations."

"It was a team effort, Sir, and my storm division leader deserves most of the credit. She did all of the mathematics. Unfortunately she no longer works for the bureau and has left the country."

"That is unfortunate, can't you get her back?"

"The truth is she seems to have disappeared. A few months ago her mother and father were both murdered by Libyan terrorists and I suspect that she has returned to her family."

The President hesitated for a second before he asked

"Was her mother a lawyer at the UN?"

"Yes. And I do know her father was a surgeon."

The President picked up the phone on the small mahogany table by the side of his chair. He wanted the head of the CIA on the line. He asked about the UN lawyer who had been killed in Libya. John couldn't hear the reply but it seemed the agency was well informed about the murders.

"Is he available?" the President asked and the caller must have replied that he would call back.

The President smiled at John and invited him to help himself to more coffee. John declined; no breakfast and three cups of coffee already was more than enough. The phone rang. The President answered it with a brief; "Hi" followed by "get him to come over as soon as possible, I will arrange security at this end."

The President put the phone down,

"It appears that the CIA was very concerned that a lawyer with the Libyan delegation had been murdered. There was a theory that she had information that could be prejudicial to the improving relations between Libya and the USA. We sent a Major Ed Schick to Libya to investigate; he's on his way over and will be with us in thirty minutes. Please help yourself to a Danish. I need to sign some papers. I will come back when Major Schick arrives. With that the President left the room by a side door which opened just wide enough for John to see it lead into the Oval Office.

Immediately after the President left the room John was on the phone to his office. His secretary answered with her usual; "Hi John". She had seen his number come up on caller identification.

"I need the very latest on the three storms that are crossing the Atlantic now. I need the information in the next fifteen minutes and I don't care what it takes but call me every five minutes to update me."

He put away his cell phone and for the first time noticed a television receiver in the corner. Dare he switch it on; at least if he saw the weather channel he could have a better feel of things. He put his head around the door through which he had entered the room. A secretary was working across the corridor.

"Would it be possible to turn on the television in the President's ante-room?" he asked politely. The young woman looked up and smiled.

"Of course." She stood up and walked across the corridor with him.

"Which channel do you want to see?"

"The weather channel, please".

She pointed the remote at the screen, pressed 47 and the weather channel appeared. At least the commercials appeared. Here he was, in the White House, watching an advertisement for free fries with every flame-grilled whopper at Burger King this weekend while the President prepared to see him. The commercials seemed to last forever. Then it was the local seven day forecast that was suggesting only high winds and rain. At last the presenter appeared. It was Paul Goodlove, explaining the current unseasonably warm weather. But nothing about the storms. John's cell phone rang. It was Jack. He didn't waste words on courtesy

"These three storms are gathering force. They will become hurricanes and are forecast to hit anywhere from Miami to Virginia. The first hurricane is about three days away and getting stronger by the hour. The other storms are about two days after each other and slowing down but gathering in intensity."

"Thanks, Jack, keep me posted on any change and I need the very latest on the probable landfall site."

The door gently opened and a man's head appeared around the corner.

"Mr John Williams?" said the head and the door was slowly pushed open.

A tall ramrod of a man stepped into the room, hand outstretched. John shook the hand.

"Major Ed Schick from the CIA. Very pleased to meet you, Mr Williams."

Both men sat down and engaged in small talk, each unaware of what the other knew. Within minutes the door from the Oval Office opened and the smiling face of the President appeared.

"Glad to see you two are getting to know one another; let's get down to business and, by the way, John knows about the ransom note".

Before the President could continue John spoke.

"Mr President I have made enquiries about the pending storms. It is our view that they will each become a hurricane. The most likely place for landfall is Maryland and Washington DC and at the most it is only seventy two hours away. We must take all possible measures to prevent a very serious disaster. The last hurricane to hit Washington was in the last century. The city is not well prepared and the emergency services are going to be heavily stretched. I urge you to start preparing now."

"Don't worry, John, a meeting of the Joint Services Committee is meeting as we speak. Already the National Guard is setting out its plans as are the emergency services. In fact I would appreciate you staying around for the next few days, we may need your experience.

The President turned to Ed.

"Tell me about Alissa Sanussi".

Ed moved almost as if to stand up when addressing his Commander-in-Chief then sat bolt upright, his hands in his lap.

"You will recall, Mr President, that at the time of Mrs Sanussi's death that there was suspicion that terrorist forces in Libya were trying to disrupt the new friendly relationship that had been developing between our country and Libya for the last few years. I went to Benghazi to investigate and made contact with Mrs Sanussi's daughter on the plane to Tripoli."

John's eyes nearly popped out of his head and, forgetting all protocol;

"Was she Saida Sanussi?"

"Yes she was" replied Ed "but I didn't get to know her very well. She only spoke to me in the last few minutes of the flight. We lost contact with her in Benghazi. You may recall, Mr President that we quickly concluded the Sanussis had been shot by US Army personnel. It was an accidental shooting during their pursuit of terrorist suspects. The individuals involved have returned to the US and are serving punishment duties in a military prison. The complication was that the Libyan authorities didn't want it to be known that American soldiers were involved and for that matter neither did we. So the shootings were attributed to terrorists which gave the authorities good reason to increase the pressure on a group of militants led by, of all people, a member of the Sanussi family named Habib.

"The group are thought to be behind the explosions at the Great Man-Made River Project. Habib Sanussi has since disappeared and is thought to be hiding out in the Southern Desert. The daughter returned to the family home and set about renewing her research into the formation of rain at Benghazi University. She hired a personal guard who appeared to be always at her side and local police enquiries led them to believe that he was a known criminal involved in people trafficking. After about three months the daughter bought a Toyota Landcruiser, fitted it out for long distance travel and disappeared. The authorities are still searching but so far no luck."

During the conversation John's mind had been working overtime.

"Mr President, Ed, I have to tell you that Saida Sanussi is one of the foremost mathematicians and meteorologists there has ever been in the bureau. She trained under Professor Lorenz and it was her work that pinpointed the landfall of Zoe and the height of the storm surge. Saida used to work for me at the bureau and I'm afraid there is one further complication. She was my fiancée until she walked out on me, her job and the country."

Ed chipped in. "Don't worry, we already knew that."

John continued,

"If ever there was a person capable of developing a formula for the conditions needed to create a hurricane, it is her. It is not in her nature to be violent or aggressive and I would doubt that she would embark on such a venture unless she was under duress."

Ed looked at him intently.

"What if she found out that American soldiers killed her mother and father? Would that change her view? Perhaps she has come under the influence of this Habib guy."

The President was thoughtful for a minute and the other two men fell silent. The seconds ticked by for what seemed an eternity then the President spoke. His face took on a grave expression.

"Let's get these hurricanes out of the way and then, if there are signs that more storms are forming we will have to consider the ransom demand. We can go along with it until there is an opportunity to take them out. And I want them taken out without exception. I want this threat to our national security to be met with the most powerful response. This is priority level one, and all necessary resources will be available to you. Do we understand each other?"

"I understand, Mr President."

"John, we will need you to go with Ed to be able to make

a positive identification of Miss Sanussi, I suggest after the identification you leave whatever country you're in and let Ed take care of the details."

John felt he knew exactly what the President intended and shuddered at the thought of what might happen to the woman he loved.

CHAPTER THIRTY-SIX

This would be a story to tell his grandchildren. That extraordinary day had begun with a private audience with the President of the United States. And here he was, ending it by talking about state secrets over dinner with one of the most senior men in the CIA. They were in agreement as to their first task. They needed first of all to identify the source of the storms. Their position off the coast of Africa was readily pinpointed and John was able through his laptop to monitor the first signs of the storms as they started out from the coast. To calculate the origin was a little more difficult and could require a detailed review of satellite images from the American orbiting space station. This was a matter of mere routine to Ed. NASA had the material they needed within minutes.

John noticed that although Ed was designated a Major he clearly had much more influence than his rank suggested. John was beginning to realise that he needed to speak to Amelia about her work with the development of tornados and perhaps Ed could fix it. Two phone calls later John was speaking to Amelia.

"I'm glad you called. When are you next in Washington?" was her opening remark, "I'm missing you."

John quickly interrupted her.

"You are on speaker phone and I have a colleague, Major Ed Schick, with me. I'll call you on our committee business in the next few days." Ed joined in and got straight to the point.

"Have you received an email from the Pentagon this morning?"

"I'll have a look now".

They could both hear the sound of her computer booting up. After a few seconds she came back on the phone.

"I've got it, what do you want to know?"

"How successful have you been with your experiments and how did you go about it?"

"Our success so far has been very limited" she replied, "we have tried a number of ways. Our most promising involved a jet making tight circles and another plane hovering overhead, dropping ice particles into the vortex that the jet was creating. Sure, we got a mini-tornado but it quickly faded. We are moving to a new location to try it on water but none of us have been able to produce comprehensive models of the flow patterns that would give us the exact parameters we need. I think it is down to finding the very small variations that contribute to the whole. But it's eluding us at present."

Ed quickly ended the call. There was no need for her to know more.

After dinner John finally had the chance to talk to Jennifer. It had been a long day and tiredness had begun to creep up on him. She was taken aback when John told her about his visit to the White House. He had thought of a cover story for the visit. He was to observe the impending hurricanes and their potential for serious damage.

"The President has asked me to stay around for a few days and at least I will be able to witness the hurricane at first hand."

They exchanged declarations of love. After he had put the phone down John felt a twinge of conscience knowing the time was coming when he would have to be truthful and he let his mind drift to the time when he would return to Miami. He thought about how he would break the news to her over the next two days. John was still thinking of Jennifer and Saida when he was brought back to reality by his cell phone ringing. It was Jack. His words spilled out without stopping for greetings.

"The first storm is now hurricane force 2 which is not too bad but the second hurricane is already at force 2 and looks as if it could make force 4 by landfall. Maryland and Washington are going to take one hell of a hit. The storm's direction is north westerly and it looks as if it will go straight up the Potomac River."

"Thanks, Jack, I'll switch the television on and see what's going on.

The television commentators were full of dire warnings and people were being advised to take shelter or leave the city by the easterly route 66. The pictures flashed to the Chesapeake Bay Bridge which joined Cape Charles with Norfolk. The bridge was closed to all traffic and people in Maryland were being advised to drive north towards Philadelphia. John looked out of his hotel room window. The traffic was flowing normally. People were still on the streets and the shops remained open. The first splashes of rain appeared on the window and umbrellas started to go up. Within minutes the wind started blowing and he could see people leaning into the wind. But no sign of panic, no desperate scramble to escape. Perhaps the people of

Washington, who had never suffered a hurricane before, were taking this too lightly. John called his Washington counterpart at the Weather Bureau. It would be useful to assess the storm using the data they were collecting.

"Sure anytime. Take care coming I think the cabs have stopped running."

"No problem" replied John "I'll walk, it's only thirty minutes away."

John was glad of his raincoat as he stepped out of the hotel foyer into the wind and rain. He was amazed to see some shops still open. If this had been Miami everywhere would be boarded up and the stores emptied of water and supplies days before.

By the time he reached the bureau all his clothing was wringing wet. As he battled the wind and rain he remembered the last time he had been in a hurricane when he had searched for Saida. It tugged at his heart as he recalled how he had to stop himself from holding her in his arms and kissing her, like a romantic moment from an old-time movie. Surely she could not be responsible for this, no, not Saida. John knew Paul Murphy, as the two bureau bosses often had cause to speak to each other in the daily line of work. He knew straight away that Murphy had only bad news to impart.

"Come and look at this," he said and led John to the operation room where banks of television and computer screens were streaming out information from all over the region. The hurricane force winds were already hitting the land east of Chesapeake Bay. Uprooted trees littered the streets of Salisbury but at least there the streets were deserted. Paul spoke to John without taking his eyes off the screens.

"I'm really afraid that this hurricane has not been taken seriously. Very few people have left and many have not taken precautions."

As he spoke he heard the sound of breaking glass as a shop window was hit by flying debris. The cameras at Chesapeake Bridge clearly showed a storm surge pushing up the river in a six foot wall of water. That would bring flooding in its wake. Much of the land was low-lying and very few defences were in place. John turned his attention to the second storm. It appeared to have speeded up and was less than twenty four hours behind the first. Local television was beginning to show graphic pictures of the flooding and a helicopter rescuing a family from the roof of their home. The darkness of the night added to the fear of people trapped in flash flooding and a beam of light from the underside of a helicopter caught the reflection of a small car being washed away down river.

As dawn broke the eye of the storm passed by with a short period of calm and morning television's main item was the Mayor appealing for calm. Some looting had taken place overnight and the news had plenty of pictures with armed police patrolling the main streets. The White House appeared unaffected and a slightly shredded stars and stripes flag still fluttered from the flagpole. The storm soon unleashed its fury as the eye left the area. Winds up to one hundred miles per hour were reported from some parts of the city but it was the flooding that had caused the major damage.

The second storm swept relentlessly in, its winds stronger and the surge even higher. The whole city and the machinery of government were paralysed. The President appeared on television, pledging support from the National Guard and promising aid where it was most needed. John had slept for two nights on a sofa in the reception area of the bureau. A young office assistant had managed to make coffee. At least they had a generator and lights. Most of the city was without electricity, phone lines were down and the cell phone lines were constantly engaged. In the gap between storms John had managed to return to his hotel to shower. The message light was blinking on the phone in his room. It was a terse message from Ed,

"We need to get our plans together. We leave as soon as these storms are through. Make sure you pack something cool. I will call you in three days time. Be ready."

He rang Ed straight back.

"I need to go to Miami for my passport otherwise with a little bit of shopping I will be ready to go."

"Don't worry; I've got a passport for you.

How are you finding the storm?"

"We're holding on so far but it's tonight when the second one comes through that I'm worried the surge will be at least twice the size of last night. The flooding could even reach the White House", he replied ominously.

The third storm ripped through Delaware and severe damage was registered in Georgetown. The storm surge had just about engulfed the whole of Cambridge. Washington continued to be paralysed and the President

was back on television appealing for the nation to pull
together. Rescue teams from across the country descended
on the area. The National Guard were at full stretch
patrolling streets in the towns and cities across an area of
two thousand square miles. After six days of storms the
weather began to settle down and the authorities counted
the cost in damage and loss of life. Six hundred people had
died in flooding or storm-related accidents. The whole cell
phone network was jammed and the storm had caused
one hundred and twenty billion dollars of damage,
according to the insurance companies. Many of the dead
were from the poorer areas where precautions had been
least effective. Twenty people had been shot by police as
they looted the up-market stores of Washington DC.
Electricity supplies were cut off to most homes and only
those buildings with generators were functioning. The loss
of telephone lines meant that food stores could not accept
credit cards and in one small town in Maryland a mob had
rushed the supermarket and stripped the shelves of food.
Police had stood by impassively as the looters departed
weighed down with liberated items, many pushing them
in the store's own shopping carts. The banks remained
closed and most gas stations couldn't pump fuel because
of the lack of electricity.

The President toured the area and was taken aback by
the extent of the damage and even more worried about the
lawlessness taking hold on the streets. The National Guard
was under pressure and regular army soldiers were being
rushed in to the area and in some places were patrolling

the street with bayonets fixed, a sight not seen since the conflict over desegregation of schools in the 1960s. The President ordered the recall of thousands of troops back from overseas to help with the disaster recovery operation.

CHAPTER THIRTY-SEVEN

The two hundred million dollars ransom paled into insignificance compared to the cost in lives and property that the storm had brought with it. That the terrorists meant business and had the means to carry out their threat was no longer in question.

Ed reported back to the White House almost hourly as the crisis deepened. The American satellite surveillance had identified three possible points of origin and at one there were signs of a small campsite. It was decided to move immediately. John was part of a group which would be sent to Senegal on the pretext of a goodwill mission. From there they would enter Mauritania, covertly, as the country's government was hostile to the USA. Ed was choosing his best men for the operation. But he made it clear he felt John would be a burden. And the fewer witnesses to the action, when it came, the better.

The President called together senior members of his administration and the inner circle of White House advisors to announce his strategy for dealing with this, the most serious threat to national security since 9/11. His message to them was uncompromising.

"I've reached a decision. I have sent a message to the terrorists that I will not deal with them. That will unquestionably prompt them to launch another attack, compelling them to remain at their current location. We are monitoring their position by satellite. I have a team going in there on the ground, and if we know where they are and can keep them there, we can get to them. There will not be a major show of force, because they will use that as a pretext to portray our actions as those of an invader bent on intervention in the region. For that reason my team is a small one, but it is well-qualified to take on the task. My orders are that every last one of this cell of criminals must be eliminated. These terrorists will not be allowed another chance to threaten the American people".

The military executive jet took off from Dulles on a bright sunny morning. The devastation of the last few days was clear to see from the air and John marvelled at the thought that only six hundred people had died. The area looked as if an atom bomb had hit it and there was scarcely any movement. No cars, no trucks and very few people. They arrived at their destination ten hours later.

The airport was small with a short runway. Two experienced marine officers had been selected to join the mission and clearly they were resolute in the task that lay ahead. The plane landed with a jolt. The runway was peppered with holes and the nose wheel sent a shock wave through the whole plane as it hit a large pothole. John looked out of the window. Ed leaned over to him.

"We've landed at a disused airport. Apparently the authorities were not happy to see a US military plane so we had to come by the back door".

The jet came to a halt in a dark isolated part of the airport. Within seconds the stairwell was out and the four men hurried out. The heat and the smell of the tropics hit

John almost before he set foot on the ground. Within seconds beads of perspiration were on his forehead and down his back.

Out of the night a small figure appeared. He was an African in a long robe-like garment. John was surprised to hear him speak with an impeccable English accent.

"I am David. We must be on our way quickly. No unnecessary conversation please."

A Toyota Landcruiser appeared across the tarmac and parked next to the jet. The hold door was already open and the four men passed the contents to each other and into the vehicle. John noticed several submachine guns and other weapons along with provisions, flashlights and a case of hand grenades. David had disappeared into the dark but returned driving another truck. Apparently he was to be their guide to take them across the Mauritania border and on to Mbout, a journey of about eight hundred miles.

David hurried up the team. The longer they were close to the airport the greater the danger. The jet was already taxiing down the runway, the pilots happy to be on their way to a friendly airport so that they could refuel. The two vehicles left the airfield perimeter in convoy stopping only to change drivers. The plan was to drive through the night, get across the border and then review their plan of action. John marvelled that no one seemed tired except him and he closed his eyes and dozed. His turn for driving would come.

CHAPTER THIRTY-EIGHT

Aktham and Habib sat huddled together over their computer. The response from the Americans was due any time soon if they intended meeting their deadline. As they talked Habib's laptop chimed to indicate an email had been received. The message was terse and to the point. The United States of America does not respond to blackmail by terrorists. No signature, no encouragement, no doubts. Aktham and Habib looked dismayed. Aktham broke the silence, his voice in a whisper.

"It is clear that the USA needed another dose of our particular brand of medicine to bring them to their senses".

Saida spent the evening with Brian and Mustapha before returning to her communications tent. She switched on the satellite tracking device and managed to pick up the Al Jazeera television station. The news was on and it was showing the devastation caused by the hurricanes. Even the Arab commentator seemed genuinely grieved to see the toll in human life that had been inflicted by the storms. One poignant scene, captured by an amateur video, showed two small children being washed away holding onto a broken door. Suddenly the door disappeared and the children were screaming in terror. Their mother ran into the flooded river but couldn't reach them as they disappeared under the swirling torrent. The news coverage continued with many more similar scenes, each one filling Saida with horror. These innocent people had nothing to do with her parents' death and she felt the first signs of misgiving for the part she had played in the devastation. She thought of all the lives she had saved by predicting the landfall of Zoe. Now she had sacrificed even more lives for a cause in which she was increasingly losing faith. Brian and Mustapha stood behind Saida and watched the news in silence and when it finished both left without comment. Saida made her way back to her tent as Habib and Aktham came out of theirs.

"We need to talk to you, Saida, about when can we start our experiments again. It appears that our enemy has not responded well. Perhaps another series of hurricanes may change their minds."

Saida interrupted,

"But we have achieved what we set out to do. The Americans have taken large numbers of their troops back home. We have all but removed them from our country. I've just heard it on the news."

Habib and Aktham looked at each other and Habib said gently,

"I think it is time we told you of our new plan. We believe the Americans must pay for their past deeds. So we are demanding a ransom from the American Government to stop the hurricanes and so far they have rejected our generous offer. We need to send a little more unhappiness their way. When do you think conditions will be right for our next adventure?"

Saida looked at both men in horror. This was not why she had embarked on this venture. She believed they had been acting for the good of the Libyan people. Now she was to be an accomplice in some money-driven extortion scheme to enrich these two men. All along they had used her for their own financial ends.

"We of course will give you your share when we receive the money."

Saida answered angrily.

"I don't want or need your money. I feel remorse about the misery and torment we have caused many innocent people, but I believed it was for a just cause. Now I see your reason for coming here. Well I will have no more of it. I am returning to Benghazi and I will continue my research work on the formation of rain. I would like to leave as soon as possible."

With that she turned and walked in a determined fashion back to her tent.

Aktham looked at Habib,

"You must tell her the facts of life. She is going nowhere until we have sent more storms across the Atlantic."

Habib knew Saida was a determined woman. It would not be easy to change her mind.

"I'll talk to her but I think we may have to resort to a little more gentle persuasion than conversation," he said.

Habib waited a while before walking across to Saida's tent. She had already undressed and was in a long white robe. Habib called out and Saida put her head outside the tent holding the lower flaps together concealing her body.

"Saida, Aktham means business. He is not a man to mess with as you already know. Please reconsider. At least one more attempt, then we will review the situation."

"Habib, my mind is made up. I will not cause any more harm to innocent people."

As she spoke she let the flaps of the tent slip and her dressing gown was partially open. Habib looked at her and felt a growing desire; a desire he had contained for weeks. He felt his breathing rate increase as his heart beat a little faster. Saida saw his eyes looking at her body and she quickly covered up, said goodnight and firmly zipped up the tent from the inside.

Habib reported back to Aktham on his failure to convince Saida to change her mind. Aktham wasn't surprised.

"We will have to take harsher steps tomorrow," he added without explanation.

The following day they all watched the television coverage of the American disaster. The numbers of dead were growing and the pictures of the children drowning were repeated over and over again. During the afternoon Aktham asked Saida to walk with him. As they strolled along the rough track made by the SUV he talked gently to her, asking her to reconsider her decision. His voice although gentle was persistent and more than a little menacing. Eventually he came to the point,

"You will help us, Saida, you are our prisoner here and I would hate anything to happen to your family in Benghazi. We need you to start your work tomorrow. We need to know when conditions will be right to strike again."

Saida thought about her two brothers and their children. How vulnerable they would be. She was trapped. After a few moments Saida nodded in agreement. She would buy time. Perhaps the weather conditions might not return for weeks and Aktham would become weary of the wait. That night after dinner Mustapha asked if he could watch the television news again so they both walked across to the information tent. Saida set the satellite dish into the correct position and switched on the computer. The generator outside rumbled on, drowning out the noise of the crickets and bullfrogs. Mustapha looked at Saida and put his finger to his lips. He looked out of the tent. Brian, Habib and Aktham were talking around the small camp fire. Mustapha turned to Saida,

"In Kufra, Aktham promised me one million dollars to look after you and make sure you did as he asked. So you will see you have been a precious commodity to me. I have been with you now for six months and over that time I have admired you greatly and I care for your welfare. I am worried for your safety. Aktham is not a man to be underestimated and life is a trivial matter to him. I have a plan to help you escape. I know where the key to the truck is kept and I know the route from here better than anyone. Tonight meet me at the truck at two. I will be sitting inside waiting; I won't start the engine until you are with me. I've found a route that they cannot follow and the helicopter cannot fly at night. Bring nothing with you, we need to travel light. We can be in Mbout by mid morning; we will avoid the airport and get a ship to anywhere as long as it is away from Mauritania."

Saida listened, her heart beating faster. Mustapha seemed sincere and she had taken a great liking to him. She agreed with a small nod of the head. The entire conversation had taken place with them both looking at the television screen.

That night Saida lay in bed wide awake, gripped by fear

and waiting for the appointed hour.

At two Saida left her tent by the back and silently made her way to the SUV, keeping in the shadows. As she approached the 4x4 she could see the silhouette of Mustapha already in the cab of the vehicle. When she opened the door of the cab there was a creak where a hinge needed oiling. She hesitated and waited, not daring to move. Nothing stirred and she breathed a sigh of relief She slipped inside and said quietly,

"Let's go."

Mustapha didn't speak or attempt to start the vehicle. Saida put her hand out to him and he slumped forward on to the steering wheel. His head turned towards her, eyes staring and his face covered in blood from the bullet hole between his eyes. Saida turned to get out of the vehicle. Aktham was standing directly in front of her and made her jump and cry out aloud. He had the suspicion of a small smile on his face as he held out his hand to help her down from the vehicle. She ignored his hand and made her way back to her tent not speaking but trembling in fear. There was no chance of sleep that night. Her brain worked overtime but to no avail. There were no alternatives, tomorrow she would start looking at the world weather maps again.

The following day all signs of Mustapha's death had been removed. Brian was informed of the events of the night and was clearly shaken. He resolved to himself to get out using the helicopter as soon as possible even if it meant losing his five million dollars of the ransom, but he would have to choose his time. At least he was an invaluable part of the business. Shooting him would achieve nothing.

Saida computed that the next favourable weather pattern for starting a storm would be in two or three days time. The time passed uneasily and Habib seemed particularly edgy. In the evenings Saida felt unable to speak to Aktham and sat alone in the communications tent looking at weather patterns and when possible television programmes across the world. She retired early and read for a while. The flickering light from the bare bulb powered by the generator made her eyes tired. She slowly undressed feeling so depressed. She thought of John and her family. She thought of her work and regretted ever getting involved with Aktham. As she was undressing she remembered that the bulb in her tent was still on and quickly went to switch it off. As she did, a hand came through an opening in the tent and placed it on hers. It was a dark hand, a strong hand, the hand of Habib. He had made a short slit in the tent wall next to the zip. His hand found the zip and he pulled it up and stepped inside. He didn't speak but looked at her, his eyes wide and his mouth open. He stepped towards her and as she began to protest. His hand covered her mouth.

She fought back, biting his hand until she drew blood. She was strong but he was much stronger. He threw her onto the bed and lay with his full weight on her. She could hardly breathe. The evil smell of his breath filled her nostrils as his face came close to hers. He made no attempt to kiss her but held both her arms above her head. He could hold both wrists with one hand and with his other began tearing at her clothes. He attempted to kiss her bare breasts but she squirmed and nearly got her hands free. He managed to tear away under garments and began to use his leg to force her legs apart. He was struggling to get his abaya up; he wore no underwear, his penis erect. Saida struggled again and got one hand free; she scratched down his face until it bled. Habib spoke for the first time,

"Submit or I will kill you" he whispered.

She was spread-eagled across the bed, the smell of his unwashed body filled the tent and she felt her strength weaken. As she relaxed he managed to get his legs under hers, pushing them up and exposing her. He struggled to achieve penetration, getting more desperate each time he tried. He let go of her hands and forced himself into her. She beat him with her fists but nothing was going to stop him now. It was over in seconds; the passion that he had for her for ten years gone in a few short strokes.

He looked down at her. She was bleeding as a result of his rough penetration. Her face was bruised and red. His look at her was one of contempt. He slowly adjusted his abaya, his erection already fading, then without speaking, turned to leave the tent. As she lay on the bed Saida's hand stretched out and she felt something hard and remembered her gun. As Habib bent his head to duck out of the tent, she slowly raised the gun and took careful aim. The shot hit him in the middle of his back. He turned with a puzzled look on his face. A second shot penetrated his chest and blood trickled from the wound staining his white abaya a bright crimson. He fell towards the bed, dead.

In seconds Aktham and Brian were at the door of her

tent. Saida crept into a corner, a blanket wrapped around her. She slowly started to sob that gave way to a wailing cry of anguish. Brian tried to console her but she still had the gun in her hand. She waved it at him so that he stood back putting both his palms towards her as a gesture of submission. Aktham dragged Habib from the tent and Brian backed away. The noise of the generator slowly died away as it ran out of diesel. The sounds of the jungle re-emerged unnoticed by Saida. She sat in the corner of the tent not moving, still holding the blanket in her mouth. Her eyes were open but not seeing. Aktham nodded towards the tent door suggesting they leave but Brian bent down on his knees and gently held out his hand. She gave him the gun. Brian gently tried to help her back to the bed but she pulled back like a frightened animal. Aktham whispered.

"Let's leave her for a while. I'll come back in an hour and maybe we can persuade her to take a sleeping pill."

As Aktham and Brian left they felt the wind change so that it was coming from the south east.

"Looks as if Saida was right again" murmured Aktham, almost to himself. He turned to Brian.

"We will try again tomorrow but this time I will fly with you. I don't want you deserting me now. Saida will be okay on the ground. I will have the vehicle keys; she will have nowhere to go".

The next morning Saida appeared at the door of her tent. Both Aktham and Brian looked up and waved a greeting. She ignored them both and set off down the track to the lake. At the lakeside she undressed without modesty. She was past caring about someone looking at her and she plunged into the lake, the bruises and scratches stinging at the touch of the water. The blood on her legs had congealed and took a gentle rubbing to come away. She immersed herself in the water not caring if there were crocodiles or snakes around. She scrubbed herself clean and as she did she remembered doing the same thing after she had made love with John. This wasn't the same; the terror of the previous night was still with her. The cool water slowly brought her brain back to some sort of normality. Her first thought was the need to pray and she quickly left the lake, dressed and made her way back to the camp site. Aktham and Brian were eating a meagre breakfast and the depression of the previous night's events hung over them. Saida set her prayer mat facing Mecca and prayed for forty minutes. She swayed back and forth on her knees almost passing into a trance-like state. The prayers at an end, she stood up and gave Aktham a hard bitter look. He gave half a smile and Brian stood and walked towards her. Her face was a mask of hatred. Brian held out his hand which she gently took and led her to the campfire.

"Saida, what happened last night was not of our making. Habib was an animal and you had every right to shoot him. He deserved all that he got."

Saida stiffened and stood up ready to run. Brian calmed her down again and told her that the plan was to leave that evening but first there would be one last try to create the fourth storm. He and Aktham would ride the helicopter and she would be the guide. Without saying it, he implied

that her co-operation was a condition of her leaving the
camp site alive and Saida was aware enough to
understand the message.

CHAPTER THIRTY-NINE

John sat up front in the leading vehicle with David. David had had an eventful life which started out in the Congo where he had been dumped on the doorstep of a catholic mission. Hence he was named after one of the saints. He had no idea who his parents were but, thanks to the mission, he had a good education which took him to university. From there he had entered the civil service in the Foreign Office of the Congo. The work had been fraught to say the least as his principal job was to demonstrate to the outside world that the military government was a benevolent dictatorship bent on restoring democracy. From there he had been recruited by the CIA.

The crossing of the border into Mauritania had been easy. Border guards maintained posts only on the main roads and a short cross-country diversion had by-passed any trouble. The convoy looked like a hunting party and they traversed the eight hundred miles without incident. John was beginning to enjoy the adventure, in particular the comradeship that developed from living rough but more than anything he was obsessed by the thought of seeing Saida again.

Ed was clearly in charge and in the evening over an army rations meal he spelled out what he expected from each of them. John had just one task, to identify Saida then he was to return to the vehicles. In no way was he allowed to advance on the camp site and he was not given a weapon.

The instruction to the others was 'shoot to kill'. Ed had explained that the destruction of the site and the people around it was of the utmost importance to the United States. He didn't explain why and nobody asked. They knew their job, it was to eliminate without question. They had all done it before and comforted themselves with the thought that whatever the reason they were saving American lives.

The satellite navigation was showing that they were close to the campsite, possibly as near as five miles. The afternoon thundershowers arrived, leaving the track deep in mud. Ed decided that they should rest and approach the camp site after dark. They could carry out a reconnaissance and formulate their battle plan ready for the following day. A dawn raid always caught people unaware, but first of all they needed to know how many people were involved. The rain hammered down and the south-westerly wind howled around their vehicles. No one smoked as the high explosives in both cabs were fragile and the last thing they needed was an accident. As the rain cleared John wound down the window of the vehicle and looked towards where Saida could be hiding. A thought struck him. He jumped from his cab and walked towards Ed who was gazing into the distance through his binoculars.

"Ed, I think Saida must be a prisoner. She would never do this of her own accord."

Ed mused for a while and turned to John,

"Tell me who could come up with the whole idea of attacking the USA through the weather. I don't think it would be your run of the mill terrorist. And even if she was forced into it presumably she could have easily made an error so that the project didn't work. You've told me that the slightest alteration to the parameters would render the project useless. After all, Amelia hasn't been able to do it yet with all the computing power of the Pentagon behind her. Face up to it, John, she is up to her neck in this and our country's security is at stake. She will be better dead than the fate she would have if we took her back to the States."

John's heart sank. But Ed was right, very few people could have thought of the idea and even fewer could have made it happen. The pictures of the devastation of Maryland and Washington was still very clear in John's mind. Six hundred people were dead and bodies were still being discovered in the Potomac.

Suddenly Ed put down his binoculars and listened; he put his fingers to his lips to quieten John and listened more carefully.

"It's a helicopter, sounds like a military chopper."

He picked up his binoculars again and scanned the horizon. He stopped.

"Got it" he said out loud, "looks like an old Lynx and it's hovering with full power on. What the hell is he doing?"

John already knew.

"They are creating a new storm. The wet conditions and the south westerly wind may be part of the conditions they need."

Ed hesitated for only a moment before running back to his vehicle.

"We are going in now" he shouted to his team, pulling his battledress together as he ran.

The men all jumped into their vehicles and were on their way in a matter of seconds. The weapons were handed out and Ed reached over and attempted to lift a large case over the seat. He couldn't manage it alone so one of the other men helped and between them they were able to take the top off and lift out the rocket launcher. The vehicle hit a bump and the launcher fell from Ed's hands. He grabbed it and held it on his knee. The vehicles were travelling along an escarpment with a view down the valley and the helicopter was now clearly visible. The vehicles screeched to a halt and Ed jumped out and within seconds the launcher was on his shoulder. The mechanism was loaded, the viewfinder in position. The helicopter was a sitting target hovering fifty feet above the ground. Aktham and Brian never saw the rocket. The explosion was spectacular and debris rained down on the camp site. Saida fled for cover. The truck with the helicopter fuel caught fire and exploded, burning the campsite tents. A plume of black smoke rose high into the air. Saida ran in panic her clothes burning and smouldering from the heat. Her final thoughts as she lost consciousness were of her mother and father. Ed took one vehicle and two men down towards the wrecked helicopter. He instructed John to stay behind. Ed's truck disappeared along an old track and David excused himself and went into the bushes to relieve himself. John looked at David's vehicle. The key was in the ignition. The impulse was too great. John jumped into the truck revved the engine and shot off down the track in hot pursuit of Ed. From the top of the ridge John could see Ed with gun in hand looking down on a body, he was not clear if the body was a man or woman but Ed held the gun as if to shoot. John breathed hard and jumped from the SUV and started scrambling down the rocky slope, rocks and debris tumbled after him and the thorn bushes tore at his clothes. John was screaming at the top of his voice for him not to shoot.

Ed looked up before looking back at the body on the ground, putting a bullet in the head. At the campsite the scene was one of devastation. When John arrived Ed was already searching the smouldering remains of the helicopter cabin. The charred bodies of Brian and Aktham were clearly visible, one with Ed's bullet in the head. Ed looked up as John arrived, an expression of anger then resignation crossed his face and he instructed one of his men to go back and fetch David. Ed didn't speak to John as he set out a pattern for the five men to search the area and within minutes one of the men called out. He had found a shallow grave. John's heart beat faster – was it Saida?

He turned away, unable to look. The body was slowly unearthed and the remains of Habib exposed. The ants had already been at work but his strong features remained. Ed took a photograph and emailed it to his colleagues back in the USA. The grave of Mustapha was found nearby and more photographs taken. The search went on. John began calling out Saida's name but to no avail. They had widened their search checking the undergrowth when one of the team called out,

"Over here".

The other four ran to his call but Ed stopped John,

"You may not want to see this".

But John was in no mind to stop now. Saida lay face down tangled in the thorny bushes of the scrub. She obviously had been running away probably looking over her shoulder. Her clothes were badly burned on the back. Ed gingerly bent down and touched her on the neck. He looked up.

"There's still a pulse – get the first aid box here quickly!"

John bent down and put his hand on the back of her head. Saida moaned and John saw the signs of a serious wound down her arm, he whispered into her ear,

"Hang on, I'm here, I will look after you."

Saida attempted to move but fell back still only semi-conscious. The first aid kit arrived and Ed began to cut away Saida's clothes. She had obviously been knocked unconscious by burning debris and had fallen into the thorny bushes. They cut away the branches and carefully removed them from her body. Saida moaned in pain as they waited for the morphine injection to work on her. With the bushes removed all five men together carefully lifted her onto a mattress and she slipped into unconsciousness again. Ed checked her pulse; it was still there and remarkably even. Between them they laid her on the stretcher still keeping her face down because of the wounds on her back. Ed gently bathed the cuts and removed the congealed blood.

"She's in a bad way but she'll live" he declared.

"She'll have some scars but I don't think that will bother her. Let's see if we can turn her over."

Between them they gently turned her on her side. It was the first time they had all seen her face. It was cut and scratched with the thorns.

"Looks worse than it is", declared Ed as John took over the cleaning and removal of thorns.

He suddenly remembered how he had taken small pieces of glass from her beautiful face when they were caught up in Zoe. He could still see the very fine scars and now she will have some more he thought. As John worked on her she opened her eyes and a faint smile crossed her lips. She tried to speak but John hushed her. He held a flask of water to her lips and she managed a small drink.

"I knew you would come" she whispered to John before lapsing into unconsciousness again. Ed took over,

"We need to get her out. I think she is badly hurt and has taken a massive blow to the back of her head and back. She still has feeling in her feet which is a good sign. The dilemma is do we take her to the nearest hospital in Mauritania and risk being arrested or do we try to get back to Senegal. The border is only seventy miles away."

David joined in.

"I can arrange a helicopter to pick her up when we get over the border."

"Okay that's what we'll do", Ed decided.

They carefully laid Saida in the back of one of the vehicles. John was beside her. Ed drove and David took the lead vehicle.

"We need to move fast. The sound of the explosion will have been heard for miles. We can expect the Mauritanian military to be already on their way."

The journey was hard and seemed never-ending and Saida occasionally moaned with pain. She lapsed into unconsciousness and hadn't spoken since the whispered words to John and he began to fear that she was seriously hurt. At last they crossed the border. David searched the sky with his binoculars for the helicopter. Eventually they could all hear the rhythmic beat of the helicopter's engine. Saida suddenly sat up and screamed. The engine noise had brought back memories of the last few hours. She sank back on the stretcher, eyes closed. Ed turned to John.

"At least her back isn't broken."

The helicopter landed and they loaded the stretcher. The pilot signalled he was ready to go. Ed called out to John to leave the helicopter but he refused to move.

"I'm going with her; I'll find my own way back to the States" he replied without even looking away from Saida's face.

Behind him he heard the click of the safety latch being taken off a gun. John looked up and Ed had his gun pointing at Saida.

"This woman is a terrorist and I have every right to kill her and if you don't leave this helicopter now then I will not hesitate to do so. Take a good look at her. It's the last time you will set eyes on her. David will see that she gets to hospital and there she will come to realise the serious consequences that will occur if she tries to cause problems for the USA ever again. I already know letting her live is a mistake but, John, you need to forget her and get on with your life."

John very slowly stood up. He could not let go of her hand. Ed's patience was wearing thin.

"She dumped you, buddy, and never even called. You need to get over her. Let's go."

John felt tears in his eyes but Ed was right. She had never tried to contact him and she was, by any definition, a terrorist. He slowly placed her hand by her side and kissed her on the forehead as he said goodbye. The helicopter with Saida and David on board slowly took off and headed south towards Senegal. John, Ed and his companions all watched in silence as the helicopter slowly disappeared over the horizon. Ed sharply brought them back to reality,

"Let's go, we need to get to the airfield as soon as possible before all hell breaks loose."

The journey took several hours over bumpy dirt tracks, crossing shallow river beds until eventually the disused airfield where they had arrived just a few days earlier appeared in the distance. John had not spoken throughout the journey, lost in his own thoughts, tormented by so many mixed emotions. How could he still love her after what she had done? But he couldn't forget her last words – "I knew you would come".

Ed broke the silence,

"You need to forget about this whole operation and that

includes Saida. If you were ever to think about speaking to anyone such as the press, then your pretty Arab girlfriend will suffer".

It slowly dawned on John that saving Saida's life was not an act of charity but a way that Ed would in future have a hold on him, After all this story was not one they would ever want to be made known. Ed was after all a true patriot.

"We will be keeping a watch on Miss Sanussi, partly because we are not sure about David. He's been with the CIA only a short time and he could possibly be a double agent. If word gets out about Saida then it can only be you or he and I don't think you want to seal her death warrant."

The flight back to the US was long and tedious and very few words were spoken. The jet landed at Dulles airport in late evening and pulled up to a discreet hangar on the far side of the airport. There were no officials greeting the plane and John was surprised to see his carry-on suitcase and briefcase standing isolated at one end of the hanger. A puzzled look crossed John's face,

"What happens now?"

Ed looked surprised.

"Nothing, you find your way back to Miami. You're at an airport so that shouldn't be too hard but I suggest you change your clothes before you leave."

With that Ed and his companions shook hands with him and were gone. John suddenly felt very lonely and depressed. The hangar echoed to his footsteps as he followed the signs to the exit and out to the civilian part of the airport.

CHAPTER FORTY

David had managed to get Saida comfortably lying on her side. She was still unconscious. There were no medical supplies on board other than a small medical cabinet that contained some aspirin. The journey took two hours and by the end Saida was in considerable distress. She talked a gabble of words that David didn't understand except for the occasional reference to John. The helicopter took them straight to hospital in Dakar. The Presidential Memorial Hospital had a rooftop helipad and its patients had included the most prominent people in Senegal, right up to the President himself. Its standards of care and facilities compared with anything in the west.

Saida was very gently lowered onto a stretcher and immediately given oxygen. The burns unit were already examining her back as she was taken by lift to the operating theatre. The senior consultant was a tall well-mannered Englishman. After examining her he decided that the burns could wait. He was more concerned about the blow to her head. Fortunately, the MRI scans showed injury at the base of the head but there was no evidence of brain damage. The doctor decided to continue with the morphine and let her rest for twenty four hours before making any further decisions. The burns unit had already decided that the severity of the burns on Saida's back was such that they needed extensive treatment. The hospital had on trial a new burns repair technique developed in the UK that used cells from the patient's own skin. They were grown in a laboratory and then implanted into the wound. There had been very little clinical work done on this treatment in the Presidential Memorial but this was undoubtedly a case suitable for the technique. The chief consultant gave the go-ahead and cells were taken from Saida within hours of her being admitted to the hospital.

After twenty four hours Saida's fever had abated a little and her heart beat was strong and steady. She remained in a coma in the intensive care unit for five days before she opened her eyes. David had visited regularly during the five days and had passed the time talking to her even though he didn't even know if she spoke English. The local language of Senegal was Wolof, which contained a few Arabic words but the official language used in business and administration was French, a throwback to the time when Senegal was a French Protectorate. David held Saida's hand and from time to time whispered to her the traditional Arab greeting, usually translated as "peace be with you".

After five days Saida opened her eyes when David spoke.

"Wa aleikum assalam", she said, giving the traditional response and wishing in return peace on the other person.

Saida slowly recovered her consciousness and after two weeks was talking normally. The burns unit had still to complete the autologus cell growth and it became clear she would be in hospital for several weeks. David was by her bedside every day, and would help with any request she made – apart from telling her what had happened at the campsite. He was vague about why he was in Mauritania and claimed he had no recollection of whom she was with.

He told her of the discovery of other bodies and Saida realised all the others were dead. Her own memories gave her nightmares and she could still remember Habib's face as he turned to leave her tent. Could she really have shot him dead? She knew she had and had felt no remorse.

As the days passed Saida grew stronger and while her burns treatment would continue, she was able to leave hospital. She rented a small apartment and was soon helping the local university in its mathematics department. Slowly the desire to go home returned. She called her brother to say her project was finished and that she would be returning to the family home in the next few weeks. Her brother was overjoyed and relieved to hear from her. He told her Habib was still a wanted man. Colonel Gaddafi had offered a reward for his capture. But there had been no trace of him. He had simply vanished after killing their mother and father. Saida said nothing. Perhaps there would be a time when she would tell her two brothers the truth but not just yet.

After three months Saida was well enough to return to Benghazi. The family gave her a huge party and made her feel at home again. She fell back on her well-rehearsed cover story when confronted with questions about where she had been for the last few months. To complete her return to normal life she returned to the university as a research fellow in mathematics. And yet she thought about John nearly every day. She tried to recall those fragmented memories of the last hours in Mauritania. He could only have come to her in her imagination.

David kept in touch with her and they spoke from time

to time on the phone. What she didn't know was that all of their conversations were relayed to Ed Schick. All told Schick was well pleased with the results of his work. As far as John was concerned, the mission had never happened. He had neutralized a very serious terrorist threat. And as a bonus, he had been able to test David's loyalty. It was a tidy job all round, and the President had made his gratitude clear.

CHAPTER FORTY-ONE

John stood on the roadside outside the terminal building. In the space of a few days he had experienced the defining moments of his life. He was there at the very heart of world-changing events. And what now? With his case, briefcase and his raincoat slung over his shoulder just as he'd left Miami, he was just another anonymous face in the crowd. He checked his briefcase for his credit cards and his phone. Everything was intact. His papers from the climate change meeting were exactly as he left them. It had all ended so suddenly. He checked his phone but the battery was dead. He could charge that up in the airport whilst he got washed and cleaned up. The flight wasn't until eleven thirty; he had more than two hours to kill so he walked to the airport hotel and rented a room. The almost forgotten feeling of having a shower made him feel better. There was still time for a thick steak with a glass of Cabernet. Retrieving his phone from the charging booth, he found a string of messages waiting. Jennifer had rung at least ten times. His failure to reply was going to be hard to explain. His secretary also called and told him to ring the bureau Director immediately and that was five days ago. Amelia had called but left no message. Too late to call anyone back now and as he would be arriving in Miami at 1.30 in the morning he decided he would get a taxi from the airport. Somehow he just didn't want to call Jennifer. The conversation they were about to have would be difficult and he would rather not face a confrontation on the phone.

The flight landed on time and the taxi rank had just one cab. John slumped in the back seat, jet lag and exhaustion quickly catching up on him. Suddenly the cab stopped and the driver was speaking. John was jarred back to reality. He had fallen asleep and was already home. As he had expected, there were no lights on in his apartment. Jennifer must be in bed. It somehow felt strange being back home and the feeling of depression again engulfed him. The lift to the sixth floor had a mirror on one side and John examined himself and gently ran his fingers over the scratches on his face, made when he ran down the hillside thinking Ed was about to shoot Saida. They were one of the many things that were going to be difficult to explain to Jennifer. He'd had time to concoct a few stories about trying to help people in the Washington hurricane, and how he got a slight sun tan from doing so...he'd just have to deal with that when the time came.

The elevator stopped at the sixth floor. John tried the key and gently tested the door to see if the safety chain was on; it wasn't. The lights were all out so he switched on the hall light. The living room was partly lit by the hall light and John could see his carefully-chosen furniture all in place. He glanced at the clock on the mantelpiece which showed 2:30. Propped beside the clock was an envelope with his name on it. He closed the door, threw his raincoat over the sofa arm and picked up the letter. It was Jennifer's writing and he rapidly scanned the few words that said goodbye. Not having had a call or a reply to her

message she had decided that the relationship had no
future. The letter didn't give a forwarding address but it
implied that she was going back to Orlando, and she didn't
want to hear from John again. John sat back on the sofa,
eyes closed, weary and sad. One part of him was glad
Jennifer wasn't at home but he couldn't help feeling low
about his apparent inability to have a relationship that
didn't end in grief. Loneliness engulfed him. He pulled
himself together and kicked off his shoes before going to
the fridge. It was well stocked but no milk. Black coffee
would keep him awake so he opted for a bottle of Sam
Adams Dark and drank it from the bottle. He switched on
the TV and an old Bob Hope film "Road to Alaska" was on.
John, fully dressed, fell asleep on the sofa. The TV was still
on when he woke up bleary-eyed the next morning, to the
sound of his phone ringing. It was Amanda, his secretary.
She was bright and breezy and was enquiring if he was
coming into the office.

"I'll be there in an hour" he said optimistically as he
slowly came round.

He looked around his apartment. It was exactly as he
had left it, neat and tidy. He picked up the crumpled letter
from the floor and read it again, more carefully. It didn't
change anything. Jennifer had had enough and could not
take any more of his casual approach to their relationship.
He put the letter in the trash bin and with that gesture she
was gone from his life.

John returned to work and faced the inevitable questions
from his colleagues about what had happened in
Washington. They had no idea of the real adventure John

had been through but there was no way he could even hint of his visit to Africa.

For a while life for John took on a semblance of normality with occasional visits to Washington. At one meeting he arranged to see Amelia and they checked into the same hotel. After the Climate Change Committee meeting was over they agreed to meet in the hotel lobby. John was there first, and when Amelia stepped out of the lift, she looked stunning at first. But when they sat at the bar together John noticed how the lines around her face were more defined. She looked older than he had remembered. She had the look of a woman trying too hard to look young and attractive. Even her hair at shoulder length was too long for a woman her age. She was no substitute for Saida. John went through the ritual of taking her to dinner and eventually found himself in her bed. After a less than satisfactory session John quickly departed and left Amelia with a kiss on her forehead. It was one of many goodbyes in his life recently.

CHAPTER FORTY-TWO

In Florida the summer season was approaching and temperatures crept up over the 90°F mark most days. The Storm Division of the Weather Bureau started monitoring the Atlantic for potential hurricanes. Jack Parenteau had been promoted to Head of Storm Tracking and still spent considerable time trying to find the key to Saida's methods of prediction but to no avail. John, now Head of the Miami Division of the bureau, found himself more and more involved with politicians and their agendas to use the weather as a lever for new taxes and political reform. It wasn't a task that suited him and he used the approaching hurricane season as an excuse to avoid meetings in Washington. The first storm of the season started in the Atlantic on Independence Day, earlier than usual. It was a year in which the hurricanes were named after a woman and as the storm intensified it became known as Ada.

Ada became a force 3 hurricane and moved towards the Caribbean at twenty five miles per hour. The bureau prediction was that Ada would turn north into the Gulf of Mexico towards the Florida panhandles but to everyone's surprise it turned instead east towards the south-western tip of Florida. The combination of an unusual jet stream pattern and a high pressure region to the north had produced an unpredictable track. The hurricane, now at force 5, made landfall in Naples, the most southerly city on the Gulf Coast of Florida. Naples, famous for its pier, took the brunt of the wind, rain and storm surge. Parts of the pier were destroyed and the main shopping areas of 5th Avenue and 3rd Street were under 3ft of water. The haven of Port Royal, the expensive suburb of Naples, was badly damaged by enormous 10ft waves and the whole of southwest Florida was declared a Disaster Region.

Ada left as quickly as she had arrived, moving up through central Florida, rapidly losing energy until she became nothing but a rainstorm. The devastation of southwest Florida so early in the season became front page headlines across America particularly as the path had been incorrectly forecast. The President visited the area to see the devastation for himself. His schedule included a private meeting with senior officials to talk over the disaster relief activities. John was to represent the bureau.

The line of men, waiting stiffly in the dark suits, gazed at the crush of television cameras and microphones outside the main entrance in the State Capitol as the moment came for them to be introduced to their head of state. Illuminated by a firestorm of camera flashes and flanked by his ring of bodyguards, the President emerged from his limousine, waving in acknowledgement to the dense crowd before being taken to the head of the line.

He came to John, greeting him warmly and looking him firmly in the eye.

"Glad to see you again, great job you did in Washington".

"Thank you sir. It's a great pleasure to meet you again, Mr President. And how is Major Schick?"

The warmth momentarily left the President's face.

His gaze was unwavering, his face gave nothing away. But the answer came with icy conviction.

"I'm afraid I don't know any Major Schick".

In an instant, John realized his error in horror. But before he had time to blurt out any form of reply, The President swiftly and skilfully switched the conversation to the forecasting of the hurricane landfall.

"Why was it not possible to predict the area that Zoe came in? Why didn't it happen this time?"

John nervously repeated the official bureau line. Without a pause the President continued.

"Didn't you have some help from one of your officers?" Then, meaningfully;

"Get whatever help you need and get it fixed now."

He moved down the line. John felt as if he had just been hit by a tornado.

After the visit, the Washington Bureau Chief wanted to know why Saida didn't come back to the USA. He replied that her parents had been murdered and she had not felt like leaving her family.

"Are you still in touch?"

"No" replied John, hoping his manner made clear that was an end to that topic. But the Chief wouldn't be deflected.

"I think the President asked you to get her back again or at least get her computer programs and to my mind that's an order."

John suddenly felt weary and asked,

"What do you expect me to do?"

"It's obvious isn't it, go and see her and at least try to get to understand her work."

When John arrived back at his apartment he noticed the light on the answer phone was flashing. He pressed the answer button and was surprised to hear Ed's voice. The message was in his usual clipped style.

"For your information Saida is working in the mathematics department of the University of Benghazi. She is conducting research into rain-making but also gives lectures to students on Wednesday and Friday afternoons during term time. She is living in D'Aosta House four miles south of the city on Gaddafi Avenue. She is living alone but has a woman maid living in. She appears to have no men friends and spends her spare time with her family. She is very well respected at the university. She gives the impression that money is not a problem to her. Finally, your comments to the President today were inappropriate. Don't do anything of the kind again".

The message ended. There was no signing-off or small talk.

The failure of the department to predict the path of the last storm and the clear displeasure of the President troubled him, but Ed had called with all this detail about Saida for a good reason.

He switched on the television almost out of habit and the programme happened to be a hitchhiker's story about crossing Africa. It took his mind to Saida. The more he thought about her, the more his depression began to lift. His mind was made up; he would go to Benghazi and find her. He started checking flights. The Atlanta Tripoli flight left at 5:30pm every day. A quick check on flights to

Atlanta from Miami told him he would have no problems getting to Atlanta the following morning. Within minutes he had booked both flights and had started packing. His sleep that night was fitful, disturbed by confusing nightmares where he was always running but not moving. He thought for a moment about calling Saida in advance but rejected the idea on the basis that she may refuse to see him.

The flight to Tripoli seemed never-ending to John. Although he had a lay flat seat in Business Class, he was so preoccupied with his thoughts that he couldn't sleep and was relieved when the plane crossed over the African coast. The formalities for entering the country were onerous. The local US Embassy had been alerted by Ed that John was arriving and much to his surprise a junior official was at the airport to meet him. His second flight to Benghazi took only two hours and John had arrived and checked into the Berinici Hotel by early evening.

The city had its own distinctive smell, a mixture of spices and what appeared to be wood smoke. After dinner John strolled along the promenade down to the harbour. The air was warm but much less humid than in Miami. He was surprised how modern and busy the city appeared. The hotel had given him directions to the university and he decided to check out the route in readiness for the following day. It was a day when Saida would be teaching and he struggled to think of what he would say to her. He had no idea how she would react. She might simply turn her back on him.

The following day John retraced his steps from the hotel

to the university and asked for directions to the
Mathematics Department. The receptionist indicated that
she had to fetch an English speaking person for help and
John prayed it wouldn't be Saida. He had decided that he
wanted to meet her where she couldn't run so the ideal
would be to speak to her in the lecture room. His tall
stature and his western clothes had already drawn
curious looks from passing students.

The interpreter led him down a series of corridors until
they reached lecture room three. The door was slightly
open and John could see it was a modern lecture theatre
with tiers of desks looking down onto the lecturer.
The door gave access to the back of the room and John
quietly slipped in. Saida had her back to the students as
she pointed out parts of complex calculations that were on
a screen behind her. The lecture room was only half full
and the students were busily writing notes. John slipped
behind one of the desks at the back of the room.
He shuffled down the seat to take as low a profile as
possible but several students had seen him enter and were
turning around with evident curiosity. Saida turned to
face her students and started to answer a question which
one of the students had asked when she looked up and
saw John. She stopped in mid-sentence and stared at him.
Regaining her composure, she brought her attention back
to the class. John looked at Saida, his heart pounding with
both excitement and fear. She was as beautiful as ever and
try as he might he could not discern whether she was glad
to see him or not. The class was ending. The students were

packing up their lecture notes and making their way to the doors, casting glances at John as they left. Saida stood motionless looking at John, her expression giving nothing away. He made his way slowly to the front of the room and Saida remained motionless. Her eyes followed his every step. As he came close to her he put out his hand. She looked at the outstretched palm and slowly, very gradually raised her own hand towards his until eventually their fingers touched. John was desperate to embrace her but felt a need to be cautious. Saida's hand was warm and he thought he detected a slight tremble. He looked into her eyes; they were shining with the first sign of tears. John broke the silence,

"How are you, Saida?"

"I'm doing fine" she replied in a tone she immediately regretted.

John caught a movement out of the corner of his eye and realised that some of the students were still watching them. Saida dropped John's hand and directed him to a side door.

"Is there anywhere we can talk?" John tentatively asked.

"We can have a drink in the refectory but I have to give another lecture in fifteen minutes time."

So far, so good, thought John as he and Saida sipped strong black coffee. They were both reluctant to speak, almost not wishing to break the moment. Neither knew what was in the other's mind and neither wanted to betray their feelings. Their silence was broken by both speaking together and they laughed and invited the other to speak first.

"There is no time to talk now, shall we meet for dinner? I am staying at the Berenici. Can we meet at seven?"

Saida, her head bowed forward, looked up at him without raising her head. It was a look that John had seen many times before and his heart started racing all over again.

"Seven at the Berenici" she said as she stood up, smiled and walked back to the lecture theatre.

John walked slowly back to the hotel. He had a large room overlooking the seafront. He watched the people strolling by enjoying the cool breeze from the sea and his mind drifted towards the evening and wondered where he should start. Should he tell her he still loved her first or leave that until later? Should he ask her for help with his storm-tracking problems and wait to see if she mentioned their relationship? He also wanted to tell her about the killings of her mother and father, but that would betray the secrets entrusted to him. The only thing he was certain of was that he still loved her and was determined not to lose her again.

Saida finished her last lecture and walked out still in a daze. Seeing John sitting in the lecture theatre had completely shaken her. She could hardly remember what she had said to the students. Differential calculus was a difficult concept for students at the best of times but, with her mind elsewhere, they must have wondered what she was talking about. News of the American sitting in her class had travelled rapidly and the female students could hardly contain their curiosity. Saida was eventually asked by one of the bolder students who he was but Saida deflected him with a story about a visiting Western academic.

There had been so much, too much, that had happened since they parted. Had he come to identify her, the terrorist who had attacked his country? He seemed friendly, more than friendly. Perhaps he was here to get information from her.

She could hardly let herself think that John was here to rediscover their relationship. She had, after all, treated him so badly, ignoring his communications and cutting him off from all contact. Deep down Saida had wanted to run to him and throw her arms around him but reserve, caution and anxiety all held her back. She shivered with excitement at the prospect of their evening together but what could she say?

At home she showered and dressed carefully. She looked for a dress that would remind John of their time together in the USA and took greater pains than normal with her makeup.

At seven Saida stepped out of the elevator. John was waiting and immediately stood up and quickly crossed the room to her. He kissed her gently on the cheek and led her by her hand to a comfortable settee away from the other guests. He turned towards her, held both hands and spoke tenderly.

"You look wonderful and I have really, really missed you".

So much for my plan for a gentle start to the evening, he thought.

They had been together for one minute and already he was almost declaring his love; the magic was still there and they could both feel it. Dinner was a ceaseless conversation interspersed with occasional attempts to eat.

Halfway through the meal John put down his knife and fork and looked straight into Saida's eyes.

"I have to tell you that I know your mother and father were killed by American soldiers and not by your uncle. The soldiers are in a military prison in the USA." Saida looked up,

"I already knew it was the American soldiers but that is not the official Libyan explanation. My confession is that I got involved in making hurricanes aimed at the USA as my way of revenge."

"I know that too," replied John. "And I was with you when you were injured in Mauritania."

At that, Saida started to cry.

"I thought you were just a dream and as time went by I convinced myself that it was my imagination."

The meal ended and both were reluctant to leave. Eventually Saida stood up and started to say goodnight. But John put his finger to her lips,

"I need to tell you that I still love you. I promised myself I would wait to tell you but I can't. I want you to come back to America and for us to get married, or we could get married here in Benghazi. I'm not bothered where, I just want us to be together for the rest of our lives."

Saida returned the gesture by putting her finger on his lips.

"Let's talk about it tomorrow. We can meet and talk again. I have no work tomorrow and I will show you some of our city."

She gave John a light brush of her lips on his cheek and turned and walked to the elevator.

She faced a choice she never thought she would have to make. Returning to Libya had restored her to her family, she felt at home. In America her Islamic background would always single her out, and yet being with John made her so happy. She felt complete when she was with him and she really did love him. Saida couldn't sleep; she watched television for a while then simply sat staring into space waiting for guidance to tell her what to do. When dawn broke she listened to the sounds of the city waking up, the call to prayer echoing around the streets and the gentle noise of traffic in the distance. As she did her mind became clear and she knew what she had to do.

John arrived early at the café where they had planned to meet. He had already had two cups of coffee when Saida arrived. He looked at her face and thought how tired she looked. They kissed on the cheek and held hands. The waiter hurried over. They both waited for the coffee to be served before speaking. John sensed what was coming. Saida didn't smile and from time to time looked down at her hands. She started to speak hesitantly at first, a quiver in her voice and tears in her eyes.

"I feel at home here. I don't think I want to spend the rest of my life in America. I want to be near my family and live in the house that was my mother and father's home. I want to continue my research into rain-making and my experiments are coming to fruition."

Tears started to stream down Saida's cheeks. She felt frail and vulnerable but knew she had to be strong. John started to protest but knew it was to no avail. Saida looked up and smiled through her tears.

"We can still work together. I will help you with your storm path predictions and we will be in regular contact. I will teach your staff how to understand my programs. I could even visit from time to time."

John nodded, despite feeling his world was falling apart. The coffee remained untouched and cold perhaps symbolic of their love affair.

John paid the bill and they made their way together to the Berenici in silence. John's voice was sad and heavy,

"I think it would be best for me to go home. I'll catch this morning's plane to Tripoli, Could you run me to the airport?"

She braced herself against her emotions, hating to see him hurt.

"I'll get the car and wait for you outside reception."

John disappeared inside, collected his belongings from his room and minutes later they were heading to Benghazi International Airport. Saida silently cried most of the way and what words were spoken didn't reflect the inner torment they were both suffering. John interrupted their silence.

"I don't want you to wait, just drop me off, this is just too hard."

Saida pulled up at the kerbside and John retrieved his luggage from the trunk of the car. They embraced and John strode into the departure area without looking back. Saida stood by the car watching him go, somehow hoping he would turn and wave but he didn't.

Suddenly she felt a raindrop then another and then rain started, a gentle rain, the first for five months.

Her experiments were working. She jumped back into the car and took great delight in switching on the windscreen wipers. Her excitement almost overcame her despair. Perhaps life would be worth living after all.

ABOUT THE AUTHOR

Doug Liversidge CBE has enjoyed a long and successful career as a businessman. Born in Sheffield, he studied science at the city's university before serving as an army officer in Libya, where he became head of desert navigation. After working in the steel industry, he held senior positions in a number of organizations and today remains Chairman of two public companies. His list of achievements and honours is long and impressive. A member of Sheffield's ancient and prestigious guild, The Cutlers' Company, he has served as Master Cutler and also holds honorary doctorates from both the city's universities. His business skills have earned him three Queen's awards for innovation and export, the title South Yorkshire Businessman of the Year, and the CBE. Although he still lives near his native city, he spends much of his time in Florida, where he has often experienced the effects of a hurricane at close quarters.